TWENTY CENTAVOS

TWENTY CENTAVOS

by

JOHN SCHERBER

A Mystery Set in San Miguel de Allende,
México

San Miguel Allende Books
San Miguel de Allende, Gto., Mx

ACKNOWLEDGMENTS

Any book starts as an idea and by its completion becomes a joint effort.

Thanks to my readers: Dianne Aigaki, Patti Beaudry, Joan Columbus, Lou DeRonde, Bill Dorn, Bill Hammond, Donna Krueger, Marcia Loy, Lois Scherber, Lynda Schor, and Ivan Schuster.

Cover Design by Lander Rodriguez
Author Photo by Gail Yates Tobey
Web Page Design by Julio Mendez

This is a work of fiction. Any resemblance to actual, living or dead, is entirely coincidental.

ISBN: 978-0-9832582-4-7

San Miguel Allende Books
San Miguel de Allende, Guanajuato, México

Website:www.sanmiguelallendebooks.com

Also by John Scherber

FICTION

(The Paul Zacher Murder in México Mystery Series)

Twenty Centavos
The Fifth Codex
Brushwork
Daddy's Girl
Strike Zone
Vanishing Act
Jack & Jill
Identity Crisis
The Theft of the Virgin
The Book Doctor
The Predator
The Girl from Veracruz
Angel Face
Uneasy Rider
Lost in Chiapas
The Jericho Journals

(The Townshend Vampire Trilogy)

And Dark My Desire
And Darker My Wrath

The Devil's Workshop
Eden Lost
The Amarna Heresy
Beyond Terriorism: Survival

NONFICTION

San Miguel de Allende: A Place in the Heart
A Writer's Notebook
Into the Heart of Mexico: Expatriates Find Themselves off the Beaten Path
Living in San Miguel: The Heart of the Matter

FOR KRISTINE

PROLOGUE
THE VISITOR

Tobey Cross opened the door, and with an unconsciously elegant gesture, invited his killer inside.

What a fraud, the visitor thought, an Ivy League fake. Fingering the .22 caliber Beretta automatic in the pocket of his Burberry trench coat, he stepped through the doorway. Cross always kept the entry to his gallery locked, might as well post a sign that said, "Sophisticated Clients Only." Suckers Only might be better. The visitor stared at the back of Cross's gray suede jacket as they walked across the garden, imagining a bullet hole halfway between collar and vent. Maybe two. But it wouldn't be in the back—he wanted to see the look on the antiques dealer's face.

What kind of name was Cross anyway? English? Irish? Or just something that fit his sanctimonious personality?

The late afternoon sun of a Mexican January teetered at the edge of the high garden wall. With any luck Cross's wife would be at the market getting things for dinner. If she was home and came into the gallery it would be her problem.

"I've got some new things in," said Cross, over his shoulder, "however, they're still at the warehouse. But there is that head from Copan you were considering." There was a mildly hopeful note in his voice, promising that satisfaction of sole possession that any collector coveted, but without going more than a degree beyond, "Take it or leave it." The visitor had never been able to read the dealer well, despite his years of business experience.

"I'm not here for another piece," he said, suppressing a quaver in his voice. Cross didn't respond.

They passed up the steps from the garden, through the loggia and into the great room beyond that housed the gallery. The visitor felt a wave of desire pass over him as he always did upon entering the room. The shelves of Mayan ceramics, the colonial paintings and silver, the gold and silver shipwreck coins and jewelry never failed to stimulate his collector's instinct, in spite of what he now knew.

"What can I do for you then?" said Cross, his custom-made shoes moving over the fringe of an opulent Shiraz carpet onto the tile. As he leaned against the edge of his desk he plucked a speck of dust from his cuff as he waited for the visitor to reply.

"They're fakes," the visitor spat out. "A bunch of damned fakes."

Tobey Cross regarded him coolly. "Surely you can't be serious."

"I dropped one of the ceramics on the floor. It shattered."

"Regrettable, I'm sure." He folded his arms and looked across the room at something else, something more reasonable, maybe more interesting than a client working himself into a rage.

"I want my money back on the whole batch, all of it, even the one I dropped."

A look of genuine puzzlement passed Cross's face. "I don't know what you're talking about. Look, I'm sure you're very knowledgeable about business, but I doubt you know much beyond that. As for coming in here and thinking you're able to pass judgment on my offerings, the idea is nothing less than laughable. You're just a businessman, nothing more. I offered you the same arrangement as the rest of my clients. You have a week after you take a piece home to decide whether you want to retain it. After that, all sales are final. Now, if you should wish to sell back a couple of pieces, at wholesale rates of course, I might be interested, although the market is a little soft right now. I can think of two I might be interested in, the others probably not, for quality reasons."

"Odd, isn't it, that they were all top notch items when I bought them?" His index finger found the trigger inside his pocket.

"As you will recall, the choices were all yours," Cross said.

"Write me a refund check for the lot and I'll have them brought around in the morning. No one else need know about this. You can go on just as before." Despite himself, the visitor found his voice shaking. He already knew what the answer would be.

"Don't be a fool." Cross turned away, as if the meeting were finished. As he was staring at a display case of seventeenth century silver coins from the Lima mint, he heard the faint click of the hammer being pulled back on a pistol. He whirled and took two steps forward as the visitor raised the gun to his face and fired once.

Tobey Cross fell straight backward, his head striking the tile, and didn't move, the dull thud echoing in the room. His open eyes and mouth held an expression of surprise, but not outrage. The visitor watched him for a few seconds, listening for a response from further inside the house, but there was none. The only other sound had been a slight ping as the ejected shell casing struck the coffee table, then dropped to the floor and spun away out of sight. The visitor sank to his knees, reached into his pocket, and withdrew a small object and dropped it into the dead man's mouth. Then he pocketed the pistol and sat down at the desk, searching for a ledger or book of sales receipts, but saw none. He picked up the Rolodex, tried to jam it in his coat pocket but found it too wide, so he simply held it in his hand as he searched for the spent shell casing. He was on his knees before the sofa, just about to bend over to look beneath, when he heard the door on the other side of the garden open and then close firmly. He was instantly on his feet.

From the third set of French doors on the far left of the loggia he watched as Marisol Cross traversed the garden to the kitchen entrance at the right. When she entered and disappeared from view, the visitor slipped out through the garden along the fountain wall and opened the street door. A chorus of mariachis came from the main plaza two blocks away. A sharper note sounded above the music, the sound of a woman screaming within the gallery. A string of firecrackers went off, covering the sound as the visitor closed the door silently behind him and briskly walked away into the deepening shadows.

CHAPTER ONE

My Mexican girlfriend, Maya Sanchez, was seated nude with both legs folded beneath her on a low hassock in my studio, facing right.

"Turn a bit to your left. Give me a clean profile."

The upper line of her thigh formed the base of the painting I was starting. Her right arm hung at her side and from the elbow her forearm was angled downward toward her knee, palm facing up and open. Her eyes were closed.

Normally she wore her hair tied back, where it fell just below her shoulders. Today she had drawn it up on the back of her head to frame a single orange hibiscus blossom fastened behind her ear. Her neck was long and graceful.

Mixing a thin wash of yellow ochre and burnt sienna, I sketched in her profile with a dozen quick strokes. Touching in the shadow between her arm and her side, and below her breast, established the strongest darks. Behind her body would ultimately squat the Maize God of the ancient Mayans facing left, rendered as if in stone relief, and all around the two of them, a vigorous stretch of the Yucatan jungle. I began to work next on her face. If you don't get the face right, you can forget the rest.

"You can put your arm down, but hold your head still if you can. Lift your chin half an inch or so. That's it. Are you getting tired of doing these?"

"No." She spoke without moving her head. "Each one is different enough."

I was working on a series for a June show in the Yucatan, in the city of Mérida. Each picture used either Maya or a Yucatan girl posed with a Mayan divinity behind her. It would be my second show there, and because the first had done well, this time the gallery had made a banner to hang from the top of the building. It said, PAUL ZACHER: GODS AND GODDESSES.

I got up—I always work sitting down—and took a few steps back from the canvas and regarded it critically, then went over to Maya and bent close to her face. I touched her lips with my fingertips.

"You look great today. I'm looking at the way your hair comes up off your neck and it's an interesting curve."

"Remember about my nose."

She moved her head this time and her eyebrows went up.

"Of course, but I'm doing your eye next."

"But you will remember when you come to it?"

"Always."

Maya had a thing about her nose. She believed it was too wide and had too much of an Indian look. I couldn't see it. We were surrounded by Mexicans of mixed blood every day. They made up most of the population and were usually darker, shorter, and thicker than Maya. She was tall for a Mexican woman, almost five-foot-six, with long legs and a slender build. She did not have the substantial butt that some Mexican men admire. Hers had a sensational curve to it, but it was no wider than her hips. I had come to know it well, since I'd painted it twenty times or more. But her nose? I thought it was fine.

Later we took a break. She pulled on a short silk robe and we went downstairs for lunch. I mashed some avocados, chopped an onion and a small tomato, mixed in some roasted green chilies with a bit of chopped serrano chile and added a dash of Worcestershire sauce and a spoonful of mayonnaise. Not exactly traditional, but the last two were my secret ingredients.

"I like the line of this one," I said, sitting down and passing her the chips. "The inward curve of your back is the exact reverse of the Maize god's thigh."

"Sometimes you get lucky." She gave me a tolerant smile. Maya had probably heard more talk about painting that she ever expected to in a lifetime.

"It's never luck. Maybe you think it's easy?"

"I know it isn't, but it's what you love."

⌘⌘⌘

We had a productive painting session that afternoon, and her eye and ear were working well. When I had the ear done I brought a lock of her hair across it that mostly obscured it, but nonetheless you knew it was there.

When she dressed for dinner she left her hair up and the orange hibiscus was still fresh. We walked through the cool evening to the Villa Antigua Santa Monica, where there would be wonderful food and good margaritas. Strings of firecrackers exploded around us, many more than usual. The narrow sidewalks were crowded with people moving in the opposite direction, back toward our main plaza, the *jardín*.

"Do you know what day this is?" she asked. I'd lived in San Miguel de Allende for twelve years but I wasn't always current on what holiday it was, there was one practically every day.

"Friday?" It wasn't the anniversary of our meeting, that was in December, and it wasn't her birthday, or mine. "It's January twenty-first," I said.

"It's the birthday of Don Ignacio Allende. There will be a parade soon." The sun touched the upper edge of the hills and long shadows crept through the streets. The fireworks didn't distract me, I was holding the hand of my favorite model. January can be a tough month some places, but never here.

The restaurant of the Santa Monica spreads under the arches along three sides of the interior garden. Behind the walls along the tables there are half a dozen rooms with high ceilings and colonial style furnishings that have their own courtyards behind. By the time we got there darkness had fallen and the only light came from the wrought iron lanterns at each room door and the candles on the tables. This was our favorite place to eat. A seventeenth century fountain, once a well, bubbled softly in the center of the courtyard and, lit by small lamps on the ground, we could see the bougainvillea and jasmine vines along the edges of the roof tiles. In a month or two the jasmine would flower again, crowning the tops of the arches, and the courtyard would fill with the scent. The bougainvillea never stopped blooming.

The waiter set down chips and guacamole and we

ordered margaritas. Having guacamole twice in one day is not considered excessive here. Maya was toying with an earring, which I took as a signal that there was something on her mind. She took one of the chips and nibbled the corner. When the drinks came I lifted mine and said, "Here's to my favorite person in the world."

She smiled and took a sip. "What do you think about the series so far?"

"I like it." This is strong praise from me. "The mix of you and the Mérida models is good. I'll have some nude and some clothed." She gave me a broad smile. I'd been unable to persuade any of the Yucatán girls to pose nude, so I had used folk dancers' costumes on all of them. It gave potential buyers a choice.

"You don't think it's too much of me?"

I shook my head as she scanned the menu, although she always ordered the same thing—chicken breasts with a sauce of *flor de calabaza*. How long had we been coming here? Not long enough was the first answer that came to mind.

We live in the historic part of the city, what they call here *el centro*. In the mid 1500s San Miguel de Allende was built in a basin at the edge of a vital cluster of springs. It was originally called San Miguel el Grande, and it rests in a setting somewhat like a cupped hand among the not terribly formidable mountains. Four hundred years later American expatriates began to filter down to México to study art here on the GI bill at the two major art schools, the Instituto Allende and the Bellas Artes. Some stayed and more came and they began to restore houses in the central part of San Miguel and build more up the slopes. So at night, as Maya and I relax on our rooftop garden sharing a bottle of Chilean wine, we can see into some of our neighbors' walled gardens, but our view to more distant parts of the city is mostly up.

In 1993 I was one of those Americans who filtered down to San Miguel, although the GI Bill was history at that point. After I finished my degree at Miami University in Oxford, Ohio I came for a few more art classes in an exotic setting and never got beyond it. Not that I tried very hard. At first I rented a bedroom with a studio and tiny kitchen and that was about as much as I could afford. When my grandmother died in 1996 she left me the money to buy this house on Quebrada and put a new roof on it. The rest of the renovation I've done piece by piece, room by room, when I've had the money. One of the first things I did after the roof was tight was convert the largest bedroom for my studio, adding first the north glass and then the south shortly after, when I discovered that in June the sun was far enough to the north to shine directly in. The quality of that light (every painter says this), and also the quality of the people, and the lush colors of the culture have kept me here. At thirty-five it seems to me like the best place in the world to live.

Less obvious, although I was aware of it, was the way it had gotten under my skin. Whatever I had been driven to do when I came down here had been driven away. I still worked hard, but without ever feeling I had to. I found time to hang out in the *jardín*, to watch the sunsets with Maya and to sit and talk. After six or seven years I could no longer remember what I had been, and I didn't care. I didn't quite feel like Gauguin in Tahiti, but I understood why he stayed.

Eventually I made friends with Ramon Rivera,

who owned Galería Uno on Calle Jésus, and began to show there. It was toward the middle of 1997 that I had my first successful one man show in San Miguel and from the proceeds I acquired a big round table with six chairs to put out in my *loggia*, the outdoor covered living room facing the garden.

One night, at a gallery opening just before Christmas of 1999, I saw Maya. I didn't call her Maya yet; it turned out her name was Maria Sanchez. I was not unaware of the Mexican girls around me at that point, but my Spanish was not yet fluent and how to make contact was not always clear.

There are many art galleries and thus many opening nights in San Miguel, and I don't go to all of them. Many of the modern things don't appeal to me; I had embraced the return to representational painting after it began in the eighties. But on this particular Friday evening was a collage show and I am clueless about collage, I mean conceptually. I do know about clear acrylic medium and things. This show was a knockout. Who knew collage could be a powerhouse of color, shadow and texture? Many of these had a depth of four or five inches, so the shadows changed every time you shifted your viewpoint. They were like a combination of painting and sculpture. They made me think hard about what I was doing, which is what I look for in any show.

I was mumbling to myself when someone touched my elbow.

"Are you all right?" I turned and looked into the face of a Mexican girl with a wide mouth that seemed ready to laugh, and large black eyes. When she smiled her upper lip dipped slightly in the center. Her thick glossy hair touched her shoulders, and her teeth were perfect. Her English was close to perfect. "You have a passion," she said. I looked for a moment at her fine skin and the shape of her eyebrows, and the line of her jaw and how it related to her neck.

"Yes, well I never have seen collage like this. I'm practically speechless." I had even tried this in Spanish.

She was wearing snug jeans and a teal blue sleeveless top. On her left wrist was one of those micro-beaded *Huichol* bracelets that you could find in a few shops in San Miguel. Instantly she made me think about doing figure painting again. I missed it.

"Are you an artist?" she asked.

"Yes, are you?"

"I'm a historian. Do you know that right next door to this gallery was the home of Ignacio Allende? I came here to write a book about his youth." Allende was the local hero of the 1810 War of Independence.

"You have a passion too."

"I do. I can almost feel his presence here. What do you paint?"

"I'll paint anything, I guess. Right now I'm doing still lifes, mostly ordinary things. I just finished a stack of tennis hats. I also do some figure work, the occasional portrait, now and then some landscapes."

"Do you ever paint girls?"

"I've painted a few girls."

"How many?"

"Lots, actually. Not too many lately," I said.

"Are you very good?"

"Very. I could capture you, if you'll to pose."

There was something irreverent about her,

and that's how it began. Much later she confessed to me that she had picked me up at the gallery because she thought I had an erotic response to the collages. Although she had a master's degree in history from the Autonomous University of México in Mexico City and had never taken an art class, she turned out to have a good eye and quickly became an eager critic of my work.

We began to see each other often and she showed me places near San Miguel that were good for landscape painting. I did a small oil of the reservoir above town and gave it to her as a birthday gift. She was touched although she later gave me back the frame. She had replaced it with something much more elegant, and I had to admit it did more for the picture than my frame had. She would disappear from my life for days at a time, immersed in her book, I assumed. I connected with this because I got involved in painting the same way. As time passed I didn't try to deny to myself that I was falling in love with her.

It wasn't long before she began to pose for me and I had to instruct her in the protocol of the painter's model. Instead of just dropping her clothes in front of the easel I asked her to change behind the screen in my studio, put on a robe, and then come out and take the robe off when we set up the pose.

"Why is this?" she asked with a startled look.

"Because for you to undress in front of the painter is a sexual invitation. The model tries to avoid that."

"I thought you liked to sleep with me?" She placed her hands on her hips.

"Of course I do. But painting is painting and our love life is something else. That's all. Besides, I don't want to get paint on you."

After that she changed behind the screen.

She moved in with me in September of 2000. I felt like a college kid with his first serious girlfriend when she pulled up in her Volkswagen beetle with all of her things. She took her laptop computer out first and then gave me a big hug and a kiss and said, "I am here now." And she has been ever since.

⌘⌘⌘

Our lives settled into a sweet spot that lasted more than four years. Sitting across from her at the Santa Monica that night I could see no reason why it should ever change. We had finished dinner and she took my hand, leaning forward across the table.

"What are you thinking about?" she said.

"You, art, life, the usual. What are you thinking about?"

"You. What's the best thing about you?" she asked. The waiter took away our plates and brought coffee. Maya was studying my face as if she already knew the answer. I wasn't sure I did. She liked to do these little checks now and then, as if to see whether we were still on track. I thought if we weren't we'd know it without checking, but I always went along.

"I'm a good painter. It's taken me a while, but I know I'm there. If I'm not any good at anything else I'll always have that."

"I know that."

I wondered what more she was looking for. As a painter I deal in surfaces, that's my comfort zone. Even in a portrait, where the viewer may think there's depth and character in the subject, it's most likely only the spaces within the mosaic of color she's seeing. It's never anything more than illusion. I sensed Maya was looking for more.

"Well, I'm a fraction over six feet tall, 175 pounds, thirty-five years old, and I still have all my hair. Even some of the curl."

"Besides that."

"I still take chances. I'm not afraid to fall on my face. You lose that, and you start to repeat yourself."

"Did you take a chance on me?"

"That was about the smallest chance I ever took."

I still wasn't sure where she was going, but I'll always recall the look on her face as I said this, because at that moment her cell phone rang and that statement became the final words of the first part of our lives.

Immediately I could hear the caller's high-pitched Spanish, mingled with wailing that seemed tiny and far away because of the phone. "*Que pasó, que pasó*?" Maya was sobbing. She covered the receiver. "It's Marisol Cross. Tobey was murdered this afternoon!" I signaled for the check as she resumed her rapid Spanish.

Marisol was an old friend of Maya's who had married an American named Tobey Cross, an elegant man in his forties who had a gallery specializing in colonial and pre-Columbian antiques. It was a by appointment-only kind of business, set up in the great room of their home. I had seen him a few times at gatherings in Los Balcones and Atascadero, expatriate neighborhoods up on the hill at the eastern end of San Miguel.

After a few moments Maya hung up. Tears ran down her cheeks leaving tracks edged with her eye makeup. She pulled out a tissue.

"The police just left. Someone shot Tobey in the head at the gallery. Marisol found him when she returned from the market about five o'clock. When the police put him on the stretcher to take him away a coin fell out of his mouth. Twenty centavos."

⌘⌘⌘

I don't sprint well after a dinner and a margarita or two, but we headed across the corner of Juarez Park to Diezmo Viejo, upsetting a flock of egrets that had just settled down above us in the trees. Then up Tenerías and as we approached Umaran we started to slow. She wasn't breathing hard but I was. Why were we in such a hurry? I wasn't unsympathetic to Tobey Cross but it seemed like he'd still be dead when we got there.

"Twenty centavos? In his mouth?" I wheezed, thinking of the phone call. It immediately seemed like a stupid thing to say. Like it should have been ten, or fifty.

"Marisol wants you to look around. You know, to see if you can tell what happened."

"Why me? I mean, I'm happy to go over there with you, but what would I be able to do?"

"Because you are a painter she says you will see things differently than the police. Maybe in the detail, I don't know. Find a notebook. Write things down. If nothing else, maybe it will make Marisol feel better. Anyway, nobody trusts the police here, you know that."

I was about to protest that, having no experience in such things, I was not likely to see anything the police had not seen, trustworthy or not, but everything seemed to be decided.

Twenty centavos is a change coin, one of no significance. It doesn't appear much in circulation anymore. Less than two American cents, using it in the murder might suggest the victim was of no significance either, a cypher. As time passed would the murder of Tobey Cross still evoke the usual comments reserved for people who did matter, such as "deeply shocked, saddened, untimely loss," and so on? Would the writer for *Atención*, our local bilingual newspaper, refer to Tobey's roots in the expatriate community, his charitable contributions, his support for the arts? Of course there would be a brief profile of Marisol, his widow, and of his antiques business, Galería Cruz. Maybe the writer would speculate about whether anyone could take his place. Probably he wouldn't make any reference to Tobey's personal warmth.

The truth was that while Tobey Cross was not overtly enigmatic or veiled, neither was he a person most people knew well, even his customers. His usual manner expressed an elegant reserve and I didn't know anyone who was close to him, other than Marisol. He usually kept his suit jacket buttoned, and the few times I saw him it was hard to imagine him being anything but unruffled. I wondered if his killer had ruffled him at the end.

What Maya and I didn't anticipate on that night of January 21 was how everything would change for us, the way our life would be subtly divided into before and after this event, and how it would force us into roles which were sometimes neither comfortable or even appropriate.

CHAPTER TWO

Winter evenings in San Miguel are rarely threatening; it felt like the temperature was still in the mid fifties as we hurried over the rough stone sidewalks toward Umaran. Traffic was light and as usual, the facades of the houses gave little away. In the historic center of this town it is forbidden to alter anything visible from the street, and each house front is nothing but a long wall joining its neighbors in a mute, anonymous procession. The colors change from one to the next, the intent does not. The facades may have several grilled and shuttered windows or none at all; some have a wider door to admit a car or a carriage, dating from before the design controls, some have only an entrance for the occupants. The state of repair of these walls tells you nothing. Sometimes a deteriorating front masks magnificence inside, and I've always thought the owners take a perverse pleasure in surprising people when they walk through the door. These houses unfold into their gardens. All is inward looking, private. Easily private enough to conceal a murder.

At the corner of Umaran and Quebrada we turned and stopped at Marisol's door. The facade was wider than most and painted a deep ultramarine that would have raised eyebrows in the States, but here it read as elegant and cool, like Tobey. A light gray marble tablet beside the entry announced Galería Cruz in gilt letters, lit from above by a crisp modern fixture recessed into the stucco. Maya rang the bell. I heard nothing from inside and then the door swung open and Maya and Marisol were wrapped in each other's arms. Twelve years I had lived in Mexico and their Spanish was still too rapid for me. I waited for them to separate, not comfortable with what my role was going to be. After a few moments Marisol's wailing eased and she took my hand.

"Thank you for coming to help me. I hope you can."

"I'm sorry about Tobey," I said. "I'll do anything I can."

We stood in a small reception room opening into a deep garden. In the center was a cluster of eight ficus trees trimmed into cylinders. It had a formality that ours did not. Across the garden from the entry was the *loggia*, a long outdoor room also open toward the foliage from the opposite side and roofed in tile. At one end of it, past a group of wicker sofas and chairs, stood a massive cantera stone fireplace. Crossing the garden, we went through one of the three pairs of French doors into the great room beyond. Frescoed angels blew trumpets in greeting on the double-height vaulted ceiling. At the second floor level, openings let in light from what must have been bedrooms. I had never been up there. On our left an archway with recessed doors led to the dining room. Opposite a tall fireplace projected into the room. Behind it, stairs descended to the lower level at the right and upstairs on the left.

Marisol led us to the middle of the room, her footsteps soft and soundless on the tile. "When I found

Tobey I still had the broccoli and lettuce in my arms." Details like this would be engraved on her recollection of the murder scene for the rest of her life. Her chest began to heave again and Maya put her arms around her.

"Marisol," I began, after a while, "If I'm to help I'd like to ask you some questions, things about Tobey's business, his friends, anything that will help me understand this. But wouldn't it be easier for you if we did this tomorrow?"

"No, please. Now is good. I already talked to the police and it's better if I can try to help you now. I don't want to be alone yet."

"Show me where he was when you came in."

She walked to the main fireplace. Like the one on the loggia, it was ornately carved cantera stone in the manner of the seventeenth century. With courses of columns and pilasters, it reached almost to the double-height ceiling.

Marisol stood at the edge of the hearth. "It was just here. He was partly turned with one leg over the other and one arm was stretched out ahead, so. The police said he was shot one time." She turned away.

The stone had been cleaned of blood and was still damp in places.

"Where was the coin?" Maya asked.

I wondered why this mattered, but she was searching for a way to approach this too.

"Just here." Marisol pointed. "His face was toward the fireplace. The police took many pictures and then they set next to him the stretcher and turned him onto it, on his back. His mouth was open and the coin came out. It rolled on the floor."

This was evidence of a sort, but I was trying not to picture it. "I'd like to look through his desk," I said. I was supposed to be seeing what the police had missed but I was mainly seeing what a stretch this was going to be if I was any help at all.

"Please. Whatever you need to do." I felt her eyes on my back as I turned toward the desk. She was wearing a midnight blue jogging suit that looked like velour, although I knew from Maya that she never exercised. The top was unzipped to reveal a pink tee shirt that said, I (heart) Charleston. Well, we all hearted Charleston, I thought, and while the pink and the midnight blue were OK with each other, the pink did not suit her skin tones. Many Mexican women and girls wore pink as if it always worked. I realized my mind was wandering.

There was a quality of thorough exhaustion about her. Drooping at the shoulders, her arms hung limp at her sides as if waiting for instructions that didn't come. I thought of her as the same height as Maya, but now she seemed shorter. She had always been attractive, but today it was starting to blur. I realized I was looking at her as a painter looks at his subject, and a wave of sympathy came over me. Cut her some slack, I said to myself, she didn't dress this morning to lose her husband, she thought she was only going to the vegetable market.

A large eighteenth century mahogany desk anchored the center of the long wall to the left of the French doors, flanked by display cases on both sides. The cases housed hundreds of small items; Mayan jade carvings and fragments of masks, three trays of gold and silver coins of the colonial period, a few spurs and ornate knives. A brace of pistols in wood, ivory, and silver mounts. In the center of one tray were earrings and pendants; I didn't know enough to tell whether they were colonial or earlier. The only antique I had ever owned was my house. So much for seeing things differently, I thought.

Two low piles of books and an angular Art Deco bronze lamp occupied the desktop. Large in format and glossy, the books were all devoted to Mexican antiquities. One on top was called *Ancient Textiles of Oaxaca*.

The center drawer held a leather-bound notebook. Inside was a pad of good quality unlined paper. I flipped through the pages. All were blank. Holding it angled to the light revealed no impression of earlier writing. Next to it was a six-inch round magnifying glass with an onyx handle and a small flashlight. In the front of the drawer a curved felt-lined tray held three expensive-looking fountain pens and a few pencils that looked like they hadn't been used since they were sharpened. Maya and Marisol watched hand in hand. Their expectations were silent but unmistakable.

A string of firecrackers erupted outside. They sounded like gunshots and Marisol flinched, although she must have known what they were. A chorus of dogs howled back in answer. Power outages are frequent here and dogs are the equivalent of burglar alarms.

The upper left drawer held a tray of business cards, gray rag stock with a subtle brown fiber in it. They said Galería Cruz, with the Umaran address. In the lower left corner they read, Tobey Cross; in the right, Antiquities. The next two drawers were empty, but in the bottom drawer on the right I found a dictionary of Mayan hieroglyphics and a package of Galeria Cruz stationery in the same color paper as the business cards. Next to it lay a bundle of matching envelopes and three spiral notebooks. The top two had entries recording wages for cleaning and gardening help. The third was empty.

In my role as instant detective I took out the blank spiral notebook and laid it on the desktop. When I came in I had imagined myself listing all the things I noticed, as if I possessed some system that would make sense of this. But what I wanted to do now was list all the things I didn't notice; it was a much more telling group. I looked at Marisol; she watched me with raised eyebrows.

"Is this where Tobey did his business?" I leaned back in his chair thinking that no one but Tobey ever sat there. "Because I don't see any business here." It sounded a little too final, even harsh, but there it was.

Maya came over to the desk and looked over my shoulder. "What do you mean?"

"Well, you know how my painting business is. I keep my sales files on a computer. I know where every one of my pictures has gone. There's a Rolodex file of all my customers; and on the computer, what they own, what they're interested in, and so on. I have my expense and travel records. I have my tax information for years and the galleries where I show now or have shown, together with what they've sold. I have a record of all the galleries I've approached unsuccessfully and what slides they've seen. Do you see? There is nothing like that here. Where is Tobey's business?"

Marisol sat down in a leather chair opposite me, placed her elbows on the desk and her chin in her hands. Whenever I had seen her in the past she was nicely turned out, but tonight her face was puffy and her makeup smeared around the eyes from crying, although her hair, cut shorter than Maya's and with the ends curled forward just under her ears, was still in place. I wondered if it made her uncomfortable for me to see her like that. Beyond a certain point, Mexicans are usually private people and I didn't know her well.

"Did the police take away anything from the desk?" I asked.

"I do not think so. I did not see them, but Tobey's Rolodex is not here. It is usually by the books."

"Other than that, is this the way it was? Did you ever go in the desk, like to dust or put things in order?"

"Well, to clean we have Luz, but the desk is never a mess. It is always like this, on the top. Just the books and the lamp, and the Rolodex. I think there was also an appointment book inside, but I am not sure."

"I didn't see it."

My eyes traveled around the room. It was set up like the great room of a wealthy gentleman collector. Lit niches in the walls held important-looking Mayan clay figures and vessels. There was no gallery lighting from overhead, but with four sofas in the room and accompanying lamp tables and floor lamps the ceramics were all washed in a subtle light. Normally I would have examined them more closely to get a sense of the ancient artisans who made them, but tonight I was more interested in what might be missing.

Maya was moving about among the cabinets, looking at the paintings, doing what looked like a mental recording of the room's contents.

On two tables against the wall were artful arrangements of massive colonial silver and religious figures. Spaced along the walls above hung religious paintings with costumes elaborately gilded, and portraits of early notables. I tended to think of these as the "brown gravy" school of art, but that didn't do justice to the color designs. It was just that they took themselves so seriously.

Tobey could have been a curator of a small museum. The wall surface was rag rolled in shades of pale gold, and two huge wrought iron chandeliers hung on chains from the double-height ceiling. It was all about display. I tried to think if that had been my impression of Tobey as well, but this was one of a hundred things I couldn't remember about him.

"Marisol, is there an office in the house where Tobey did the routine parts of his business? I realize this room is mostly for display. But where did he do the paperwork? Perhaps the same place he kept his computer?"

She shook her head. "He has no other room here for his business. And I don't know of any other office somewhere else. I am sorry. We don't have a computer here, but I have one in my office. Tobey always said a computer was too much of a concession to the twenty-first century."

I didn't let my face betray it, but this statement had the sound of nothing more than a desire for concealment to me. Perhaps Tobey wished to make himself seem like an old-fashioned curmudgeon when it came to business technology, but there were no ink pots with quill pens, no ledger books.

"When you went to the market this afternoon, what time did you leave?" I asked her.

"Just after three o'clock, I think."

"Was Tobey here then?"

"No, he had gone out earlier to meet a client."

"Did he say who he was meeting?"

"No, and I did not ask."

"But when you got back the door was locked; there was no break in?"

"No. And there are no windows on the street, as you know."

"Do you think any of the antiques might have been taken? As I look around, all the niches are full. But the cases of smaller things, the gold or silver...?"

She shook her head. "It looks the same, and the pictures too. I checked these things with the police."

There were no obvious blank spaces on the walls. I looked at the phone by one of the sofas. It was the kind with a built-in answering machine. The cord on it was long enough to reach back to the desk. "Have you listened to the answering machine?"

"No, and the police took the tape."

"I'm sure they asked you this, but was Tobey having any problems with anyone? Were any customers angry with him?"

"He did not say." She shrugged. "I don't think he would tell me. He never spoke much about his business except to show me new things when they came in."

"Was there anyone who visited him often?"

"None more than others. But I am usually not here during the day. I have my interior design studio to look after."

I tried to think how long had it been since I'd seen Tobey. Six months at least. It could have been eight or nine. Brief conversations with him didn't have much impact; they were too superficial. I tried to picture him, the way he dressed and carried himself, as if I were painting him. I was mainly painting nudes now, but I had completed a series of clothed figure studies a year ago and clothing had been a revealing part of the effect. All I could recall about Tobey's clothing was the way he always kept his jacket buttoned. I hardly knew anyone else in San Miguel who wore a jacket.

"I'd like to look at his clothes," I said.

We left Maya bent over the display cases, her arms folded as if to make sure she didn't touch anything, and went up the stairs behind the fireplace. From the largest of the bedrooms upstairs Marisol led me into a long dressing room next to the bath. The walls were lined with shelves of dark wood. "I will go back downstairs," she said, backing out the door, her hands palm outward to me as if I had been about to pull her in further. "I can't look at his clothes now." She left me alone.

I ignored the neat stacks of underwear and the rows of shoes each racked with those wooden forms you stick in them to help retain their shape. I'd never owned a pair of them, most of my shoes had no shape. Nor did I bother with the ties. There were no jeans, which may have been a major statement about him. Or perhaps he stored them elsewhere, possibly with his computer. There was nothing in the pockets of his slacks and suit pants. I had gone through seven suit and sport jackets, all with American labels, when in an inside breast pocket of the eighth, my fingers found a key. It was large with a circular top, but most interesting, stamped into the face on one side were the numbers 132. I put it in my pocket and continued to go through the clothes, but there was nothing more of interest.

Downstairs Maya and Marisol were sitting

together on one of the sofas, an arm around each other. I held out the key to Marisol. "Do you know what this one is for? Or what the number refers to?" She looked at it on both sides and shook her head as she gave it back to me.

"I have not seen this one before. The other keys of Tobey are on a ring in the tray in the entry. The police asked me about all of them."

"Can I take this one? I'm not sure why, but maybe something will come to me. I'm just trying to think why he wouldn't have it with the rest of his keys. He was methodical that way, wasn't he?"

"Always, like with everything else. Please, take it with you."

I slipped the key in my jeans pocket and sat down across from them on one of the deep armchairs. The notebook was on my lap. "I'm trying to remember when Tobey opened the gallery," I said.

"It was almost nine years ago. He had been living in Texas, in Austin, working for one of the big dealers there. That's how we met. I was visiting my sister and we were out shopping and looking at antiques. I was hoping to find something for my business here. Tobey helped us in the store. He was very handsome."

"And he wanted to have his own shop?"

"Yes, one day. He was spending some time in Austin learning the business, he already seemed to know about the objects themselves. We went out a couple of times and then I had to come back here and he came down to visit me. It was then he got the idea to open a gallery here, because of all the gringos. He thought his business might fit well with mine. There is much money here, as I think you know."

"Do you know what he did before that?"

"Something with money." She shook her head. "Was it banking? I think I never knew exactly. He seemed to not want to look back on that time."

"Did he say that?"

"It was mainly that he would change the subject if it came up."

"So you were married here?"

"Yes. His family lives in Minnesota. They came down for the wedding, and then once again, later."

"And did he have the money to open a gallery?"

"Oh yes, he didn't have to get a loan, like from his family."

"Did you work with him in the gallery?"

"Well, at first I did, but I had limited time because of *Estilo San Miguel*, my studio."

"You already had this when you met him?"

"Yes, for two years already at that time. He thought he could be a source of antiques for my clients."

"And did it work out that way?"

"Very much. I would tell him that this or that client wanted a particular look and often he was able to find things that worked. It was a good connection for him when he was getting started and later as well. There was no other place like this in San Miguel." Her hand made a sweeping gesture that took in the space. "*La Fábrica Aurora* hadn't opened yet. Having his gallery available helped my business grow more because I always had first choice of the better things, even before his other clients saw them. After a while I was so busy I had little time to help him."

"But he didn't hire anyone else, did he?"

"No."

"What sorts of things did Tobey supply to your clients?" I said.

"Mostly pictures, but sometimes ceramics and silver as well, like the tall candlesticks you see here. They are very popular." She gestured to the display table against the wall.

"I don't mean to suggest there was anything wrong with your business, Marisol, but were any of your clients unhappy with things that were furnished by Tobey?"

"No. Never."

I had no follow up question after that. "Marisol, thank you. That's about all for tonight. I'll talk to you again tomorrow after I think about this for a while. I have a friend who is a retired detective from the States. I might ask him to help us with this, if that's OK with you?"

She nodded.

Maya asked if Marisol wanted her to stay, but she said she just wanted to try to sleep now, and thanked us for coming. When we got back home it was after midnight. We sat in the *loggia* for a while, not ready or able to sleep.

"I don't know that I can be much help," I said. "I'm sorry, but this is so far out of my depth." I gave her my best Mexican shrug, which in its nuances can express anything from the most minor of uncertainties to the complete incomprehensibility of the universe. It's much in use here.

"Just to come with me is a help to her," said Maya, who had a way of embracing another person's problems with an iron grip. It didn't happen often, but I could see that she was taking this case seriously. "Now she feels it isn't only the police working on it. She said before she was afraid the police wouldn't try very hard because Tobey was a gringo. Sometimes it seems like they don't try very hard at anything. Aside from that key, did you get any ideas?"

We had turned the lights on in the garden, mostly small wattage ground level things that lit the bottoms of the leaves. You didn't notice them in the day.

"Well, what we have is a business that's just a facade. No customers, no records, no accounting. I was struck by what she said about Tobey's view of computers, and I didn't buy it. There was also no appointment book for today's meeting with whoever killed him. Just inventory, and from the look of it, first class inventory. Where does he get it?"

"Marisol has said he is gone a lot either on buying trips or to see clients."

I put my feet up on one of the wicker chairs next to me. I had no idea what time it was.

"Of course the 132 must be an address," I said. "I suppose in the morning we should start looking, but I'd like to paint a bit first. If it is an address it's going to be on the edge of *centro*, so let's walk the town afterward." Street numbers radiate outward from the *jardín*, but by the time they reach a point halfway between one and two hundred, the street name is often changed and they start over at one. "We can get a duplicate made and I'll take east/west and you take north/south, trying the key in any door with a 132 number."

"And if someone comes to the door?"

"Act confused, say you are looking for someone. Say you met a guy who gave you a key last night in a bar but you forgot the street name."

"And is that something I would do?" She folded

her arms.

"No, but people might like to think that about you. They won't argue if you say it."

We got a late start in the morning. Maya was a little weepy when she realized that the nasty reality of the night before was still with us, but I got her seated on the hassock and finished her face and began working on her body. The line of her back was not right so I had to pull that in a bit and I'm not sure I was at my best either. Neither of us had much to say, which is good for painting because for the artist at work the conversation-making part of the brain is mostly shut down anyway. After I got her back right I didn't have the momentum to go on to her shoulder, which requires a lot of subtle shading to get the modeling right, and we knocked off with a shorter session than I wanted. While she was dressing the phone rang. It was Marisol. I told her our plan for the day and she said someone had called for Tobey. The caller would not say his name, and when she said Tobey had been killed he was silent, and then hung up without saying any more.

"A Spanish speaker?" I said. It would have been an odd lapse in *cortesía* for a Mexican to hang up like that.

"Yes, but by his accent he sounds Yucatan, I think."

"Has he called before?"

"I am not certain. Maybe he reached Tobey if he did. There are two phone lines and he called on the one in the gallery. I usually didn't answer that phone during the day, when, you know, when Toby..."

As she struggled with this I passed the phone to Maya and finished cleaning my brushes while she asked Marisol how she was doing.

We had a quick and early lunch and put on our walking shoes. I had the key copied at a little shop on the edge of *centro* down on Hidalgo, and we split up, each with our cell phones. In about two hours I found six places with the 132 street number, but the key fit the lock to none of them. Trying the key and then walking away brought me a few strange looks. I had not heard from Maya. I was hoping she was a better detective than I was when my cell phone rang.

She had found eight places to try but turned up no lock that fit the key either and was headed back to our starting point. We stopped for a coffee at Las Terrazas, a small restaurant overlooking the *jardín,* our main plaza. It looked like another perfect day for everyone but us. Tourists sat there and watched the balloon and ice cream sellers. A few were reading *Atención*. I was shaking my head as I stirred my coffee.

"Nothing," I said. "More nothing."

"I had one thing. A man came to the door at one house. I said I'd been given the key by a man I met in a bar. He said he had a bar at the edge of his garden if I wanted to come in for a drink." She smiled without irony.

"Did you?"

"No. I said I was high on life. Then I called again to Marisol. She is going to her mother's in Guanajuato tomorrow. She needs to be away from the house for a while."

"I can see that."

"I thought we could visit her before she left. Give her a report on the key search."

"Not much to tell," I said.

"I think she'd like to see us, to make her feel like

something is happening."

"OK."

"You know, there's Perry Watt's party tomorrow night. Are you going to be able to forget about this and have a good time?" Maya was always our social director, even in crisis.

I thought for a while. "Could it be a locker at the bus station? You know, locker #132? Or are we just blowing smoke here?"

"You would be seeing Barbara Watt again," she said. "She always gets you going."

CHAPTER THREE

Perry and Barbara Watt's house suggested an attraction from a colonial México theme park. The low, dense foliage around the horseshoe drive within the walls, masked floodlights that illuminated the facade, throwing the architectural details into deep relief. It might have been the mansion of an eighteenth century silver baron. When the Spaniards settled central México in the mid-sixteenth century San Miguel had grown and prospered as a transfer point for silver from the Guanajuato region, especially the great Valenciana mine.

From the look the house might also have been a *hacienda*, except that nothing agricultural had ever happened there. It was less than ten years old. The neighborhood, Los Balcones, was a gringo enclave that ran for half a mile along the northeastern rim of San Miguel and crept slightly down the hill. Similar, but less grand mansions stretched along the crest as well. If the silver barons ever returned, the local builders would be ready for them, better than ever. The old skills don't die here.

Maya and I were dwarfed as we walked through a pair of wrought iron gates set in the ten-foot high wall. At the house the door must have been ten feet high as well, crafted of thick mahogany planks and studded with more wrought iron. Four scrolling hinges snaked across almost the entire width of it. Going through it felt like entering an important place. The house was two stories high, done in bull's blood red stucco, and the sills and casings of the windows were all carved from *cantera* limestone. Two huge wrought iron lanterns flanked the door, and on the left were large bow windows on both floors. Just below the parapet, iron gutters with gargoyle heads projected three or four feet from the house. They reminded me of those on Notre Dame Cathedral, but the Watts probably worshipped something else here, possibly money. Everyone needs religion. Within the main floor window on the left we could see the crowd milling around a grand piano as we rang the bell.

There is a large group of artists in San Miguel that I don't hang out with much, but this was not my normal social set either. Maya was a social director with a business head and we had done some schmoozing with this group before. She doesn't mind working the crowd if there's a sale to be made. With a little urging, I don't either, although I don't toot my own horn as readily as she toots it for me.

At that moment Barbara Watt opened the door and stepped out.

"Oh I'm so glad you could come!" She pecked us both on each cheek and took my hand and pulled me in. I hadn't seen her in some time but I hadn't forgotten how stunning she was. She was a genuine blonde with milk and rose petal skin, and lips that seemed about to whisper enticing secrets in your ear. Or mine. She was wearing a sheer periwinkle blue dress that clung to her in the right places as she moved with an animal elegance. Barbara was about twenty-seven or twenty-eight to Perry's forty-five. It was his second marriage, and although I'd never met his first wife, this time he appeared to have gotten it right.

"Let me get you a drink. What would you like? Perry's making *mojitos* tonight—you heard he snuck off to Cuba again, didn't you? It's his new thing. He tried to meet Castro but I guess he's too old now. Not Perry, Fidel. But he did bring back about a dozen boxes of Monte Cristos too. I know you like those, Paul." Her fingers touched my cheek as if accidentally.

"We'll have *mojitos* then, right Paul?" said Maya. She was nodding too vigorously which told me she was not fully at ease. Barbara led us toward the bar. Her dress was open to the waist behind and her back was smooth and firm and all one color.

I spotted Perry behind the bar in the great room. It seemed odd to me that he would be mixing drinks when he had staff, but maybe it was some new expertise for him. Maybe he didn't trust a Mexican bar tender to mix a Cuban drink. He was immaculate, as usual, with an even tan and smooth, brushed-back hair just going gray at his ears. His jaw was firm and authoritative, and his motions quick and exact. You felt he rarely dropped anything; once something was in his grip it stayed there until he chose to let go of it.

"Hey Paul, Maya, how about a drink? You've got to try these *mojitos*. Simple syrup, fresh mint, a little club soda, and I brought back the damnedest Cuban rum. Got it up in Santiago, in Oriente Province. Same family's been making it since 1820. Fidel drinks it himself." Standing behind the marble-topped bar Perry began crushing fresh mint into two glasses. Then abruptly he stopped.

"My God! Of course you've heard about Tobey Cross. You were friends, right? I'm so sorry." He stood with a glass in one hand and his head cocked to the left. Although he was below average height he was dressed in an old fashioned velvet jacket that defied fashion, that said fashion was a concern of people with less money than he had, and had the kind of strong presence that made you see him at the head of a boardroom table. People probably jumped out of his way when he entered a room. "The whole community is just reeling," he said. I was looking over the crowd. No one appeared to be reeling. Maybe later in the evening, after a few more of his mojitos. At the side of the piano a large woman I had never seen before began to laugh in a voice that must have been audible outside. I wondered who she knew to get in. This was clearly the best ticket in San Miguel that night. Two couples were dancing nearby.

"I didn't know Tobey very well, but Marisol and Maya are good friends," I said. Maya's eyes were starting to well up. "We spent some time with her today before she went to her mother's place in Guanajuato." Perry nodded sympathetically.

"What are the police saying? Was it a burglary? I know he had some great things there."

"It's hard to tell. Marisol said she never knew much about his antiques business. She didn't know what he had, or what was valuable and what wasn't, or even if anything is missing, but nothing was obviously gone. She asked me to take a look at it because she's not sure how much the police will do, since Tobey was a gringo, and people here don't trust the police much anyway. She thinks I might see things they might not; you know, being a painter."

Perry looked at me speculatively. "Well, I'm sure that's true."

"Oh, it is true in a way, but maybe not the right way. What I usually see are the colors in shadows, the levels of contrast, the relationship of curves to each other." My eyes came to rest on Barbara, who had a lot of curvy relationships on view. "It's not so clear that I can see a murderer five hours after he's left the crime scene, or see a reason for the crime. Tobey had his inventory arranged in that great room just as a collector would have it. If there were two or even three pieces missing I'm not sure it would be obvious. Plus, Marisol says he never kept any money in the house, not real money anyway."

Perry nodded. He must have known what was meant by real money. Probably not the same thing I meant. Three zeros on a check were a lot for me. I thought about the twenty-centavo coin in Tobey's mouth, but I didn't bring it up. Although I couldn't get the murder out of my mind, this was a party and I didn't want to be on duty. I felt like I'd already had too much duty in the last couple of days.

Perry was still staring off somewhere when he discovered the unfinished drink in his hand. He turned around and pulled a cut glass pitcher out of the Sub-Zero refrigerator. I didn't know you could get Sub-Zero in México. Most of the ones I had seen here were made by Mabe, which I always pronounced "maybe." Sometimes they worked, other times they didn't. It was usually when you had just bought fresh meat that they didn't. Mexicans thought of this as fate. I turned to look at Maya but she was being led off toward the piano by a slender sixtyish guy I knew from the English Library crowd. This was the group that ran a tour of San Miguel houses every Sunday. The tourists flocked to it at fifteen bucks a head. His name was Walt Teller. I took the drinks from Perry and threaded my way through the crowd.

Maya had recovered her composure now and wore that look of slightly formal cheerfulness she used with the expatriates she didn't know. She looked better than ever tonight in a black broomstick skirt she had gotten on our last trip to Santa Fe and the finely knit sleeveless turquoise top that set off her form and coloring. Simple things worked best for her. On her right wrist was one of her *Huichol* bracelets, a rainbow of colors done in superfine glass beads. I think it was the same one she was wearing when we met. A necklace of alternating beads and seashells in old Mexican silver graced her neck. I passed her the drink. The young piano player was working his way through the Thelonius Monk songbook.

"It's you, isn't it! I know it's you," Walt Teller was saying to Maya as he pointed to a picture on the wall behind the piano player.

It was an early full length nude of Maya from about four years ago, not long after we got together. Her hair was shorter then and had some curl, but not a lot, and came just over her shoulders on both sides. She stood with one hip thrust out and both hands meeting over her pubic hair, one over the other. There was a saucy glint in her eye that seemed to say, "Guess what I've got for you?" It didn't require much speculation.

This picture is a favorite of mine, although I think now I might use less chrome oxide green in the shadows that fell directly on her skin, but that's the way I painted then. You can't go back. A picture either stands up over time or it doesn't. In this case it's still fun to look at. I wish that were true of all of them. In our house there were pictures I'd kept for years, and the test for each of them is always the same—did you continue to look at it when you walked past? If one started to become invisible, I sent it off for Galería Uno to sell and hung something else in its place.

"Of course Perry wishes she had her hands behind her back." Barbara's voice came from behind us. I felt her hand on my shoulder. Maya was beaming now, even to Walt. Modesty was never her thing anyway, that's why she's such a great model.

Walt led Maya off to introduce her to someone else and Barbara took my hand. Her palm was warm and dry and her thumb probed the pulse in my wrist, which immediately picked up speed. Her left hand hung at her side, weighed down by the emerald cut diamond on her ring finger.

"Perry is really concerned about Tobey's murder. He almost canceled the party, but then I persuaded him it might raise people's spirits, so he went ahead with it."

"He's a civic-minded guy; he wants to support morale in the gringo community." I said. I was listening to something in her voice. She was from the deep South, and from the way she spoke, well educated. Even as she held my hand she touched my other arm, then my shoulder. She looked earnestly into my eyes as if I was about to say something important that she couldn't bear to miss. I couldn't think what it would be.

"Alabama," I said.

Stopped in mid-stride, she smiled as she paused

just an instant, and said, "Montgomery."

We passed Maya with a different English Library ex-pat. "So tell me about your book," he was saying. We paused close enough to listen.

"Well," she began. "It's about Ignacio Allende, one of the revolutionaries of 1810, but it hasn't been published yet."

"Mel," he said, "It's Mel."

She nodded.

"OK, Mel, It's about his early years. Not much has been written about his life before 1810. It took a lot of research and more time than I wanted, but there's a wonderful archive in Dolores Hidalgo."

"Didn't he end up with his head on the corner of the granary in Guanajuato?"

"Yes, with three others. It was a short life, but very important to México. Now I'm doing some research for an old professor of mine. He's working on a book about the role of the Indian groups during the War of Independence."

"Are you still posing for Paul?" Mel was already focused back on the picture. He probably didn't read much history.

"Oh, yes. He's doing a whole series set in the Yucatan. He's having a show in Mérida in June. You'll have to come."

"I'd love to."

When Barbara excused herself to greet some newcomers Bob and Sarah O'Brien drifted over toward me. I nodded to them. "Still spending most of your time in México City?"

"I am, but Sarah's here most of the time."

Bob was about five-ten, a couple inches shorter than I am, with a red face and iron gray hair. "How's the merger going?" I asked.

He worked for the Burlington Northern Santa Fe Railroad and had spent the last couple of years mainly in México City overseeing a merger with a Mexican line.

"It's OK. It's taken a little more time than I had hoped, but what doesn't in México? Lots of paper work. Greasing the rails here and there." He waited to see if I'd gotten the pun.

"How's your Spanish coming?" I asked.

"Not coming at all, really. They all speak English anyway. You don't speak English, you can't do business here. Right, Sarah?"

"I guess, Bob." Sarah had a lot of gray blonde hair that fanned out toward her neck as if each strand was demanding its own space.

"Still liking México City?" I asked.

"Love it," said Bob. "I haven't been kidnapped or mugged even once. We just bought a house there. I can't make up my mind whether it's better there or here. Might as well have two houses. No reason to decide."

"Maybe if you factor in the air quality and the traffic," I suggested.

Sarah was scanning the crowd, as if looking for someone more important than me to talk to. "I'd like another one of these," she said to Bob, holding out her glass toward him. Crushed mint leaves clung to the bottom.

Bob went off toward the bar where Perry was still mixing drinks and I crossed the room in the direction of the terrace. Outside there was a lower level, as well as the upper terrace to the Watts' house. I went down the broad stairs to a garden full of low palms, none high enough to block the view from the terrace, mixed with bromeliads and split leaf philodendrons. I thought I might be able to use it as background for one of Maya's Yucatan series. Past the low wall at the edge of the steep slope was the tile roof of the house below, about twenty feet down. Along the side wall was a swimming pool with a pool house that had the same detailing as the main house. Inside the pool house hung a still life of mine, showing a precarious pile of colored canvas tennis hats. I had titled it *Stacked*.

Three or four people bobbed in the pool. The surface captured curls of light from the house and the garden lights as the swimmers moved. The sudden violence of Tobey's death had kept me from getting into a party mood. Besides, Maya and I were not part of these people. We weren't golf club people and we weren't gated community people. If the arts community hadn't been valued in San Miguel more than in most places, we wouldn't have been invited. We lived with our Mexican neighbors, and they lived with us. We weren't business movers and shakers, or merger managers. Another *mojito* and I might be able to figure out which people we were. Painters never quite fit in with this crowd, and Mexican girlfriends were rare among the expatriates. I couldn't think of a single one besides Maya.

"Paul, there you are. Come on up. I want to show you some new things."

Perry was standing backlit with three others on the second floor terrace above the garden. I couldn't see his face but I knew which one he was because he was the shortest of the four. Short in stature, big in business, I thought. Barbara was about five-eight, model material, but

Perry was two inches shorter. I wondered how they met.

Coming up the terrace steps, I passed through the great room and went to the second floor. I heard Perry saying in his soft Houston voice, "So I just have a few more recent things I wanted to show you. Come on in, Paul. You're going to like this." Walt was next to me, with two others. One was Bill Frost, who had been an investment banker in Canada, and next to him was a man named Clare Mason. I had met him before and remembered he was from Kansas City.

"Well," Perry was going on, "you know how it was in the later days of the Roman Empire." Like we all did. Like we thought about it at night when we couldn't sleep. "Everybody wanted to get their money out. These coins are aureii from Yugoslavia, or what was until recently called Yugoslavia. Anyway, the Romans had a major town around Split on the Adriatic Coast. These are from a big hoard there. They were excavated just inside the wall of a country estate."

Perry pulled a tray from a rosewood cabinet. Three dozen gold coins were evenly spaced on a green crushed velvet background. They bore the effigies of the bullnecked, thick-jawed military emperors of the later empire. They were perfect models for Mussolini macho. The condition was unbelievable for coins 1800 years old, but then they hadn't circulated much as they waited for their owners to return and dig them up. Perry caught my eye.

"Paul, take a look at these."

"Wait Perry, what are coins like these worth?" said Bill Frost. "I mean, where have they been for the last 2000 years?"

"Well," said Perry, in that voice of the ultimate connoisseur that none of the rest of us could hope to match without a lifetime of study, "they've been in that small hole in Yugoslavia until about eight years ago. Coming out, in this condition, they're basically worth three to twelve thousand dollars apiece. A few might go higher."

"Jesus," said Bill. "What do you look for when you're buying these?"

"Well, rarity, of course, but also quality of the strike. They were all made by hand, with the celator, the striker, if you will, holding the cast metal disc between two dies and hitting it with a hammer. Quality was uneven from the day they were made. Naturally for your collection you want the best quality strike with the least wear."

I was amazed at their survival in this state but they still reminded me a lot of World War II propaganda. The psychology of brute force hasn't changed much.

"Paul, you'll connect with these." Perry pulled out the second drawer. "Here's where the connoisseur's eye really comes into play." The others were looking at me as he said this, but he must have been referring to his own expertise.

More gold, but of a different mindset. Maybe twenty coins, smaller in diameter, but thicker. The faces glowed with the flash of galloping horses, and the reverses were crowded with ripe heads of wheat, bent over in the wind, the motion palpable on the surface. The style of each leaped out with its own individuality. These were not from people who ever marched in formation or wore uniforms. I had never seen anything like them.

"Think one word: the Celts. The untamed spirit

of the British Isles, mostly around 40 to 60 A.D.—I never use that 'Before Current Era' bullshit. It's B.C. or A.D. These were the people the Romans were running down. This was the soul of a different kind of England, one before welfare checks and housing estates, and dowdy old queens. And young ones. The original Brits had a lot of nerve."

Sometimes Perry surprised me. Barbara had once said to me that he thought of himself as a Renaissance prince, a collector on a grand scale, a true patron of the arts. Perhaps from the Houston branch of the Medici.

"Most of these came from the estate of an Englishman named Mossop," Perry continued.

"He must have been quite a connoisseur," I said.

"Actually, his primary claim to fame was that he was the first man in Britain to own a metal detector. It was right after World War II and they had adapted the technology from hand held mine detectors. He didn't know much about anything, but he had one great idea. Sometimes that's all you need. He traveled to all the ancient sites and dug up whatever beeped. He had everything made of metal, from belt buckles to door knobs."

All of us looked blankly at Perry. I was trying to picture a Roman doorknob and not having much luck.

"I went to the estate auction in London," he continued. "The British Museum had first refusal on a lot of it."

"So," I said, "that means the British Museum has a better example of all these coins, and that's why they let you take them?"

Perry looked chagrined. "Yes, unfortunately. But I guess if you have to be second best to someone..." It must have been a new experience for him.

From below us on the terrace I could hear a group of *mariachis* singing an old Cuban song about two gardenias. We were in Perry's study, a large room where the walls were old gold as well, and hung with seventeenth and eighteenth century devotional paintings and knightly ancestors of a kind fairly common in México, but rarely seen in this condition. No paint was chipped, and none of the canvases were bulged or dimpled. The frames were correct and of the period. They were as perfectly restored as the ones I had seen in Tobey's Galería Cruz. On another wall four Navajo rugs tried to fit in. I guess quality complements quality. Perry's glance followed mine. I thought the scale of the rug designs overwhelmed the room.

"All natural dyes, mostly late nineteenth century. That one on the left end is a very rare Two Gray Hills from about 1905."

In a tall cabinet near the door were six fine Mayan ceramic pieces. Most were of the same quality as I had seen at Tobey's. A couple were a little more beaten up, missing minor parts here and there. I wanted to take a closer look, but Perry was still holding court at the coin cabinet. Something occurred to me.

"Perry, have you ever thought about being an artist yourself?" I asked, thinking that collecting might be a substitute for artistic ability. You could own it, even if you couldn't make it yourself.

"Well," he hesitated a moment as if recalling a former state of mind, "yes I did. But Dad needed me to go into the business. I was the only son."

"I suppose he wouldn't pay for art school." Just like mine, I thought. I'd gone on my own dime, working as a part-time cabinetmaker.

"Actually, he didn't pay for any school. He thought that if I was going to run Watt Industries I needed to show I could make my own way. See, Dad had some oil drilling equipment patents that dovetailed nicely with what Hughes Tool was offering. He had worked for Howard when he first started out, and in the process he developed some good ideas of his own. I took up lock-smithing and put myself through a degree in petroleum engineering. But the closest I ever got to art was being a collector. I guess it's OK. You didn't cross Dad. Maybe if my family had been poor I'd be a painter now."

"And still be poor."

"Possibly. It's a long time ago, now. You make your choices."

"And collect your regrets?" asked Bill Frost, looking him in the eye. There was something I liked about Frost, and not all of it was on the surface.

"Let me put it this way," said Perry, after thinking about it for a moment. "When I took over Watt Industries after Dad died, it was like taking over someone's truck full of goods, you know? The inventory was all there, the route was determined, all I had to do was drive it, make my deliveries and collect the money. But at that time it still said Del Watt Industries on the side of the truck. That was OK, but I wanted my own truck. In the end I drove Dad's truck anyway, and I've done all right. The company stock's tripled since he died, and it's only been seven years. But I always took art and collecting even more seriously. I've reached the point where my eye is as good as anyone's on this planet. I don't mind saying that it's really what I do best. Watt Industries is there to finance my habit. I dropped the Del part a year after he died. It's a subsidiary of Perry Watt now. I'd set myself up against any so-called expert in any of the fields where I collect. Check my library some time; I've got more than twenty-five books on Navajo rugs alone, most of them out of print."

Bill Frost nodded, as if he were seeing a new side of Perry.

Clare Mason was shifting his weight from one foot to the other as if this was more than he wanted to know. Walt Teller said nothing.

I felt an arm curl around mine. "Can I talk to you for a moment?" Maya said in my ear.

"Excuse me, Perry. Wonderful collection." We headed back down to the piano room. "You're the most beautiful woman here," I said to her.

"Better than the *güera* (blonde)?"

"Even on her best day." This was not quite true, but it may have reflected the fact that I was more interested in Maya than anyone else.

"If it's all right with you, I'd like to go soon, I'm feeling bad about Tobey and Marisol."

"OK. Let's dance to a couple of these tunes for a moment because I want to check on something upstairs when the crowd thins." She gave me a puzzled look, but then the piano player launched into *These Foolish Things* and we moved across the floor, although there was not much that was foolish about Maya. She was an unusual mix of higher education and the kind of practicality that people with nothing needed to survive. I pressed her close and my hand moved up and down her back. Barbara drifted past on the arm of a gringo I didn't know, and then he took her hand and they began to dance. The room was big enough for thirty couples if they avoided the sofas.

After ten minutes I saw Perry and the others come down the grand staircase and he went back to the bar and started mixing mojitos again. There was a satisfied look on his face as he worked. As much pleasure as he took in what he owned, he clearly needed to share it as well. It was important to him that we knew how much he knew, if we did.

"Talk to Perry a little," I said to Maya. "I don't want him coming back upstairs. You know how you always say you can be very charming?" She nodded, smiling now. "This would be the occasion to turn it on."

"Show him a little skin?" But she knew that wasn't what I meant.

"I don't think that will be necessary this time. He's already got that picture." I nodded at the wall over the piano.

No one was watching me as I moved off to the kitchen, knowing that in a house of this size and pretension there would be a servants' staircase. In the pantry, platters were being assembled with tiny sandwiches and miniature quiches. There were trays of champagne glasses. The kitchen was vibrating with activity. No one had time to look at me as I headed for the back hallway and climbed the stairs.

On the second floor I emerged from a doorway that looked just like three others. I took note which one it was and crossed the corridor to Perry's study. No one else was in view. I slipped into the room through the partly opened door and closed it behind me. The lights were still on and the coin trays were back in the cabinet. I scanned the two walls of bookshelves where Perry stored his expertise when he wasn't showing it off, then took a survey of the room, trying to record the detail. I had a good visual memory from the exercises in art school where the model would take a break but the students would all keep painting from recollection. The trick was to focus on a particular detail, say the shape of an ear or a mole on a hand, and then place that detail in context. Some people thought it was voodoo, but with enough practice it could be done.

My context this time was the desktop, and I felt a twinge of anxiety as I sat down. I opened a few drawers, but they contained nothing unusual. The top held a notepad with a leather cover, a thick fountain pen with an opalescent finish and gold nib, a phone with three lines, a Rolodex, and a silver framed picture of Perry and Barbara. She wore a voluminous wedding dress, her hair up and she was not much younger. They were standing next to a vintage Bentley, older than she was, in front of tall wrought iron gates. Through the gates the entry of a massive Georgian style brick mansion was visible at the end of a long drive. It had to be the Watt family compound. Georgian architecture always means old money, especially when it isn't.

I lifted the lid on the Rolodex and flipped through it randomly. The usual expatriates with phone numbers and spouse's names in a neat masculine hand. Stopping at C, however, there was no card for Cross, Tobey. Under G, nothing for Galería Cruz. Under Z, no Zacher, Paul. But under S, I found Sanchez, Maria. It had our current phone number, not her old one.

I wasn't sure what this meant. The Watts' acquaintance with Maya and me dated only two years back, but I was beginning to feel more like a common snoop than a detective, poking around in other people's business when they had graciously invited me into their house. I had come back upstairs to examine the Mayan ceramics, which Perry glossed over when he gave his tour.

I stopped and listened, then crossed to the cabinet. It was not locked. Of the six pieces, all but one were vessels. Two were cylinder forms, one squat and the other about twice as high. The shallow one had two minute chips on the rim. The exposed clay looked dark and earthy, not like the pale interiors of our own crockery. There was one figure, whether human or divine I couldn't tell for certain; it may have been a vessel as well. I didn't want to handle it to see whether the top came off. One was a shallow bowl or deep plate with incised animal figures. The other two were deeper bowls also with figures, one with jaguars, one with humans.

I studied the incised figures in detail on each one, and it confirmed my first, cursory impression. Looking at them this closely, I wished I had examined the ones at Galería Cruz better. But from what I remembered these could easily be from the same area and period.

Everyone knows that fingerprints are unique. The combination of hand, eye, and mind leaves a distinctive mark too, but one that is not as well understood by the police and probably not admissible in a court of law. I had the strong feeling that these ceramics were all made by the same hand. As little as I knew about Mayan pottery, I still had little doubt about their common authorship—they had the same feel to me. I can't explain it better than that. As I pushed the cabinet door shut I heard the creak of the parquet floorboards outside on the stair landing.

I whirled around. To the right of the cabinet was a door fit flawlessly into the paneling; I slipped through it and found myself in a powder room. I locked the door and turned on the light. It was done in Perry's understated style. Gold faucets rose like trumpets from the onyx counter and gold towel bars held mahogany-colored deep-pile towels. Liquid soap was available from a Baccarat crystal dispenser. I was straining to listen to someone moving around in the study, and as I turned to press my ear to the door I glimpsed something shocking in the mirror over the sink.

Being a painter requires a fair degree of confidence and an outgoing temperament, since you're also a salesman. But what I saw tonight was a nasty sheepish look on my own face, as if I had been about to slip a few of Perry's Roman coins into my pocket or poke around in Barbara's underwear drawer. It was not a look I had ever seen before in a mirror and not one I ever wanted to see again. I couldn't imagine that a detective ever had that expression as he worked, and decided I had to change my frame of mind. A drawer in the study closed and then the hallway door opened and closed again. Then welcome silence.

I waited a while without any idea whether the visitor had been Perry or just another snoop like me. When I opened the hallway door from the study a crack there was no one on the landing and I slipped out and went back down through the kitchen. In the great room more couples were dancing and I got no strange looks. No one had missed me. Perry was no longer at the bar, and Maya was at the piano talking to Clare Mason. I touched her shoulder.

"I think I'm ready now. Let me say goodbye."

Maya looked relieved. As I moved off I tucked a fifty-peso note into an oversize brandy snifter by the music stand. The piano player smiled and nodded while he played. I found Walt and shook hands, promising to come to the house tour again soon. It was probably time for us to put our place on it. Suddenly the *güera* was by my side. She grasped my hand in both of hers and looked into my eyes. Her index finger was rubbing my pulse again, which didn't fail to respond. Then my index finger was rubbing her pulse. This was her game. Some people would stick their face too closely into yours to make a point, Barbara would find something to touch. It felt like intimacy, but it was more like power. Whatever it was, it worked. Maya watched us narrowly from the doorway.

"I have some business for you, something I think you'll like," Barbara said.

"Hmmm?"

"I'd like you to paint a nude of me, like you always do of Maya. Just for a record, you know? In case I don't always look like this. What do you think? Perry will buy it, of course."

"Call me," I said. "We'll set something up." She kissed me on the cheek, lingering half a second longer than necessary. "Great party," I said. "I look forward to seeing you." It wasn't small talk, I already knew how to do the shadows. The skin tones would be challenging; I'd never painted a blond nude in México.

As we moved toward the door something that had been bothering me all evening came into focus. San Miguel is a gossipy town. The gringo population of 8,000 acts like a town within a town. News travels rapidly. If Tobey had sold his gallery for a million dollars everyone would have been talking about it tonight, but no one had said a word about his death, except Perry as we walked in. The silence was as big as a billboard; the underlying message was clear. Tobey had not been robbed, therefore he was murdered by a gringo. One of us. Maybe someone at the party. That was why no one brought it up, other than Perry's brief mention.

Outside the night was black. San Miguel after hours didn't generate enough wattage to light the sky, although possibly Barbara did. I kissed Maya and we walked down the hill toward our house on Quebrada. The street name means broke or bankrupt. It seemed like a good choice when I bought there. Some months it still is, but it seemed like this wouldn't be one of them.

I thought about Perry and the difference between making and collecting. When I was first starting out I copied pictures I wanted to own, as a kind of test, I suppose. Some Georges de la Tour and other old masters, an Alfred Sisley, and a couple of Juarez Machado, a Brazilian painter whose show I had seen in Paris before I came to San Miguel. Even two Diego Riveras. I found I could copy just about anything, but it wasn't the same as doing original work. Just collecting was probably even less satisfying. Maybe Barbara was part of Perry's collection; one of the more satisfying parts.

As for the Mayan ceramics portion of his collection, I couldn't see how you could assemble six pieces by the same maker. Perhaps if they all came from one dig, or if the excavator had come across a buried potter's studio. Or maybe the Mayans themselves had been collectors, and this group came from some wealthy household that had patronized a single preferred artisan. Unfortunately the only expert I had ever known was no longer available for consultation.

"Did anyone else, besides Perry, mention Tobey's death to you?" I asked, as we came down Calvario to Calle San Francisco.

"No. That's odd, isn't it? Maybe the gringos don't talk about death at parties like we do."

"It's probably a little of that, but I would have expected something, nonetheless. Did you sense a particular discomfort about bringing it up? Because I did."

"You're thinking they were imagining one of them had done it and looking around to see who it might be?" she asked.

"It did cross my mind."

Maybe it was because she sensed my discomfort as well that she waited until we were almost home before she asked what I'd been doing upstairs.

CHAPTER FOUR
RAMON XOC

At ten minutes after four in the morning in the ancient Mayan city of Izamal, his home town, Ramon Xoc stood outside the bus station. A small, neatly dressed man in his mid thirties, he was waiting for the four-thirty bus to Mérida, the capital of the state of Yucatán. He wore a *guayabera*, the traditional white sisal shirt of the Yucatán native, and a fine Panama-style hat, woven by one of his cousins from a minute hamlet not far out of town. In one hand he carried a battered suitcase, that more than twenty-five years before, when his father had purchased it, had nearly passed for leather, and in the other, a custom made wooden case, nearly the same size as the suitcase, but thicker, and covered in canvas. Ramon had made this himself.

The dim light from the station barely lit the faces of the few people waiting with him for the first bus of the day; two women who could have been mother and daughter, sitting on a bench with a sleeping boy between them, and an older man with two plastic bags and the same slender build and sun-darkened skin as Ramon. But where this man's hands had the coarse, roughened look of field work, Ramon's were long and graceful, with only traces of some residue under his fingernails to suggest he too worked at manual labor, but of a different kind.

Since Izamal was the first stop of the morning, the local bus was on time. Ramon checked his suitcase in the compartment below, but kept the wooden case beside him on the seat. His face was impassive and he avoided looking at the other passengers. His wide cheekbones and intelligent eyes spoke of his Mayan ancestors; his thick black hair came neatly to a widow's peak on his forehead, but his looks were marred by teeth of uneven quality. On a black cord around his neck was a jade pendant of the Sun God, invisible beneath his shirt. From time to time, as the bus threaded its way over the narrow road through the jungle, slowing here and there for the inevitable tricycle drawn carts, Ramon's hand moved to feel its form under the cloth. From a dozen years of research he was sophisticated enough about antiques to know it dated from the eighth century. He had discovered it when he was seventeen, in a mound of ancient stones less than two miles from his house.

The bus maintained an unhurried pace as it bounced along the road. Ramon kept the impassive look on his face, even though he was worried this morning.

After three brief stops in smaller villages, the bus pulled onto the Periférico, the circular highway around Mérida, just after six o'clock. The glare of the sun was creeping downward through the buildings, knifing along the narrow streets, and the temperature had already climbed into the mid-seventies The dense humidity was unchanged from the night.

Because Mérida was the state capital, Ramon was able to catch the Mercedes Benz expreso bus direct to México City—a luxury he could afford. He did well (in

Mexican terms) in his business, but the expense was also a necessity, because Ramon was in a hurry. He had even considered catching a plane, but that required showing identification, and until he knew what was going on, he wanted to leave no record of having made this trip. This anonymity was costly; it would be eighteen hours before he reached México City, and from there it would be another four hours to Dolores Hidalgo.

Despite the top-of-the-line comfort of the Mercedes bus, Ramon slept fitfully. Once in México City he struggled through the crowd at the bus station, full of travelers even at midnight, bought the ticket for the last leg of his trip, and settled down to wait for an hour, trying to stay awake.

Izamal, where Ramon had spent his entire life, was an ancient city of about 14,000; much less important today than it had been to the Mayans in the fourth century, when it was founded. Originally a major ceremonial center, it was now a market town for local farmers. People called it the Yellow City because for block after block the buildings were painted a vivid shade of ochre. On the property of Ramon's family generations of the Xocs had lived, first in the old Mayan house with the palapa roof of palm leaves on the back of the lot. After that, with their walled garden in front, they had lived for the last hundred years in the newer house, facing the street. His two older brothers had started families and moved on, and only his mother remained. To her embarrassment, he had never married. When Ramon was sixteen his father had been injured when he was thrown from a truck full of agricultural workers. He lingered for two days in the hospital in Mérida, and then died without regaining consciousness.

His older brothers filled the void financially while Ramon remained in school.

For several years before his father's death, Ramon had been fascinated by the Mayan ruins that still dotted the city. The church and convent complex of St. Anthony, at the center of Izamal, sat on an immense platform that had originally held an enormous pyramid, one of the largest in Central America. In the sixteenth century the pyramid was leveled and the dressed stone was used to build the church and convent. Lesser sites in the city had been ignored and allowed to mound over as they became covered with vegetation. Ramon and his friends became amateur archaeologists and chipped away at the edges of these ruins, bringing home pottery shards and bones, occasionally a tool. When he was fifteen Ramon found an engraved Spanish spur that became the centerpiece of his collection.

Over time, the pottery fragments captured more of his attention, and by doing some detailed research in the Mérida library he was able to separate and classify the types he found. His parents let him take over the abandoned old house in back for his "laboratory" as he called it. They repaired the thatched roof and made it weather tight. He borrowed a book on conservation and learned what adhesives to use when he found shards that fit together. His sense of kinship with the makers of these artifacts grew and he laughed when he came across passages in the books on Mayan civilization that told how the Mayans had abandoned their cities and simply disappeared. He knew they were still there, all around him. He, too, was one of them.

The steaming jungle lay on all sides and Ramon

began to venture further afield in his search for treasures. South of Izamal he came upon a small mound no higher than the surrounding trees. Official excavations tended to focus mainly on the larger sites that offered the possibility of pyramids. Ever mindful of the snakes, he worked to chop away the foliage and dig at the edges. He gradually learned that most of the snakes were either nocturnal or liked to hunt in the cooler mornings. The most feared was the *fer de lance*, whose bite was nearly always fatal. It was typically from two to three meters long, disappearing easily among the vines that choked the trees. Less threatening were the jumping pit viper, the hog nosed viper, and an odd rattlesnake called the *Cascabel*. He preferred to work in the heat of the afternoon when they were at their *siestas.*

After two days at this site he was rewarded with the best finds he'd ever made; two vessels, one in a cylinder shape with two wedge-shaped feet and a clear space where a third had been. Even after digging all around he could not locate the third foot. The sides were elaborately incised. The other vessel was also on a tripod base, but with all three feet present. It also had no lid. The sides bore elaborate painted figures of Mayan dancers.

Ramon was stunned at his good luck. At this early point in his career, he was neither archaeologist nor forger, but his first thought was how to restore the damaged piece. He knew he would have to attempt to make a replacement for the third foot, something he had never done. It was a challenge. The clay would be no problem; he had already discovered several hollows nearby where clay had been dug in the distant past. He could make the replacement foot fit perfectly to the space on the bottom of the vessel. But then he would have to fire it and get the color right before attaching it.

⌘⌘⌘

The bus stopped, and people began to stand up around him, pulling down packages and luggage from overhead racks. The bus station sign said Dolores Hidalgo. He found his suitcase above the seat ahead of him, and with the wooden case he descended from the bus. Ramon had been on the road for more than twenty-four hours. He felt in his pants pocket for the address where he had been shipping his merchandise and pulled it out. He had it memorized, but he read it again anyway. Independencia 132. It was just after six in the morning.

A few steps from the bus terminal there were several small, inexpensive hotels. Ramon took a room away from the street noise and unpacked the suitcase, pulled off his clothes and took a shower. Afterward he lay on the bed for a while but was too agitated to sleep any more. He would have felt better if he'd had a plan, but he did not know what awaited him on Calle Independencia. He ate a mango from a plastic bag in his suitcase and then sat on the bed and opened the wooden box. It was divided into two compartments and in the right compartment were tools rolled inside a wide canvas belt. In the left was a sample of his work. He wrapped the belt around his abdomen, pulled on a nondescript shirt and checked himself in the mirror. It made him look only a little thicker than normal, but there were no obvious bulges. He combed his hair and locked the door behind him.

On the way out of the hotel Ramon obtained a free map of the city from the desk clerk, then stood outside to study it. Calle Independencia began near the main square and ran roughly west for about eight blocks, when it changed its name to Calle de Los Padres. It looked like about two kilometers to the plaza from his hotel. Ramon started off at a brisk clip. Traffic was starting to thicken around him, an intimidating tangle of buses, taxis and cars. It was far more hectic than he had ever seen in Izamal, and reminded him of Mérida, the farthest place from home he had ever been until now.

At the plaza he located Calle Independencia, but the first building number was 2. After the tropical climate of Izamal he was shivering in the thin shirt. Apparently not all of México shared the climate of the Yucatan. As he passed 120 he began to slow down. When he saw his destination he crossed the street and turned to look back at it as he considered what to do.

Calle Independencia 132 was a narrow apple green facade between a house on the right and a large two story structure on the other side that announced itself as a boys' school. The school wrapped around the corner, and Calle Independencia went on to become Calle de Los Padres, across the intersection. Perhaps the Padres ran the school, he thought.

The building was not wide enough to be a house and possessed no bell to ring. It had only one story and there were no openings other than the door. He came back across the street and tapped on it but got no response. He didn't expect any with Tobey Cross dead. He had briefly regretted hanging up the phone on Marisol, but he'd been so shocked when she told him that he could think of nothing more to say.

Ramon passed by the school, looking in as he

went. The paired front doors were open and inside, the school resembled many other buildings in México; a central courtyard with a fountain but no garden since the space was probably used for assembling the students. Two levels of arches surrounded the courtyard with shaded classroom doorways set back within. In one corner Ramon could see a staircase leading to the second floor, and further, to the roof. His left hand adjusted the tool belt beneath his shirt.

There were no students in view; classes had just begun. Inside the entry a janitor's cart stood against the wall. Ramon stepped quickly inside, lifted a mop and an empty bucket from the cart with a single gesture and walked swiftly to the staircase on his right.

Once on the school roof he leaned the mop against the parapet, set down the bucket and crossed to the common wall adjoining 132. One story below a small, untended roof garden displayed dead potted plants. Along the common wall a covered staircase projected above the roof to within a meter and a half of where Ramon stood. He slipped over the parapet and dropped to the angled roof over the stairs. Initially he slipped, then caught his footing as he held his breath, listening. No noise came from the school except a muffled droning from the students. Dropping to the flat part of the roof he examined the door at the top of the stairs. It was steel, hinged from the inside, with no window, knob or handle. If he got in, it wouldn't be from this exit, and in this position he knew he could easily be seen from the school roof.

On the opposite side of the small roof a drain pipe led from the gutter at the edge to a cistern about six feet from the back wall. When Ramon tested his weight, the cast iron held him without sagging and he slid down to the top of the cistern and jumped to the ground.

It was at this point that a plan would have been useful, since if he did not get into the building and out the front, he was not going to get out at all. The yard he was standing in was no more than five meters deep to the back wall, and as wide as the building. It was littered with chunks of concrete and broken tiles, a few sections of pipe, and stands of long dry brush.

The rear of the building presented the same faded apple green as the front, stained by years of rust below the drainpipe, with a single-width door in the center and a large square window to the left. This window was the only source of natural light to the interior. The door was as unpromising as the one on the roof.

A six bar iron grid blocked the window, with cross bars at the top, center and bottom. All three of the crossbars were fastened at both ends with heavy bolts into the masonry at the sides of the window. Ramon lifted his shirt and untied the canvas tool belt. From the tool kit he selected a socket wrench of the right size, attached it to a ratchet and began work on the lower right bolt. As he leaned all his weight into it he heard a noise from the school roof and quickly faded into the corner between the back of 132 and the common wall of the school. His heart was pounding against the canvas tool belt, but no faces appeared at the parapet.

The fourth bolt, at the left of the center bar, was the most difficult. Ramon could feel his shoulder almost dislocating and he had to rest several times before the bolt began to move. He picked up a short length of pipe to extend the wrench. When the bolt finally came out, all that remained were two at the top, which he could not reach anyway. With one of the longer pipes from the yard, he levered the entire grid outward from the bottom and then jammed the pipe in, to keep the grid away from the sill. With a pry bar, he popped the interior latch on the steel casement windows. Hoisting himself up, he pulled the grid back into place, but it did not return all the way back to the window. He smiled to himself. It was not a bad outcome for a man without a plan.

Moving forward in the dim interior he found the light switch. The light couldn't be seen from the street. He moved past stacks of familiar boxes bearing his own return address, past a small bathroom, toward the front of the building. The last space at the front was an office enclosure.

Ramon sat down at the desk, surveying the room. Everything was immaculate; the pale bluish gray walls displayed a few old architectural engravings framed in black lacquer. One depicted a moonlit ruin of a pyramid in the Yucatan that Ramon recognized. The desk lamp was sculptural in design and made from a pewter-colored metal with a light amber glass shade. The rosewood surface of the desk looked like the kind that grew in the jungle around Izamal. Small planks of it were available in the market two blocks from his house.

He ignored the computer and the expensive stereo set behind him. Computers made him uncomfortable, and although he had some minimal skills, he believed most personal data was protected by password anyway. He went drawer by drawer through the desk. By the time he left at lunch time, he had everything he needed; the customer lists, the sales records, and the sale prices (these greatly surprised him). He stuffed everything into a small briefcase he found on the computer desk, pulled the front door shut and walked briskly down Calle Independencia.

With *Señor* Cross dead it was time Ramon Xoc took his business in his own hands. Although he thought of it as simply marketing his own work, Ramon was effectively going to be an antiques dealer.

CHAPTER FIVE

Three days after the party Barbara Watt came for her first sitting. Every day I felt like I should have more going on with Tobey's murder investigation, but I didn't know what to do next. Marisol's comment that I might see things differently sounded plausible, but in practice I was mostly seeing nothing and sometimes I wondered if I wasn't avoiding the whole thing. I preferred to think about what pigments to mix to get Barbara's coloring right.

Maya had gone to the revolutionary archive in Dolores Hidalgo to begin the research on a new book. It was not her book, she had signed on to do research for a former professor of hers who was now teaching in Albuquerque. She had taken the artmobile, my older Chevy van that I had fitted with a canvas awning that unrolled from the side over the sliding door and was supported at the other end by two aluminum uprights that could be stuck in the ground. I often used it to sit in the shade by the roadside and paint landscapes.

Maya had sold her Volkswagen beetle several years back because it was too difficult to keep two cars in San Miguel and we didn't drive much anyway. It was more fun to just hobble over the cobblestone sidewalks. It strengthened our ankles. Marisol was still in Guanajuato working through her grief and we had drawn a blank on the idea that the 132 key might be for a locker at the bus station; we had checked and none were provided. We didn't know what to do next. Tobey's family in Minnesota wanted him to be buried there but the authorities had still not released the body. I couldn't imagine what else they thought they were going to learn from it.

When Barbara came through the entry, she took my hand and went on into the garden. In the center an old well with dolphins carved on the sides now served as a fountain. In the area immediately around it, we have smaller plants, mostly bromeliads, which come in about a hundred varieties here, and then, moving outward toward the walls, we have lime and orange trees, and on one wall, a banana tree that wishes it were in a hotter climate. Bougainvillea climbs the arches at the *loggia*, mixed here and there with orange trumpet vine. The back wall has a tall stand of bamboo.

"This is very lovely," she said. "It looks more real than ours, and that bamboo going up the back wall is great. I wouldn't like to give up our views, but we're so... above it all, you know? I'm not sure it feels right." She wore a pale green halter top and jeans, cut very low on the hip. "I didn't wear much make up, like you said on the phone. Just some lipstick and a touch of eyeliner."

"Are you sure Perry's going to sign off on this?" I asked her.

"You mean, does he know it's a nude? Of course, darlin'. He doesn't own me, he only leases me." She gave me a bright smile. It made me wonder what the payments were.

The studio is on the second floor of our house and has the traditional north facing glass, but in this part of central México (we are in the Bajio, just south of the Tropic of Cancer), during early summer the sun goes far enough north to shine in directly. At that point I draw the thick curtains on the north windows and move the easel to the south. If the sun shines directly into the studio, the balance of contrasts is destroyed. The common wall against the guest bedroom has built in storage for canvas rolls and stretcher bars, as well as finished pictures, going from one bank of windows to the other, and opposite is a wet bar and a small refrigerator with a counter where I can make coffee or sandwiches if I'm in a long session. Beyond the studio on this side, a staircase separates the studio from our guest bedroom. It leads both down into the living room and up to a roof garden covering the top of the entire second floor. Our view from there frames the towers of the *Parroquia*, which dominate the town. This is the quirky pink limestone church of San Miguel de Allende, and it faces the dense green of the pollarded trees in the *jardín*.

I led Barbara up to the studio and pointed out a screen at the end by the south windows. "You can change there. There's a robe on a hook, I think." There was the sound of clothes being pulled off and she emerged a moment later in Maya's silk robe and stood by the easel. Then she untied the robe and dropped it to the floor.

"What do you think?" She held out her hands.

"Stunning." I was pulling out tubes of paint. "What were you thinking about for a pose?"

"Stunning? Just like that? I'm standing here naked and you just say, 'stunning'? Don't you want to...you know, touch me just a little? Maya's not here, is she? I hoped we could have a little rendezvous."

"Barbara," I said, squeezing out some titanium white onto my pallet, "please don't think I don't appreciate you. You're really gorgeous. But painting is just not an erotic activity for me. I tend to look at the human body as a kind of landscape; a few hills here, some valleys there, an outcropping or two of bush." I meant this.

"Look at me." There was an edgy, demanding tone in her voice.

"You may not realize it yet, but I'm going to be looking at you more thoroughly than anyone ever has before, believe me. This process may not be sexual, but it is intimate. I am literally going to recreate you."

"I thought you wanted me. I saw how you looked at me at the party. That's how I got this idea, don't you see that?" She stood with her hands on her hips, her chin thrust outward.

"Who wouldn't want you? The Pope would want you, for Christ's sake. But this isn't about that." She shuddered. She had probably never dated an old Polish guy with red shoes. "But that's another issue. You can relax. I've done this dozens of times. Maybe you're just feeling a little vulnerable because you're undressed?"

"Never. That's when I'm strongest. I'm just used to more of a reaction." I paused without one, flexing the ends of a few brushes. "Is it because of Maya?" she asked.

"Of course it's because of Maya. I love her, and she's given me more of herself than any woman I've ever known. Is that what *you're* offering? Or is it twenty minutes on your back?" I was getting angry now. This was my turf and I was used to being in charge. I don't like people messing with my studio process, and this was getting messier by the moment.

"It could be more than twenty minutes...and it doesn't have to be just on my back. I also like other positions. Besides, I was hoping you had an arrangement." She was holding her arms folded now.

"We do have an arrangement. I don't fall into bed with other women and she doesn't stick a knife in my heart while I sleep. It's worked out well so far."

"It sounds so inflexible."

"Sometimes these little certainties can be good."

She looked at me for a moment and then the stiffness went out of her.

"How should I stand? I just don't know. I want it to be classy, you know? Not cheap, but still sexy. Can you do that?"

"Do you know Manet's *Olympia*?"

She nodded. "I saw it in Paris."

"I've always wanted to try something like that. Maya isn't right for it. Just lie on your back on the day bed with your face turned toward me. Do you think Perry wants big? I've got a canvas that's about forty by fifty-six inches or so." She reclined on the day bed and gave me a winning smile.

"Perry would like big. Perry would like to *be* big, aside from his business."

I ignored this. It sounded like more than I wanted to know. "No teeth," I said. "I don't do teeth. Just a more subtle, yet welcoming, look. That's it." I set up the canvas and started mixing some washes. "Wait a minute. Let's get a prop." I dug around in a cabinet drawers and came up with a midnight-blue velvet choker with a small stone set on the overlap at the end. "Would you wear this?"

She tried it on and I gave her a mirror. "It's

perfect," she said.

"It makes you look more naked. Artists always say nude, but in your case I would have to say it's naked. That's part of what Manet was saying in *Olympia.* That this girl was no Greek goddess, and this picture is no classical fantasy of nymphs and satyrs. This is just a street girl with no clothes on. He was blowing up the phony mythology thing that the Victorians used as an excuse to ogle naked women. Not that you're a street girl."

We didn't talk for a while. I was more comfortable not talking. Once I started it was just landscape, after all. I had the masses and contours where I wanted them, and I had blocked in the foreground shadow where her body met the day bed. The picture was anchored and normally I would go on to the face but I was captured by the curve of her left thigh as it rose above her right knee. I would save her face for the next session. Faces take a good deal of focus and sustained effort and I wasn't sure how much energy I had left.

"Are you comfortable?'

"Very. This is my natural state."

"Well, it's not a demanding pose. It's not like your arms are going to get tired."

When I had finished her left thigh and knee I had run out of gas. Later, I walked her to the door. We left it that she would call me for the next session.

"I'm sad we didn't do it," she said, holding my hand. "But at least you know what you're dealing with now."

"I think I do, but it's those little denials that make life sweeter," I said. What crap. I could rationalize the feathers off a goose. At the entry she kissed me on the lips. I felt it all the way to the soles of my feet. I was flattered that she was interested in me as a diversion, but all the same I was irritated at the casual way she thought she could disrupt my studio process. It had developed over years and it was why I was any good at all at painting. There was an implicit egotism in Barbara thinking that I would just fly into her arms. Maybe no one had ever rejected her before.

After she left I was restless, and as Maya wasn't likely to be back before evening, I called my friend Cody Williams and asked him to meet me for a beer at La Vida around four. I left a note for Maya in the kitchen, in case the meeting turned into something more than a beer.

Cody's a beefy guy in his late fifties and about six-three, who still has most of his ginger colored hair. He cashed in his thirty years as a detective in the Peoria police Department for a pension that lets him live pretty well in San Miguel. His wife had stayed behind; she didn't like México.

La Vida is a little out of the way, down on Ancha de San Antonio past the Insitituto Allende, one of our two big art schools. It's a neighborly kind of place and it's fun to sit at the horseshoe-shaped bar and watch the action, not that I needed any more today.

"Hey painter boy, whatcha workin' on now?" Cody slid in beside me at the bar.

"Nothing much. Just a bit of landscape." I don't tell everything.

"I ran into Bill Frost yesterday. He said you've been sniffing around at something besides paint fumes. Like the late Tobey Cross." The bartender came up. "Negra Modelo," Cody said, "*por favor.*"

"Maya's close to Marisol Cross, and I got pulled into it. What could I say?"

"Did she ask you what your qualifications might be for the job?"

"She said she thought a painter might see things differently, things the police had missed or chosen to ignore."

"Sure. Like Picasso saw things differently. In that way?"

"Well that, but I also told her I knew you."

"I figured that. You want to tell me what you know so far?" The bartender set down a beer in front of him.

I gave Cody the whole thing, from the call at the Santa Monica right up through the pointless trip to the bus station. I showed him the key. He looked carefully at both sides of it and flipped it on the bar top.

"Well, this would never be a locker key anyway because the number is so crudely stamped on it. With a locker key the top is going to be made to hold a tab with a variety of numbers. I would have to guess this is a key to a rental property, run by someone who only has a few to manage, otherwise he'd never do his keys this way. It's too inefficient. He's got a set of dies and he's just hammering on the numbers one at a time. And if it was somebody's house key it wouldn't have a number. People know their own address."

From the corner of my eye I saw Maya come up behind Cody and put her arms around his chest. They barely met in front. His hand with the beer in it stopped half way to his mouth. "I think that would be my favorite Latin American author. Next to Garcia Marquez, that is.

How are you, sweetheart?" he said.

She came around and kissed him on the neck. "It's been like one hundred years of solitude since I've seen you."

"You are the best. Thank God my wife's still back in Peoria. She couldn't bear this."

"Will you two stop now?"

"I saw your note," said Maya. "The archive closed early in Dolores Hidalgo. And I had an idea. The 132 key maybe is not from San Miguel. It could be Atotonilco, or Santa Teresita, or Pozos, or Dolores Hidalgo, or even Querétaro. If Tobey hid his gallery business, then maybe he hid his office in a different town. That way no one who sees his comings and goings knows who he is or what he's doing. Not like here."

"So we're supposed to search all those towns, and maybe more? I hope it's not Querétaro. There are probably a thousand 132's there," I said. "There must be over a million people in that place."

"That's why they say, a dollar's worth of sweat gets you a dime's worth of information," said Cody. "It's always more sweat than genius."

"I'm increasingly thinking it's none of the above. The only thing I felt when I was going through Perry Watt's stuff at the party was that it was unworthy of me. I should confine myself to painting."

They both stared at me in silence for a moment, and I took a long pull at the beer.

"So then just because you're good at one thing that's all you're able to do?" Cody said. "How about learning new skills in an area where you already bring part of it to the table, your ability to see and remember detail?"

Maya was nodding now. "To help someone out who asked for your aid and is possibly getting the short end of the stick? As an ethical issue, I think stepping up to the plate here trumps being a sneak."

Now it was my turn to nod. "OK. I see it. I'll be a principled sneak, working to avenge the death of an antiques dealer I didn't know very well."

"You're also doing this because I asked you," said Maya, giving me a pointed look.

"Good," said Cody. "That's probably as comfortable as it's going to get for you without a badge. And since you bring it up, how well did any of us know Tobey Cross? Isn't he the real starting point? Where's he from?"

"I think Minneapolis," said Maya. "His family, anyway. I didn't know him very well. But his wife, Marisol, we are like sisters."

"Seesters?" I said.

"I didn't say that. My English is good as yours."

"All right, all right. I still know some people in the Chicago Police Department. Let me make some calls. Do you think his real name was Tobias?"

I shook my head. "It could be. Why not run it both ways?"

"Makes sense. But there's one other thing. You don't know who you're dealing with here, and you're not carrying the firepower of the police. You two have got to watch your backs. Word is out that you're looking into this. If I heard about it, then a lot of other people know it too, because I don't go very far out of my way to keep my finger on the pulse of this community. I'm retired now."

We had made so little progress it was hard to think we'd put ourselves at risk. Who could be threatened by what we knew?

"How about a girlfriend?" Cody asked. "Maybe an irate husband did this."

Maya was already shaking her head. I hadn't thought to ask Marisol about this, but in the circumstances it would have been awkward to bring it up.

"I mentioned it when you were upstairs looking at his clothes," Maya said. "She had never seen any sign of it."

Cody didn't comment. We were probably both thinking that Tobey would have been trying hard to conceal it if he was unfaithful, so Marisol having seen no sign of an affair meant nothing.

At about eight o'clock we came out into the street. Cody went home and we walked back up Hernandez Macias into *el centro*, where we paused to watch the action in the *jardín*. I always thought of it as San Miguel's living room. Three or four groups of *mariachis* were circulating around the square looking for work as the *paseo* began. In the *paseo* the boys of the town circulated three or four abreast in one direction around the *jardín* while the girls passed in the opposite direction. They eyed each other with interest. The parents, seated among the benches, eyed them with interest too. When we reached home I stuck the key in the lock, but the door was not locked. I looked at Maya.

"Did you leave it open?"

"Never," she said. "I know I locked it."

I pushed it open and we stood there in silence. There were no sounds from within and no lights were on. I flipped on the entry light to avoid being blind-sided and we slipped off our shoes and walked in. Everything looked normal. Nothing was changed in the living room or the kitchen. We checked the loggia and the garden, then went upstairs, turning on lights as we went. The studio door was open. No one was inside.

The Barbara Watt picture was still on the easel and I realized that in wrestling with my misgivings I had forgotten to tell Maya about it. The Maya painting leaned against the coffee bar, not where I had left it. It had been slashed from corner to corner both ways. Maya gasped, touched my arm, pointing across the room. On the wall behind the bar in red paint were the words, in Spanish, PINTA QUADROS Y OLVIDA LAS CERAMICAS. (Paint pictures and forget ceramics.)

I took a few steps toward it. The painting was unsalvageable. Maya and the Maize God had been finished and only the jungle background remained. The only time I had ever seen a picture of mine destroyed was when I did it myself, and with good reason. I felt sick.

Maya had paused behind me and stood now before the easel. "It's the *güera*, isn't it?"

"Yes, I was going to tell you, but I forgot."

"What is that on her neck?"

"The choker."

"I wore that, a long time ago."

"Yes."

"Did she wear my robe too?"

"Very briefly."

"You didn't...."

"No. I wouldn't."

"Is she going to buy it?"

"Perry is, for four thousand."

"Four thousand dollars. Yes."

"We need the money. I've got to do six more pictures for the Maya series before the show. Excuse me, seven pictures, now."

"I should be practical, right?"

"Yes."

"OK. I'll be practical. But I can't like her, not like that."

"No. I suppose not."

"I will not be screaming now."

"Good. You know it's only paint."

We were quiet then, for a while. There was large mound of cadmium red squeezed out on my palette, and a number twelve hog bristle brush lay on the floor, full of the red paint. Cadmium red from Winsor and Newton is a series four color, the most expensive level. Naturally the intruder couldn't have chosen something cheap, like black. Cleaning the brush and scraping the paint from the palette, I felt violated. I soaked a rag in turpentine and began to scrub the wall. Maya's hand was on my shoulder.

"I'm sorry," she said. "This shouldn't happen. Cody was right. We need to watch our backs. I'll get us a brandy." She went downstairs and locked the door.

Later we sat and sipped the brandy but there seemed little to say. I called Cody to let him know but there was no answer. I left a message for him to call me. I didn't want to say in a message what had happened. After a while we went to bed and slept fitfully, tangled in each other's arms. I dreamed the Mérida show started tomorrow and I had no pictures finished. Not my standard art opening dream, but close. Usually it was the buyers who were absent.

In the morning I pulled the staples from the

ruined canvas and threw it away, saving the stretchers. I couldn't look at it. I stretched clean canvas over the frame but I didn't have the heart to start work on the picture again. When I tried Cody again he picked up on the first ring. I told him what happened.

"This is worrisome," he said, "but there's something funny about it too."

"I'm somehow missing the humor in this." I realized now my doubts about being involved with this were gone. When the situation reached into my studio, it became personal. It felt like war.

"No, I mean the message. You notice it didn't say FORGET ABOUT TOBEY. It said FORGET ABOUT CERAMICS. Somehow that's the issue here. This guy has helped us out, in a costly sort of way. If we knew where Tobey got the ceramics we might have a lead."

"Then we're back to finding the office."

"Right. I think the ceramics must be high-powered stuff. Museum quality. I haven't seen any of them," said Cody, "but he had the reputation of only selling the best. I can't imagine how anybody can get them out of the country."

"I haven't seen anything better. Maybe he's only selling to the expatriate crowd, maybe it all stays here in San Miguel, or perhaps among the beach house crowd along the coast. There are quite a few Americans with money in Guadalajara as well."

I hung about the studio for a while, poking around in my supplies, making a few notes of things I needed to buy on my next trip to Lagundi, the art supply store on Umaran a few blocks past Tobey's gallery. It was time for another tube of cadmium red, the old one was nearly flat.

I wondered for a moment if there were fingerprints on that tube of paint. But I didn't want to involve the police. They would only try to shut me down. It was better if they didn't know what I was doing. Not that I did, beyond knowing that now I'd be doing whatever it took.

At nine Cody picked me up and we left for Pozos, an old mining town about fifty miles away. I'm not sure why we picked Pozos, but neither of us had ever been there, and we had to start somewhere. Maya had already taken the artmobile back to Dolores Hidalgo. She was going to do more research for the professor and then spend the afternoon looking for 132. I was still too upset to paint.

CHAPTER SIX

In the twelve years I've lived in San Miguel, Pozos was not a place I ever heard much about. But lately, I'd been hearing more.

Most people knew some of its history. It was a mining town that went back to the fifteen hundreds. In the seventeenth and eighteenth centuries it was a boomtown and had enough ore to stay booming until around 1900, when it went into a sharp decline, as a lot of mining towns do as the ore runs out. At that point the population had reached about 70,000, similar to San Miguel today. By the 1920s, the population had fallen to a fraction of its peak, and it continued to trail off for decades. Today it was thought to be about 4,000.

During the last year I had heard of several gringos moving into Pozos, without fanfare, and buying property for renovation. Several people told me it was going to be the next San Miguel.

Cody and I discussed this as we drove through dry but decent looking farm land on the way there. It rarely rains here in January, but some fields were green with broccoli and corn and that meant the farmer had the capital for irrigation. After about forty miles Cody turned north and we began to climb into the hills.

"I've heard there's a renovated hotel," he said.

"Hotels mean visitors. Maybe this place is really coming back. There certainly is a backlash against property prices in San Miguel. It wouldn't surprise me to see people start buying out here."

"Must be huge numbers of things for sale," I said. "There's been no property market there for years. Marisol said Tobey was in some kind of financial business before the antiques. Maybe he had real estate experience. Would it be a surprise if he were looking for a place some distance away to set up an office and picked Pozos for its potential?"

"It'd be a fair commute, though." It was about an hour's drive.

"It would, but how often would he need to go? I wouldn't think that in his business he made more than one or two sales a week. Most invoices were probably big, and I'm sure his markups were too. He could have received shipments in San Miguel and carted them out to Pozos. Or maybe he had an agent in Pozos to receive shipments for him."

The road got steeper over the next few miles and then went into a sharp curve. When it evened out we were on an urban street, but none like I had ever seen. Had Pozos been built with wood-framed houses and stores, like most towns in the States, it would have long ago rotted away when the roofs fell in. But like most Mexican towns it was built of stone and stucco and adobe brick, and so for block after block it still stood, melting away, edges rounded and crumbling. It was all the same dusty grayish ochre, a perfect match for the unpaved streets.

Most of the doorways and windows were bricked up and the roofs must have fallen in behind. Here and there an isolated house was still occupied, some toward the center were even being restored, if you call starting from virtually nothing restoration. Driving along we heard the occasional chicken, just like in San Miguel; a homey touch. No firecrackers, though, the celebrations would have ended some time ago, not within living memory.

After five or six blocks we came to the plaza, a smallish affair, but surprisingly well maintained, compared with what we'd seen coming in. If a restoration effort was getting started, this would most likely be the focus of it. Half a dozen people were in view. On the south side stood a church in decent repair that looked as if it were still operating. On two other sides was a mix of small active stores and abandoned fronts, and on the fourth side a two story, white, freshly restored building with a sign reading "Hotel Montana."

Cody parked in front of the church and two dogs came hopefully over to us and sniffed our cuffs as we got out. He pulled a bottle of water from the back seat and locked the car. Everyone in view had paused to look at us.

"Not much cover here," he said.

"Cover? You think we're going to have to shoot it out? I don't own a gun."

"Not likely. I meant for Tobey. If his office is here, everything he did would have been on view. I'm not sure he would've wanted that, even if he had made a good real estate buy. Let's circle out from here. I don't think there's any reason to separate. This isn't going to take that long."

We walked along the front of the church and continued down the street. About three blocks further the street climbed a hill to the ruins of a larger eighteenth century church. I tried to imagine the sound when the dome had collapsed. It probably felt like a minor earthquake. We turned left every couple of blocks, winding outward in a spiral from the square, but what soon became clear was there were almost no street numbers, even on the few inhabited houses. They had ceased to matter. We turned back toward the plaza.

"This is one dollar's worth of sweat that is not going to return a dime's worth of anything," Cody said. "Let's get back in the car and make a circuit of what's left."

We zigzagged through the town, seeing a few more people, a lot more dogs, and another small square, this one covered with blue plastic tarps as if it hosted an occasional market day. At the northern edge of town a large brick school building stood alone, now walls only with empty windows. Beyond that the terrain became hilly and we passed among seven or eight ruined mining haciendas, all stone and all roofless, usually surrounded by perimeter walls.

"Let's get lunch," said Cody. "I think this is the saddest place I've ever seen."

We found our way back to the Hotel Montana.

"There is no way this is going to be the new San Miguel within the lifetime of anyone now living or even contemplated," I said. We pulled up in the same place in front of the church. The same dogs met us as we got out and they were still hopeful. No one else was, except the owner of the Hotel Montana. Maybe she knew something the rest of us didn't.

Inside, the hotel was pristine; the kind of restoration that had to have been done by someone who knew where to go, and had the deep pockets to get there. From the condition of the rest of the town I could imagine what the starting point must have been like. Inside the restaurant the exterior walls were exposed stone and the inside walls magenta on smooth plaster. Arched windows overlooked a serene garden and above the wall the view took in blocks of ruins.

We ordered lunch and Negra Modelos.

"Aside from the transcendental sadness of this place, is conducting a search usually so boring?" I asked.

"Usually, and the scenery's not as strange or as interesting. Then, every three weeks or so, there's twenty minutes of excitement and thirty seconds of terror where, if you have time to think at all, you're wondering if you're going to walk away at the end. That's pretty much it, aside from writing all the reports."

"And you did thirty years of this?"

"Yup. You just have to pace yourself. Otherwise you're asleep when the terror starts. You don't want that. It makes for a short career." He sipped his beer.

"And a lot of years of pension for the widow."

"Hard on the department budget. I think we can scratch this town off the list," Cody said, reaching for a toothpick while I paid the bill. "I wasn't too hopeful anyway, but I guess we had to come."

"Lovely ruins, though."

"Something a painter would say. How far were you on that Maya picture?"

"About three quarters. I only had the foliage left."

My cell phone went off. I pulled it out of my pocket and read the caller ID number on the screen.

"It's Maya," I said.

"I'm here now," she said, "I found it! I'm sitting at

Tobey's desk in Dolores Hidalgo. Nice leather chair, tasteful old engravings on the walls. I think one is of Cortés's palace in Cuernavaca. A new-looking Apple computer behind me—so much for the guy who never used one. Ceramics and pictures stored in the room beyond. It's Tobey all the way. Pretty good stereo too. I put on some Mozart. It's like you say, bingo."

I covered the phone as we walked back to the car and leaned over to Cody. "She's there. She's found 132 in Dolores Hidalgo."

"So you used the same tactic we used in San Miguel?" I asked her.

"Exactly. It was on the fourth street I tried. But Paul, someone's been in here. I can't tell if anything is missing, but the bars are loose on the back window. Tobey could never have lived with that. And there are all kinds of boxes and crates still here. They seem to be full, but I didn't check everything. Can you guys come now? This is making me nervous."

"Give me the street name and stay right there. I think I know the number. It might take us a while."

In an hour and half we were on the outskirts of Dolores Hidalgo. The town is widely known for its ceramic tableware and sinks. Numerous shops lined the highway as we approached. Dinner sets, candlesticks, bird baths and fountains, anything that could be made of clay. Brilliant and startling colors. We had caught a break and we blew past them all.

We found the square, facing the church where Padre Hidalgo had uttered his cry to revolution in 1810. We picked up Calle Independencia at one corner and five minutes later pulled up before a narrow, nondescript green building. The facade featured only the door, with no windows to the street. You could walk by it a thousand times and never notice it. We had to park around the corner next to what appeared to be an old mansion converted into a school. The artmobile was across the street. Maya opened the door to us, beaming. I hugged her.

"It's inventory time," said Cody, kissing her cheek and looking around. "I don't think we should take anything away with us. Just list everything that's here. Find some disks and copy the computer records. Try not to leave any fingerprints and keep everything in its original position. The police will get here sooner or later. Maya, I hope you wiped off anything you touched."

"I was careful," she said. "I'll do the computer."

The case was finally in motion. Cody began going through the desk, using a pair of gloves he'd brought along. In the back room nine large wooden cases held pictures. All had been opened. They were the usual seventeenth and eighteenth century stuff, portraits and devotional work, all framed, and already restored. I wondered who did Tobey's art restoration because they couldn't have looked like this when he bought them. I copied the return addresses from the labels and noted the contents. There were five or six different points of origin, all but one from México, and the odd one from a convent in Guatemala. The final shipping labels all said, "Mercier" with an address in México City. Although I thought I knew, I made a note to follow up on Mercier and see what they did for a living.

Eleven smaller crates stood in a line on the floor. They had all been opened. Each contained a carefully packed ceramic piece in the Mayan style, in a condition that would bring a museum curator to his knees. They were at least as good as what Perry had and similar in style and quality to what I had seen at Galeria Cruz. Tobey was connected. I began making a list. I didn't know what to call each piece, so I settled on a brief description. The odd thing about this group was that the return addresses were all the same. In a small neat hand they read:

Ramon Xoc
14 Calle 29
Izamal, Yucatán, México

I didn't know Izamal, but Ramon Xoc had to be an unlicensed excavator of extraordinary skill and insight. And luck.

Beyond the crates a worktable held a few tools to open cases, a magnifying glass, a hammer, and a powerful lamp with a gooseneck. Next to it was a leather apron. A shelf held packing materials. Tobey had been nothing if not neat. All were systematically arranged and I did not move anything. A few empty cases stood against the far wall. I added them to the inventory and wrote down the return addresses. Most of them were also from Ramon Xoc, a Mayan name approximately pronounced "shock." Beyond this there was only a good-sized paper drum for trash. It was empty, which was too bad. Trash can be revealing.

When I returned to the office Maya was still downloading files, labeling each disk. She had a pencil tucked in her hair over one ear. Cody had finished the desk and with his pocketknife was slitting the paper backing on the framed engravings from the wall. "Can't be helped," he said. "The police will know someone has been in here anyway from the window grid in back. They just won't know we were here as well."

Maya put the computer disks in her tote bag along with our notebooks while I turned out the lights and we innocently slipped out the door, locking it behind us. The sun was angling down into the western horizon over Dolores Hidalgo; it was after six o'clock. Traffic was thick and no one paid any attention to us. Just a couple of gringos, one of them awfully big, and a brown-eyed girl with a tote bag and a wide, friendly smile. Possibly even a triumphant smile.

I drove back with Maya in the artmobile and we all reconvened in our dining room where we could spread out our findings on the long refectory table. Maya set up her laptop with a printer at one end and began printing all the documents in duplicate. None was encrypted; we needed no passwords. Tobey must have felt safe in Dolores Hidalgo. It was San Miguel that did him in.

"I thought about this all the way back." Cody said, poking the eraser end of a pencil into his cheek. "The building at 132 had already been entered. But the antiques were probably not touched, so the question is that if it was a straight burglary, why not take everything? And if it isn't, what's the motive? Information? Did someone else download the records? The expense files and all the odds and ends that you didn't find at Marisol's were there. The only missing items I can think of would be a Rolodex and a sales ledger, but the sales info would most likely also be on the computer."

"It is," said Maya, feeding more paper into the tray "I'm making you a copy."

"Good. Then there's the phone; wouldn't there be a Rolodex next to it? He's not going to want to boot the computer every time he needs to find a phone number."

"How about one of those personal organizer things?" I said.

"A PDA? I didn't find one in the office," Maya said.

"And I didn't find one at the gallery when I went through his desk, and Marisol didn't mention it among the things the police took, so it's probably safe to say that the burglar was most interested in the customer list. But, oddly, he doesn't have the antiques themselves. I mean, we can't be sure how much was in the back room when he broke in, but there's still a lot. What's he going to sell to the customers if that was the reason for his visit?"

"Maybe you are backwards," said Maya. "Maybe he's a thief and gets more inventory from the customers and stores it there? That's why he wants the customer list."

"Then it's a warehouse for him too. That's possible, I guess." Cody rubbed his bristly chin. "Then we might see more things piling up in Dolores Hidalgo. Plus, we'd hear about the burglaries, if they came from San Miguel. But I'm not sure that explains why he left all that stuff there. He must know the police would be looking for the place because of Tobey's death. There would be no reason for him to think Tobey had kept it secret. I don't think it's his warehouse."

"But maybe he hasn't thought that far and now it is. I can check 132 again when I go back to the archive," she said, "just to see if anything has been added."

I opened my notebook. "Here's an interesting thing. The pictures in back came from a variety of sources. Four even came from churches on their way to Mercier. I think that must be fairly normal. But the ceramics all came from a single address in Izamal. A guy named Ramon Xoc."

"The yellow city," said Maya, "A very old place. I've been there. It's in the middle of the Yucatan. Street after street is all yellow. And suddenly anywhere there are ruins mixed in with the regular buildings. Mayan ruins. It's like the new city is built right over the old, but the old still sticks out everywhere, like bones."

I told them about the Ramon Xoc address. "I don't suppose we should call him, it would warn him."

"Sounds like we're going to Izamal," said Cody.

"I'm not," said Maya, "I've got research to do. Someone has to put tortillas and beer on the table."

An hour later Cody called. "My people in Chicago drew a blank," he said. "No Tobey or Tobias Cross in the system."

I found Maya out in the loggia, working on her laptop from a stack of research notes from the Dolores Hidalgo archive. "Nothing," I said. "Cody's police friends couldn't find a thing on Tobey."

Her cell phone rang and Maya picked it up. The conversation was brief. "Marisol is back from Guanajuato. She is hoping we have something. I told her we'd come over to give her a report."

At Galería Cruz Marisol was more composed, but her face was still tight. She met us at the door wearing black. We sat down in the great room with the two-story ceiling. The lights were low but everything looked the same. The glossy books were still positioned just so on the desk. There are people who immediately remove any sign of the departed person. Marisol was not one of these. Chilly personality that he was, it still said something about Tobey's relationship to his wife.

"We found the office in Dolores Hidalgo," began Maya, although Marisol was looking at me, waiting for a report. Marisol's eyebrows went up, as if Maya had said it was in Afghanistan or Sumatra.

"But, Dolores Hidalgo? It's fifty kilometers away. I don't understand. What was there?"

"Yes, well his business was there," I said, "more paintings, more Mayan ceramics, a computer and records. It looks like everything, except a Rolodex and a sales ledger, if there was one. Marisol, the office had been broken into, through a window in the back. I'm not sure if anything was missing. Did Tobey have a Blackberry or something like that, a PDA?"

"I never saw one. He thought that even having a computer was too great a concession to the twenty-first century."

"I know you said that before, but I think he was just covering his tracks. He didn't want anyone, including you, to think he had an office somewhere else." I felt it was time to start bringing her along to the idea that not everything was as he led her to think. She looked away when I said this, but showed no emotion. "Well, other than that, we got everything we could from the office. I think it might be time to let the police know about it. They'll dust it for fingerprints. I'm giving you back the key. We have a copy for ourselves in case we need to go back. We also copied the computer files and we'll be going over the customer list and his sources. One name came up on the packing materials many times. Have you ever heard the name Ramon Xoc? He lives in Izamal."

"In the Yucatán? It is a Mayan name, isn't it?"

"It seems to be. Did Tobey ever mention him?"

"I don't think so." She sighed. "I'll call Licenciado Delgado and let him know. He's managing the case."

"Don't mention what we've been doing. Just say this key was in Tobey's clothes, which of course it was, and that now you recall him saying something about Dolores Hidalgo. He can take it from there. Also find out if they know anything more. They might have something we don't." What I didn't say was that I didn't think they'd tell her if they did. They tended to keep their investigations private, not wanting to arouse undue expectations, especially if they hadn't done a thing.

Marisol got up and then hesitated for a moment, rubbing her hands together. "I want to thank you so much for helping me with this. Both of you." She walked over to one of the niches by the French doors. "I want to give you this for your efforts." She lifted a large ceramic statue from the niche and placed it in my hands. My first instinct was to refuse it because it was probably quite valuable, but a quick glance at Maya told me it would be ungracious and even insulting to not accept it. What people here call *mal educado.* No manners.

"This is very generous of you, Marisol. I hope what we turn up will be worth your gift."

"I can get you a box for it." She managed a smile and moved off to a closet near the dining room entrance, returning a moment later with a container of heavy cardboard and a sheet of bubble wrap. The statue was about fourteen inches high and weighed four or five pounds, a substantial piece of work. It portrayed a godlike creature with thick lips and nose, holding some device out from his body. He wore an elaborate headdress and something in his nose. There were two fine fracture lines in one arm but the repair was nearly perfect. I wrapped it in the bubble wrap and slid it into the box thinking it could be part of a still life some day when I got back to painting.

We paused at the door. "I'm going to Izamal tomorrow to talk with Ramon Xoc."

"I hope he will speak to you. Thank you again. I will let you know what Licenciado Delgado says. I hope this can be over soon." I didn't say it but she spoke for both of us. Her expression gave me the sense that she was holding back in my presence, but if it had been Maya alone she might have broken down again.

CHAPTER SEVEN

The Aero Mexico flight went east over San Miguel and out over the Gulf toward the Yucatán Peninsula. Cody had the window position and the arms of his seat gripped him like a sausage in a pair of pliers. He struggled to retrieve his briefcase from under the seat in front of him and, with a grunt, pulled it up between his knees, the little finger of one hand looped into the handle.

Below, the water was a featureless silvery gray sheet, hard and unyielding, like I imagined some cases must be. Cody pulled out a sheaf of papers. "Did you get a chance to go over the sales records?" We could have been a couple of salesmen traveling to an annual meeting in the Bahamas.

"No. Maya and I went to update Marisol. She's doing better. I told her it was time to bring in the police now on the office, keeping us out of it. I made a point of not mentioning the picture slasher. It would only make her feel bad that she had asked our help."

"Well, we've got some interesting things here. Tobey did quite a bit of business, much of it back in San Miguel, but also a lot in Guadalajara, some in México City. It also looks like he supplied a retail gallery in Manzanillo, and one in Acapulco. Then there are a few shipments to Austin, Texas, but pictures only. We talked before about whether these ceramics could be brought out of the country and something occurred to me." He turned and tried to gesture, then gave it up for lack of space and settled for pulling off his reading glasses. "What if you lived in a beach community and had a boat? A large one that could make the trip in deep water back to LA or San Diego? Bringing the pre-Columbian stuff back home would be no problem at all."

"Interesting thought. Any names you recognize?" I asked.

"Only in San Miguel. Bill Frost bought one piece." He handed me the list. The common feature of the five names that I recognized was that they all had the money to finance expensive hobbies. I was not surprised that the most common name was Perry Watt; he had bought a total of seven ceramic pieces and five paintings, aside from a long list of shipwreck jewelry and old silver. There was a gold and emerald rosary with an eye-popping price. Perry could certainly buy and sell most people in San Miguel.

"Do you know Perry Watt?" I asked.

"Only know of him, but I ran totals on everybody. My tally says Watt spent about $385,000 with our friend Tobey over the years. That would include the seven major ceramic pieces, some pictures, a lot of jade, and some odds and ends like daggers and spurs, silver pieces from the mint at Lima, and some gold. Must be quite a collector."

"We've known them for a while, but not well. We were at a party they gave last week, two days after the murder. Barbara said Perry would like to be a Renaissance prince, a patron of the arts. I sold him a nude of Maya about four years ago that hangs over his piano. I've gotten a lot of business from it. It's very sassy."

"What's his wife think of it?"

"No problem that I'm aware of. Barbara can be a handful herself. I think she tends to go her own way." I didn't want to bring up her behavior in my studio; I still wasn't sure how to think about it. But I *was* still thinking about it.

"Where does his money come from?"

"Oil field equipment, Barbara says. I'm not sure whether it's the drills or the derricks. It's family money anyway, but since his father died Perry controls it. He goes back and forth between San Miguel and Houston, where he's got some kind of family compound. I'd like to see the art and antiques he's got there."

A flight attendant came by in a crisp blue uniform, hair coiled up on the back of her head, attractive, capable and efficient, but still friendly. Mexican hospitality travels well. We made room on the fold-down trays for some coffee.

Going back to the paperwork after a while there was no indication that Tobey had used anyone else to receive things at Calle Independencia 132. Almost always the restoration costs were higher than the original purchase price. I thought back to the condition of the paintings at Gallería Cruz, and those in Perry's house. They may have been wrecks coming into Tobey's possession, but they were museum quality going out.

According to the older records, the ceramics came from a number of sources in and around the Yucatan and Guatemala. Many of the sellers had only a single transaction. Ramon Xoc first appeared eight years back with Tobey's purchase of one item, and then with increasing frequency until from four years ago until the present, he was Tobey's sole source of Mayan ceramics. I wondered how he could be *that* good. Had he discovered a buried city that no one else knew about? But when I checked the prices he was getting for these pieces I was amazed to see that Ramon Xoc was getting only about ten to fifteen percent of Tobey's sale price, and sometimes less. I would have expected half, the kind of split you found in an art gallery. Unlike the paintings, none of the papers noted any restoration costs for the ceramics, although I had noted repairs on a number of Perry's pieces, as well as those in Tobey's gallery. This was a good business, for Tobey at least. I made a note to ask Ramon what he thought Tobey had been getting for his finds.

As the coastline came into view we could see Campeche below on the right. First there was a dry area to the north and east of it and then the solid carpet of jungle spread out as far as we could see. This was not the African variety of jungle, I knew it was more like twenty or thirty feet high, never more, full of thick scrubby trees yielding rare and exotic hardwoods in small dimensions. Then Mérida appeared. It was just past two o'clock when we got off the plane and the heat hit us like a wet quilt thrown over our heads. We picked up a small Chevrolet rental car and headed from the terminal out onto the Periférico, a belt line that circles the main part of Mérida. There was not much traffic and we made good time into el centro.

I had booked us at a bed and breakfast occupying two adjoining townhouses not far from the main square. Cobbled together from these adjacent residences, it was maze-like and confusing at first, with twenty-foot ceilings and a roof garden and bar with long views over the city. On a table in the entry was a tall candle bent over in the exact curve of a horseshoe, a metaphor for the heat.

The interior held a small courtyard, with a tiny swimming pool so enclosed by the tall surrounding walls it was like swimming at the bottom of a hole. Sunlight reached it for ten minutes precisely at noon. In my room the hot water sometimes worked, but never during my shower. I had a small balcony overlooking the interior jungle and some stairs beside the bed that led to a door to my own personal roof garden. A hand-lettered sign on the door warned, "Reserved for Walter's Mother." She didn't use it while I was there, unless she got past me during the night.

The climate dictated a small *siesta*, and the air conditioning was more reliable than the hot water. I woke up about six with Cody tapping on my door and we headed out toward the square. Automobile tires were no longer melting. We found a small restaurant on a side street where the waiters fought over us as we entered. After dinner we found the *zocalo*.

This plaza is the heartbeat of Mérida, with flower and balloon vendors and small booths with handmade clothing, most of it embroidered in the Yucatan style, usually multicolored flowers at the edges of sleeves and hems or necklines.

I had been to Mérida a number of times before and in some ways I liked it better than San Miguel, but I didn't think I could do the climate. You couldn't get away from it, and I didn't want to live in a place I felt I had to get away from for part of every year. I'd had enough of that in Ohio. We sat before a platform set up in one of the streets and the folkloric dances began, young boys and girls in white embroidered outfits swaying to the music of a small combo. The music was laid back and distinctive; it did not remind me of the *mariachis* in the *jardín* in San Miguel.

It was late when we came back to the bed and breakfast and the door was locked. One of the owners, probably Walter, had to let us in. We were not ready to turn in, so we went up to the rooftop garden. It had views in all directions. The bartender was no longer on duty and we borrowed a couple of beers from the bar fridge, wondering what Ramon Xoc might have to say tomorrow.

We left Mérida in a rental car at 8:30 in the morning and followed a narrow blacktop road bordered on both sides by the jungle, where we dodged streams of tricycle-drawn carts. In Kimbila we got confused and took the wrong fork in the road. I guess everyone knew the way to Izamal and there was no need to mark it. A woman with two small children in tow got us turned around. Cody was shoehorned into the bucket seat beside me, with his knees up against the dashboard. The jungle was low and gnarly and stopped just at the edge of the pavement.

"Steamy place," he said. "Makes me miss the crisp mornings in San Miguel this time of year."

We pulled into Izamal at about 9:45. Immediately ahead was a small square with a car park. The town traffic cop got up off a bench and waved us into the row of empty parking spaces. We waved back and kept going, passing an antiques shop on the western edge of the square.

"We might want to check out that antique store after we talk to Ramon Xoc," said Cody. "Let's see what's for sale in this town. I might have to get me some antiques." His normal idea of decor was a brace of police merit citations on the wall over his sofa.

The street ended in a T at the edge of an immense platform, edged on three sides by arches, and on the fourth by the Convento de San Antonio de Padua, which was itself fronted by the same kind of arches. The facade towered above with a square bell tower on the left and a Baroque peak in the center. Everything was yellow ochre. We turned left and circled the platform. I tried to imagine the scale of the pyramid that had once stood there. The rear of the church was sculptural, with massive stone buttresses left in their natural color. Close up you could probably see traces of Mayan carving in the stonework. Izamal was laid out in the same kind of grid as Mérida, with the odd Calles in one direction, and the even Calles running perpendicularly. I swung a left on Calle 4 and in a moment we were on Calle 29, Ramon's street.

On both sides, as far as we could see, it was fronted by yellow houses and shops. Number 14 looked much like the others, with arches embedded in the facade. We drifted on by and cruised around the block. As I expected, there was no way to see the rear of the house since the block was faced on all four sides with house fronts. I pulled back onto Calle 29 and parked down the street.

"Here we go," I said. "We finally meet the great excavator."

We stopped in front of an old door constructed of wooden panels placed at right angles to each other. A glazed clay tablet to the right of it said fourteen. There was no bell and Cody pounded briskly on one of the panels. The same knock he had used probably 10,000 times as a cop.

"Are we doing good cop or bad cop?" I asked.

"More like friends of a friend."

There was silence for a full minute or more and then a small panel behind a grid opened, and a woman in her sixties looked out at us. Her hair was mostly gray, but with a few streaks of black, and pulled behind her head in a bun. Her only wrinkles were at the corners of her black eyes and at her mouth. It must be the humidity.

"*Sí*?" she said.

"Good morning, *Señora*," I said, in my best formal Spanish. "We are sorry to disturb you. We are looking for the home of Ramon Xoc."

"He is not here today." Her tone was neutral.

"We were told he is an important excavator here in the Yucatan, and we have come from Mérida to speak with him and perhaps see some of the things he has found." Beads of sweat ran down Cody's forehead.

"Does he know you?"

"No, but we were sent by *Señor* Tobey Cross," I said, "who does business with him in San Miguel." This was a stretch, but I was betting that she didn't know Tobey was dead.

She smiled and opened the door. We entered a room that took up the full width of the house, sparsely furnished and with a beautiful ceramic tile floor in a floral pattern. No rugs. "*Señor* Cross is an important man in the state of Guanajuato. Ramon has said this."

"My name is Paul Zacher, and this is my friend Cody Williams." I wasn't sure whether to offer to shake hands, so I didn't. She was quite short, not even five feet tall, and under an apron wore the embroidered white sisal dress we had seen everywhere since we arrived.

"I am *Señora* Xoc, the mother of Ramon," she said. She moved toward a table in one corner. It held half a dozen photographs in silver-colored frames. On the other end of the table was a good-sized television set, rabbit ears cocked off to the right side. "This is my son Ramon." She picked up a photograph and showed us a man about my age, small stature, wide Yucatán features and thick hair. He smiled at the camera, standing before a well-preserved wall of stone skulls.

"We are sad we missed Ramon today. We had hoped to see some of the things he has found. Does he have a studio or a laboratory near here?" She looked at Cody and laughed as she made a gesture with her head.

"Ramon has the old house. That's where he works. Come with me, you can see it."

"Bingo," I whispered to Cody as she led us through two more rooms, the second of which was a kitchen. Outside we passed through a well-tended vegetable garden. By the back wall was a cleared area with a small Mayan style house under a thatched roof. Ramon probably had to chop down the vegetation daily to keep the house from disappearing.

Inside, modern lighting hung over a long worktable. In one end of the house was a hammock and at the opposite end, rows of shelving. I counted five shipping boxes of the type we had seen at Independencia 132 in Dolores Hidalgo.

"May we look around?" I asked *Señora* Xoc. "This is very exciting."

"Please do," she said. "I only wish Ramon had been here to greet you himself."

"Did he go to Mérida? Perhaps we can meet him there."

"Oh no. He is in the north, in Guanajuato State. I think he went to Dolores Hidalgo."

I nodded politely. Had this earnest looking young man gone there to kill Tobey? Maybe he'd found out what the antiques dealer was getting for his finds.

Two large plastic garbage cans stood at the end of the worktable. Cody lifted the lid from one of them and looked at *Señora* Xoc as if to say, "May I?"

She nodded. Inside, the container was lined with wet burlap and nearly full of clay. Cody didn't look at me. On the shelving lay an assortment of tools, some of wood and some of steel, with short handles and loops of various configurations, and others like paddles, some curved, some flat. Next to these was a group of brushes upright in a can. Against the wall leaned several squares of plywood, warped and stained, possibly platforms for works in progress. On another shelf was a large collection of cans, and jars of liquid that had to be paint or glaze. A single spade lay below the shelves.

"Perhaps Ramon took some of his ceramics with him?" I asked her.

"It could be, because he needs to send them away all the time. You are friends of *Señor* Cross?"

"Yes. We know his gallery well." As I said this Cody set a pencil sketch on the bench in front of me. It showed an undecorated three-legged vessel, and below it a series of animal figures that might have been intended to grace the sides. I took it in briefly and said nothing more.

We stepped back out into the merciless sunshine. Cody nudged me and pointed to a low brick structure at the edge of the cleared area. The edges around the top had a blackened look. "Does Ramon cook *comida* out here sometimes? Or is it for *cochinita pibil*?"

She laughed and shook her head as if to say, What silly gringos. "Ramon only cooks the clay out here."

Returning through the house we thanked her for showing us around. As she stood at the door she said, "I hope next time Ramon will be here for you."

"Thank you for your hospitality," I said.

"Well, well," said Cody, as the door closed behind us. "The man's an artist."

"You don't think it's just a hobby." I drove back in the direction of the square.

"A damned lucrative one. Look what Tobey was paying him."

"Do you think Tobey knew they were fakes?" I pulled up in front of the antiques shop on the square.

"Hard to tell now, since we can't ask him, but if you think of the difference in prices between what Ramon was getting and what Tobey sold them for, it looks to me like they went in as fakes and came out as the real deal."

"I think we need to talk to Ramon as soon as possible. He's got to be in over his head here and I bet he has no idea. Why not try to get hold of Maya and see if she can stake out 132?"

Cody chuckled. "I can just see Maya on stakeout in the artmobile. It's even got one of those cup holder deals for the coffee and donuts."

The traffic cop appeared in front of the car and again waved us off in the direction of the parking area.

"Did you notice the excavating tools?" I asked Cody. "The picks, the shovels, the fine brushes for dusting the precious discoveries?"

"I get it. The trays of shards, the bone fragments, the chips of jade. Above all, the fine screen for sifting through the dirt. That stuff?"

"Right. He may have had them at one time, but I'll bet he hung them up long ago. I think Ramon is only digging raw clay now. Instead of pyramids he's scouting clay pits."

The antique store had not been painted within the lifetime of anyone now living. Over the grilled window facing the parking area shaded by palm trees, it said, "Mercado Maya."

The interior reminded me of the collection of someone who had acquired broadly and without discipline for many years, and the result now covered the walls and every surface within the store, and hung from the ceiling as well. It had last been dusted during the regime of Porfirio Diaz, and even then none too perfectly. An American in a *guayabera* bent over a drawer in a small cabinet. He appeared to be in his mid-fifties and wore jeans and sandals. His hair was pulled back in a gray ponytail.

"*Hola*, guys. Let me know if I can show you anything."

He did have a phenomenal set of masks that covered one entire wall. I thought of doing a mask still life and I wondered if there was a mask here that an excavator would wear. Or a burly old cop, to cover a big red face. Cody was pawing through a pile of old maps. The American came over to me and held out his hand.

"Robbins, Mick Robbins. Don't think I've seen you before. Welcome to Izamal. Are you a mask collector?"

"No. But I am looking for ceramics. Old things, you know? Fragments. Got anything like that?"

"I don't think there's much Mayan that I don't have." He pulled two drawers from a tall oak cabinet and set them on the counter. Cody drifted over. The pieces were organized within the drawers in a way that I didn't understand. Nothing was bigger than three inches across.

Cody looked at Robbins. "Is it legal to take these out of the country?"

"Sure. In ceramics anything up to the size of your palm, more or less, and not intact, can leave the country. Bigger than that and you need to apply for an export permit, which goes through the Ministry of Culture in México City, and more often than not, you never hear back from them. I don't advise it."

"Do you have anything bigger than what you have here?"

"Not any more. I used to have a local guy who came up with some pretty good finds, a few of them very early. Larger pieces, too. But that dried up four or five years ago."

"Anything intact?"

"Now and then. But all that stuff flew out of here when they started talking about export permits."

"Ever see that fellow around anymore?"

"Sure, he's still around. Name's Xoc; Ramon, I think. Nice guy. It could be that he's found a better market somewhere else." He noticed Cody mopping his forehead. "It does get warm around here," he said. "But you get used to it. I've been here since '79. Used to be in a rock band before that. Now I'm a little deaf. Ever hear of the New Buzzards?"

"No. Thanks for your help." Cody put his hand on my shoulder and pushed me out. We tipped the traffic cop ten pesos for his valuable assistance and drove back in the direction of *Señora* Xoc's place. Nearby, on Calle 27 was a restaurant called Kinich Kakmo, which we had heard about in Mérida. It was time for a couple of beers and some serious analysis.

Kinich Kakmo was a charming, open-feeling place with no ceilings other than the thatched palapa style roofs, and no interior walls except at the kitchen and the bathrooms. The thatch was supported throughout by a structure of timbers lashed together. The waiter was young and enjoyed his work. We both ordered *poc-chuc*, the local pork specialty. In an open fronted hut at the edge of the restaurant the tortilla woman worked steadily, patting the corn into shape over an open fire, the traditional way.

Cody took a long swig of his Negra Modelo and leaned back in his chair. "So what do we know and when did we know it?"

I thought for a minute. "We know that our friend Ramon was once truly an amateur archaeologist, in a free lance sort of way. We know that at some point he took his place in a long tradition of Mayan artisans and became a producer. I don't think he is copying anything directly now. He is probably taking design elements from a vocabulary he's mastered, and recombining them to form a truly individual product. You're not going to open *Archaeology South Magazine* and find something exactly the same as what just went out to Galería Cruz. Ramon's creations are unique, or Tobey would never have risked selling them as genuine."

"What happens when the first gringo customer

dies and leaves his treasures to his favorite museum? The jig is up."

"*If* they spot them as fakes," I said. "Maybe they won't. Not every museum is expert in every area. If they do spot them and they come back at him, then Tobey's on the first bus out of San Miguel with suitcases full of money. Or maybe the museum stays gracious and polite and doesn't say anything, especially if the donor has other things in the pipeline that might be real and valuable. Just stick them in the archive with a lot of other phony stuff they've been given. And then there's the export problem. Most likely the ceramics couldn't leave the country even if a museum has them. Either way, end of story."

"How about the stakeout idea?" Cody dug into the grilled pork, with sides of beans and salad that the waiter had just set down. "*Una cerveza mas, por favor,*" he said to the man, who caught my eye.

"*Yo tambien,*" I said. "I'm reluctant to ask Maya to go back to 132, but I don't think Ramon is dangerous. It's only that she's not getting paid enough to get hurt." I pulled out my cell phone and dialed her number, but a message came up that said, "No Service." No surprise.

"I think we've got to get her in on this, since we're here and he's there," said Cody. "Does she check her e-mail?"

"All the time when she's in the archive. There's an Internet facility above Cafe Havana back in Mérida. We could get her going as soon as we get back. I don't think we can let this wait."

CHAPTER EIGHT

Cody had just dropped me off at home after our flight and gone on to his condo when Maya pulled up in the artmobile. We hugged and I kissed her and this time our door was still locked. We bolted it again after we got in, but there's something about a break-in that shakes your confidence in locks. When my e-mail reached her at the Dolores Hidalgo archive she folded up her laptop and spent some time hanging about near Tobey's office. Ramon had not appeared.

I made a fire in the great room and put on some Chet Baker ballads. Maya poured us each a brandy and we sat on the sofa. When I pulled off her shoes and rubbed her feet I worked over each of her toes separately. I'm not able to explain the exact medical reason for this, but it seemed to perk her up. She leaned back deeply into the cushions and groaned. "No activity at 132," she said. "Don't ever stop."

"I'm not surprised."

"Marisol called me. The coroner's office in Guanajuato has released Tobey's body. It went back to Minneapolis this morning. She wants me to come back with her for the funeral. I need to be there with her because she doesn't feel that comfortable with his family. Do you want to come?" She seemed uncertain about whether I might want to go. I'd never been to Minneapolis.

"I think I do. Maybe we can find out who he was. Cody's associates in the Chicago Police Department couldn't find anything. You know, why not talk to Tobey's friends and family? Get them to reminisce a bit about the good old times. Because unless we find Ramon, we've got nothing much here. Well, a little maybe. We're getting an idea who Ramon is."

I filled her in on what we found in Izamal.

"Not another artist," she said.

"Exactly. The bearer of a proud tradition in this case. He had it in his genes."

"His jeans?"

"No. Like DNA."

"You need to paint again and I need to pose. I'm feeling bad about the lost Maize God picture. I could take my clothes off?"

"You could." My hands were working her calves now, then moving up behind her knees. "I could help, I'm good at it. I'm not sure I'll mix any paint, though. Let me just get these buttons." Nothing like a good foot rub.

Maya was able to get an expedited visa the next day at the consulate because of the funeral. Marisol didn't need one because she had dual citizenship. Tickets were available for a flight two days out.

We settled into the studio and Maya emerged from behind the changing screen without her robe. "I'm going to wash it," she said. I knew she was thinking about Barbara wearing it.

It was strange starting again on a picture I had nearly finished, and I don't like to paint the same scene twice. I tried to tell myself it was a good thing, a chance to improve on what I had done before, but I knew it wasn't.

It was only an attempt to recapture lost work. The earlier picture seemed to belong to another, less problematical time. I was merely a painter then, with no thought of trying to solve a crime.

I don't use the word "artist" to describe myself. It's a five-dollar word to characterize what to me is only a highly skilled craftsman. Marisol's thought that I might see things differently was true; painters learn to see differently as they learn their craft. When I picked up a ceramic vessel in Tobey's gallery I didn't quite see the vast ancient culture it came from; San Miguel was too far west to have been part of Mayan country, and there are few Mayan artifacts here. In any case, I knew little about it. What I saw in the ceramics was the person who made them, and my instinctive goal in looking closely at them was to understand how they were made. They connected me to the individual more than the culture. It was the same for any handmade artifact that I touched.

"What are you thinking about?" I asked Maya. This time the line of her back was correct right away.

"About Marisol and Tobey. When Tobey was killed I thought, what if I lost you like that? But then I thought, no one kills a painter. Now I'm not so sure. If someone comes into our house and cuts up a painting, then it's not so different to think he might kill the painter. That's a terrible thing to think."

"You never told Marisol."

"No."

"Close your eyes, I'm ready to start your face."

"You won't die, will you?"

"Not for sixty years."

By early afternoon I had Maya roughed in on the

canvas and had begun sketching the Maize God behind her. I altered the position of her hand for this version, trying to make it seem like new work. Two days later we left for Minneapolis, not realizing what the last week of January meant there. We should have done a little research.

CHAPTER 9
VALENTIN GUZMAN

Valentín Guzman leaned against the locked door of a *tiendita*, a tiny neighborhood grocery store: the kind with a hand lettered sign, a single cooler and seven or eight shelves of last minute groceries. His right hand moved over the surface of the watch on his other wrist. It was a gift from the Boss, and in the right light it looked like gold. It didn't matter that the metal expansion band was flexed over his thick wrist and pinched a little in places; it was Valentín's most treasured possession. He shifted from one foot to the other and he heard the door creak as his bulk pressed against its surface.

He looked at the watch. It was 8:45 and had been dark for more than two hours. Any minute now the man with the sample case would come into view.

The grocery store stood on a corner on the eastern end of San Miguel, with one side that opened to a well-traveled street that became the road to Querétaro, and the other facing the quiet side street, hardly bigger than an alley, where Valentín now stood. The Boss had told him that the man with the sample case would be on foot. That meant he would either continue on the Querétaro road when he left the Boss's house or he would turn and pass Valentín in the doorway as he went down the street. Either way, Valentín was ready.

His hand found the gun in his pocket. He didn't like to touch it, but he wanted to be sure it was there. Next to it was the key, wrapped in a piece of paper he had folded over it. The small pistol was one of a pair the Boss had pulled out of his desk drawer, both layered into a felt cloth that smelled of oil. One was an automatic, the other, a revolver. The Boss had told him to take the revolver because they were foolproof, and then given him the key as well. Valentín didn't want to try to remember the address where he was supposed to leave the body, so he wrote it down. There were other things to think about. Even when he wasn't stressed like this it was hard to think about more than one thing at a time.

Two pairs of headlights moved down the street in his direction. He hoped the Boss had been right about the man with the sample case being on foot. Otherwise the plan was ruined. But the Boss was never wrong, or, at least, he hadn't been yet. But Valentín had never been entrusted with anything this important. The headlights passed and as his eyes readjusted to the dim light he made out a small figure coming down the street toward him. The man approached slowly, looking downward, as if he had a greater burden than the case in his hand. As he reached the opposite side of the street he paused as if to get his bearings, and then turned right. Valentín waited a moment and then crossed the narrow street and followed him.

Hastening down the uneven sidewalk, he came up behind the man and placed his huge hand on his shoulder and spun him around. There was shock on the man's face as he looked up.

"You are Ramon?" asked Valentín, pressing the

gun into his neck.

The man hesitated, then said, "Yes, I am Ramon, but what...?"

"Just come with me. Say no more."

"I have no money, nothing of much value..."

"Silence. I have a gun."

Valentin's van was parked near the corner. Keeping a firm grip on Ramon's arm, he opened the rear doors and pushed him inside. He quickly slid in beside him and pulled the doors shut to put out the interior lights. From behind the spare tire he drew out two lengths of rope and pressed Ramon face down on the floor with his knee as he bound his hands and feet. Ramon said nothing. Valentín moved up to the driver's seat and pulled away from the curb. He turned right at the corner, and then right again and up the hill to Cuesta de San Jose, heading toward the reservoir.

Five minutes later, a battered Nissan pickup pulled into the empty parking space and two women got out. The one from the passenger side nearly tripped over the forgotten sample case, but her irritation turned quickly to excitement as she examined the neatly made box, covered in thick canvas. She moved her purse to her left shoulder and picked it up. Its weight promised something interesting. In fact, it contained Ramon's tools, a sample Mayan pot, a Rolodex and a ledger. The women looked around, but saw no one in view, and they quickly entered a house two doors down.

As Valentín drove up Cuesta de San Jose his sense of dread grew. He had done many tasks for the Boss in the past, but never before had he asked Valentín to kill someone. Only the thought of the 5,000 pesos (about $450) pushed him on. It would keep him and his family going for more than a month. His wife was just nineteen and she had already given him two small sons.

Spaces between the houses grew larger as Valentín negotiated the frequent speed bumps. A sign ahead indicated the road for the reservoir and he turned in. No other cars were in sight. He moved over the potholed road a few hundred feet farther and then pulled over. As he got out of the van his stomach felt knotted and hollow.

He opened the rear doors and pulled Ramon out by the arm. The man was shaking but he said nothing. Valentín forced him to his knees facing the reservoir and pulled the gun from his pocket. He slid back the safety as the Boss had showed him and pointed the gun at the back of Ramon's head. Involuntarily he crossed himself, then returned the gun to his right hand and pulled the trigger. But Ramon had sensed it coming and wheeled around suddenly at the same instant. The bullet passed through his eye into his head and he collapsed backward onto his bound hands.

Valentín stood motionless as the sharp pop of the pistol faded away into the night. In the thick brush an animal got to its feet and fled. Nothing else moved.

He removed the ropes from Ramon's hands and feet and brought out a section of old carpet from the back of the van, placing the body at one edge. Now was the part that Valentín disliked the most. He took out the twenty-centavo coin the boss had given him and slid it into Ramon's mouth, pressing his jaws closed again. With a length of the clothesline he tied Ramon's jaw shut. The Boss had specifically told him to do this, so that the coin would stay in place until the body stiffened. It was another strange idea of the gringos, and Valentín had learned to not question such things.

Then he rolled up the carpet. Blood and brain material still seeped from the wound on the back of Ramon's head, but there was little on the face. Valentín easily lifted the carpet roll and slid it back into the van. Suddenly he realized that the sample case was not there. He considered for a moment going back to the street where he had parked, but then rejected it. How could he risk being seen there again, especially with a body in his van? He decided not to mention it to the Boss unless he asked. He rubbed the watch again and then looked at it. It was 9:15.

Valentín spent the night at home worrying about Ramon's body lying in the back of his truck. Early in the morning he drove the three miles back from his rented five-hectare farm into San Miguel, passing the turnoff to the reservoir, but not looking at it. He thought he would never go back there again. He had passed a difficult night, and now he could not wait for his task to be over. As he drove down Santo Domingo toward centro, he pulled out the key with the paper wrapping the Boss had given him and looked again at the address, then headed for Quebrada. The Boss had said the people who lived there would be leaving sometime in the morning, probably early, and after they had gone, he was to leave the body in the entry and lock the house again.

It was still dark when he pulled into a parking place across the street and down a bit from his destination. He rolled down the windows on both sides of the van to dissipate the odor that was beginning to grow behind him. At a quarter to eight the edges of the hills outside of town were starting to glow when he saw the door open. A man and a woman came out with one suitcase apiece, and both carried a strange bulky coat. He waited for ten minutes after they had flagged down a taxi and then moved the van into position closer to the entrance.

He checked the address for the last time, and went up to the door and unlocked it. Inside everything was quiet. No lights were on. He pulled the door shut again, but stopped short of letting the latch engage, and went back to the van. He fiddled with the handle for a couple of minutes until there was no one in view on the street, and then slid out the carpet roll and swung it over his shoulder. In the entry, he unrolled the carpet and left Ramon's body at the top of the second step.

Opening the door a crack he surveyed the street. No one looked his way. He locked the door and loaded the carpet back in the van. He hoped the Boss would be proud of him, since he wasn't very proud of himself.

CHAPTER 10

Living in México makes the idea of intense cold somewhat abstract. It is a real thing, of course, like world hunger or the AIDS epidemic and global warming, but it exists at a comfortable distance; you can talk about it at cocktail parties (although we rarely do because people who live here don't want to recall it), express deep feelings about it and you don't even shudder. Before we left San Miguel I looked up the temperature on the Internet. It was twenty-one degrees below zero in Minneapolis. Of course, that was an early morning temperature. With any luck at all I was hoping it would be up to maybe eight or even seven below zero when we got there. San Miguel, on the other hand, experiences a light frost once every couple of years, depending on how far up the hillside your house is. We throw another blanket on the bed and Maya pulls out her long nightgown.

It took me a while to remember where I had put my winter coat. When I found it in the armoire in the guest bedroom it resembled a curious bulky thing from another life. I felt like John Glenn coming out of retirement and retrieving a space suit from storage for another trip into orbit. With a sheepskin lining that came all the way up to a tall collar meant to cover your ears, it closed with little solid plastic barrels on cords that went through the buttonholes. It smelled like something I should have thrown away long ago. It had been high style twelve or fifteen years back. A pair of gloves with a hole worn in one finger was jammed in the left pocket. The only hats I could locate were a Panama and a baseball cap. I chose the baseball cap. I wasn't expecting a sunburn. Maybe Tobey had a lot of old friends who were athletic. Maybe I'd fit right in at the cemetery. Give 'em a few high fives. What about those Minnesota Vikings! I didn't own any boots.

Maya had nothing like this of her own, and had only seen such things in movies. Marisol provided her with a long olive-colored coat that came six inches below Maya's knees and looked like something the Cossacks would have worn skating across the Don River in 1870. If there was a time when this style was popular I had missed it, and I didn't mind that I had. It had a fox collar that went well with her dark hair as she modeled it for me in the bedroom. I guess we both looked kind of retro. We picked up Marisol on the way. Three rubes from central México going up for the funeral. Maybe retro was in. We wouldn't know until we got there.

Carrying the coats as we boarded the Continental flight in Leon, which at sixty miles away is our nearest airport, we got some looks of sympathy from the gate attendant who saw our destination. After Customs in Houston we switched to Northwest Airlines and got more sympathy. They knew what we were in for.

Living in México also makes you take the sun for granted. It's one of thousands of small changes you undergo that you're not aware of until you leave. We got off the plane in Minneapolis after traveling all day to find a sky the color of dishwater gone bad. Maya and Marisol both gasped as the cold hit us like a wall of spikes, probing every surface of our skin and clothing. "I had forgotten this part," said Marisol between clenched teeth. "Last time we were here was five years ago and it was summer."

The airport cab started a long freeway ride, passing the Mall of America, and continued past miles of motels and corporate headquarters. None of it had the friendly worn crumbly look of old México. I saw no buildings with the stucco falling off. Everything was bright, glassy, cutting edge, and above all, cold. I missed the oldness of San Miguel, where every time you place your foot on the ground you touch a place where someone put his foot three or four hundred years ago. It looked as if Minneapolis was dedicated to rushing ahead, and in the process, had chopped off and leveled the past, only two or three paces behind.

Tobey's parents lived in a near southwestern suburb of Minneapolis called Edina. We checked into the Sofitel Hotel and it wasn't bad. There was a French restaurant right off the lobby, which was fine with all of us because we were beat from the trip and we would have seized any excuse to avoid going outside again. After a clean up and a change of clothes we met at the bistro. The tables all had wrought iron bases with white marble tops, with banquet seating below brass luggage racks. It reminded me of a comfy neighborhood place somewhere in the French Antarctic Territories.

"*Bon soir*," said the blond waitress, wearing a crisp black uniform with a white apron, something like a French maid's in the movies, only the skirt was longer. I saw two tired faces across from me, Marisol's tightened by apprehension of what was to come tomorrow. There seemed to be more lines around her eyes now.

"I never knew it could be so cold," said Maya. "It's like hell with ice. How could Tobey live here?"

Of course, he had escaped as soon as he could. Marisol didn't answer and her shoulders began to shake as she put her face in her hands. "I'll come back when you're ready," said the waitress, and moved off to a more upbeat table.

⌘⌘⌘

The next day came up hard and bright with the glare from fresh snow cutting into our eyes at a low angle. Maya and I pulled out sunglasses simultaneously as we approached the cab in the hotel drive. Marisol had gone ahead to ride with Tobey's parents to the service. I stuck my baseball cap in my pocket as we pulled away from the hotel.

The service was held at St. Stephen's Episcopal Church in Edina, across the street from a country club on West 50th St. Only about thirty people occupied the church, and judging from their age, they were mostly friends of the parents. The coffin was closed. The minister managed to paint a picture of a cultivated man cut off in his prime. He talked about Tobey's love for antiques and his respect for the historic past of México. It was clear he had never met Tobey, or if he had, his recollection of a much younger Tobey had faded. He made no reference to the manner of his death.

I looked at the memorial card. The cover showed an effeminate and unthreatening Christ in pink and sky blue robes. Judging from the grooming of his hair and beard, he knew a good barber and tipped well. Crook in hand, he led three sheep toward a misty undefined sort of place. It could have been Heaven, or it might have been a summertime Minnesota pasture in poor focus. Inside, the card read, "Abbott Cross, May 5, 1960 — January 21, 2005." *Abbott* Cross? What the hell! No wonder Cody's background check had come up blank. I thrust the open card in front of Maya, tapping on the word Abbott. My eyebrows were up. She looked at me and shrugged. Several people around me turned and glared at me.

"There will be a gathering at the Cross home following the interment," said the minister. "I hope to see all of you there." He gave the address. There was space for us in the second limousine to Lakewood Cemetery.

Lakewood occupies a couple of hills closer to the center of Minneapolis and some of the plots there have a vista toward a frozen lake. Tobey, or Abbott as I was trying to think of him now, had one of these. Although not as cold as the previous day, the wind was vicious and constant on this slope, and I didn't feel I could put on my baseball cap, so I was miserable. My skin felt seared as if by an iron and it made my eyes tear up, the drops freezing on my lower eyelids before they reached my cheeks. Maya looked like a turtle with her neck pulled into the deep collar. No other Cossacks appeared. Marisol and Tobey's mother leaned into each other. As they lowered the coffin into the ground Maya whispered to me, "How can they dig up the ground when it's like this?" I shrugged.

The minister said some final words and we each threw a white rose into the grave, frozen before it could wilt. Marisol sobbed quietly. Tobey's father was taciturn. People stood and consoled each other, then moved off toward the cars as the mortuary people collected the flower assortments from around the grave. The most desolate part was ten minutes later when everyone was gone. As I climbed into the car I looked back; it was just a rectangular hole next to a pile of frosty dirt covered with a green cloth. For the first time I understood why we were here.

The Cross home on Browndale Avenue was a sumptuous stucco Tudor from the 1920s, with deep Persian carpets over dark stained floors, and an interesting group of eighteenth century antique furniture in the living room. The woodwork was dark oak, and there was a mahogany highboy chest that looked like the real deal, and splat back chairs in the corners of the room. A good cove molding edged the ceiling, not too wide, and from it delicate plaster tracery reached out to a medallion above the chandelier. From the living room I looked through French doors to see the back yard sloping downward toward a wide frozen creek. The snow was brilliant. Half a dozen mature trees, skeletal without their leaves, framed the view. It would be a sweet place in summer. Now it was mainly a daytime view during the dark half of the year.

A caterer stood at the end of the long table in the dining room and a server was moving back and forth from there to the kitchen. I disposed of our silly coats. When I returned from the closet I found Tobey's father at my side.

"Brent Cross," he said, holding out his hand. "I don't think we've met."

Like Tobey, Brent Cross was tall, with an aggressive nose. His white hair seemed all there. He appeared to be in his early seventies, wearing a dark suit that was almost black with a subtle maroon thread in the weave. Given his ruddy coloring, a green thread might have been a better choice, but I said nothing about it.

"Paul Zacher," I said. "I'm very sorry about your son."

"Thank you. Were you close friends?" He put his hand on my shoulder, as if to console me.

"I really didn't know him well, but Marisol and my girlfriend Maya are close." There was a small pause. "You have a beautiful place here. Did Tobey help with the furnishings?"

"Actually, some of these are family things from my mother's house in Connecticut. But the highboy was something Tobey found for us in New York, when he was in graduate school there. We're not really collectors; it's just nice to have a few things around with some history. I always wanted to have one of the Mayan pieces that Tobey sold down there, but it's nearly impossible to get them out of México."

"I didn't know Tobey's name was really Abbott. I probably should have."

"Well, he never used it. We have a tradition in my family to always use last names as first names. That's how I ended up as Brent. Funny old habit, I guess, but it goes back four or five generations. Anyway, my mother was an Abbott. Of course Tobey never wanted to use it as a kid. Then in the brokerage business he decided to use it for a while, but stopped after he left Wall Street. When he started dealing antiques, using Tobey seemed to work just fine. What kind of work do you do, Mr. Zacher?" He took a long pull at a glass of white wine.

"I'm a painter," I said.

He nodded as if this were a noble calling. "Interior? Exterior?"

"Canvas, mostly. I paint pictures."

"Really! Have you seen this?" Without missing a beat Brent Cross led me to a small portrait of Tobey in the entry hall. I had walked past it on the way in without noticing it. He looked like he might have been a senior in high school. There was the same prominent nose and narrow face. His hair was parted in the middle and long over the ears, in the style of the late seventies. The brushwork was tentative and all the shadows were in the same warm tones of the highlighted skin, only darker, so that they didn't recede properly and sometimes looked like bruises or rotten spots, the color design remaining dull and lifeless. I wondered if the painter had ever heard of *terre verte* for skin shadows. It was the kind of painting that when the subject was forgotten would end up in an antique shop priced at $30 because the frame was good.

"Local fellow, Roswell Baker, I think his name is. Ever heard of him?"

"No, but I've never been in Minneapolis before."

"This is Edina, really. What do you think?"

"Very chilly. I looked up the temperature before we left México but I still couldn't believe how it felt when we came in."

"I meant the portrait."

"It's good," I said. Good is a strong word of approval from me, because not that many things are. I probably shouldn't have used it this time, but I was on my best behavior and I wanted him to talk.

"We love it," said Brent Cross. "Of course, we're especially happy to have it now."

"I had heard Tobey was in some kind of finance, but I didn't know it was the brokerage business," I said, wanting to get away from the subject of the portrait. I did have the vague "banking" guess from Marisol, but I wanted more specifics. I hadn't eliminated the possibility that the murder was connected to something in the distant past.

"That's where he made his money. That gave him the capital to get into antiques, which was always his first love. I was a broker myself for quite a few years. Municipal bonds, mainly. Tax exempt, you know."

"Right." I nodded. Taxes had never been much of a problem for me. I was OK with paying them when I had to because they meant I'd had income.

"We were down there in San Miguel two years ago to see him and Marisol. Interesting town, with everything so old. He had a wonderful place, fantastic garden. I'd love to have that here. But we're so limited by the growing season. Imagine being able to sit there and look out on that all the time."

"I can."

"Of course. And we do love Marisol. I never thought Tobey would marry a Mexican girl. When he dated...well there she is over there." He nodded subtly to indicate a tall slender blond woman across the room who appeared to be in her early forties. She was still attractive. "Gail Stone; she was a couple years behind him at Edina High. I thought for sure they'd get married, but then one day, quite suddenly, they weren't together anymore. She married a doctor later, but now she's divorced. She got the house, it's just down the block here. Gail was a client of mine until I retired. I think she's done OK for herself," he finished, ending on a positive note. I wondered whether it was the divorce or his investment management that had set her up so well.

Maya was coming toward us with a plate of food and a glass of white wine. She was restrained but elegant in a straight black skirt and beige silk blouse. I rarely saw her so formal. Brent leaned over to say something to the passing server and I whispered to Maya in Spanish, "Did you pump the mother?"

"Pump her?" she looked alarmed. Some things don't translate well and I didn't get an answer. She stayed to talk to Brent Cross while I filled a plate and made my way over to Gail Stone. There were mushroom caps stuffed with something like crab, vegetable sticks, little sausages in a spicy sauce, triangular pastries filled with cream cheese.

I introduced myself. "Gail, Brent Cross was telling me you were an old friend of Tobey's. I wonder if I might ask you a couple of questions? Marisol has asked me to look into the circumstances of his death. She wants a different perspective from what she might get from the Mexican police. I've been trying to learn more about his background and I think it's fascinating that he could make the transition from finance to antiques."

"Well, it didn't seem odd, for him. Tobey and I went out for several years. Almost three, I think. I hardly knew him in school, but when he came back from New York, after the Parson's School, you know, someone got us together again and we just hit it off. I remembered him as kind of a nerd in high school, a budding connoisseur of just about everything. But when he got back, and we were all a little older, he was very polished and knowledgeable. He seemed to wear it better at that age. I guess no one likes a sixteen-year-old expert."

Her coloring was dark for a blonde in midwinter.

Scottsdale, I thought, or maybe Florida. She had pores that marred the total effect this close, but her b eyes were beautiful and her hands elegant. Of cou you'd never paint individual pores, they'd look like po marks. Surprising for January, her dress was short-sleev and her arms were covered with the fine hair blondes often have. She wore no rings.

"Was he in finance then?"

"Yes. It seemed very exciting at first. Brent got him into a firm in St. Paul. It didn't take long before he was making some impressive money. That was when I began to think I might marry him. But the hours were long and he started to change in ways I didn't like."

"How was that?" I didn't look directly at her as I said this, but it made me think we might be getting into something interesting.

She turned away from me to the left and didn't meet my gaze. "Oh, I don't know. I hate to talk about him now, especially, but he began to get kind of cold. Like the business was taking something out of him, some of his humanity, I guess. I know he wished he had gone into the antiques business instead. Anyway, then it started to blow up."

"Blow up?" I kept my voice neutral but her comment sounded like a door opening.

"Well, I really shouldn't say anything more. Brent is starting to look at me. It just ended, OK? And I married someone else after a while, and that didn't work out either." She still looked around the room, not at me, as if we weren't having this conversation. "I don't remember you from Edina. Were you an old friend? You seem too young."

"I only knew him in México. My girlfriend Maya is a close friend of Marisol."

"Are you in the antiques business?"

"No, but I'm looking into it." She nodded. Probably there was an opening in the field now. I wondered if she was seeing herself in Marisol's shoes. Gail Stone would be the widow had she married Tobey instead of the doctor.

We talked a little more about the weather and the Crosses' house and then she excused herself and went into the dining room. I had the feeling I had raised some painful memories. Or maybe the funeral itself had.

How had Marisol connected on a personal level with this stylish connoisseur with his elegant clothes and tasteful engravings? I wanted to think it was more than just his prospects. Apparently she had humanity enough for both of them. Looking around the room I didn't see her.

I was standing next to a shoulder-height bookcase with glass doors. Four photographs of Tobey stood on the top. In the one that caught my eye he looked about eight years old, wearing a tweed jacket with a bow tie. His right arm was around the neck of a perky young Airedale. He wore a toothy grin and his teeth seemed too big for his mouth. Now he was in the ground, frozen solid. It seemed like an odd thing to think about, but given the weather I couldn't avoid it.

The minister came up and introduced himself. "Forsyth," he said, "John Forsyth, like the actor. Are you from out of town?"

"Central México. I'm Paul Zacher. I knew Tobey in San Miguel de Allende." I wondered if I should have said Abbott.

"Of course I hadn't seen him in many years, since he was a kid, really. But Brent is a long time elder in our church. He used to manage our portfolio before he retired." I wondered why a church would need tax exempt bonds. Of course, investments were not my long suit; I mainly took positions in things like food and electricity, gasoline, tequila. A box of Cuban cigars was a major offshore holding, one that usually didn't last long.

Later I found Maya and took her hand and we said our goodbyes. How good it was to have her and just be together. I wondered if we were unduly complicating our lives by being in the middle of this. I didn't know who killed Tobey, but I suspected the name was somewhere on the customer list. Or maybe it was Ramon Xoc? Did he feel cheated? As a creative person it didn't seem like he could be a killer, although that may have been nothing more than my personal prejudice. We'd probably never get to ask him.

Four blocks down on West 50th Street was a restaurant with a small bar we had noticed driving past on the way to the church. The wind was down now and I put on my baseball cap as we braved the icy sidewalks. I wished it had room for my ears. Maya gripped my arm the whole way. Marisol stayed behind to finish out the day with the Cross family. I knew the conversations they'd have after all the guests left. The parents would remember him mostly as a child.

The restaurant was called Tejas, which we both knew how to pronounce, and it had a southwestern ambiance that might have been Albuquerque or Laredo. We each had a coffee with a stiff shot of Irish whiskey in it and we didn't speak for a while. Sitting near the front windows, which was a chilly mistake, we watched scattered flakes of snow drift past.

Maya blew her nose and said, "I want to go home now. It would be bad just to be here this time of year, but to be here for a funeral, it's too much. I want to work on my research, I want to think about the Indians in the Revolution, I want to sit in the Santa Monica and have a margarita. I want to be in my garden and watch the bamboo grow. I want you to be painting me and I want to be in bed with you after."

"You don't ask for much." I took a sip of the spiked coffee.

"No. I don't. I am ready to be screaming quite soon now."

"Maybe later in the cab. This looks like a nice family place."

She screwed up her mouth and looked at me across the table. The sun was so low it came sideways into the restaurant and lit her hands, which were together, but working strangely as if trying to escape from each other. The funny Cossack coat was over her shoulders and dragging on the floor. Her thick glossy black hair looked out of place against the snow outside.

"The mother didn't have much to say," she went on. "She is very sad and she does not understand what happened. She thinks México is a dangerous place now."

"But she doesn't blame Marisol?"

"No. She doesn't think Marisol could have stopped it."

"I didn't learn much, either," I said. "But I think something bad happened to Tobey back here, years ago.

No one wants to talk about it. I guess I can understand, especially now that he's dead. But I feel like his dying was the end of something that began here, not in México."

"There is one thing we need to do, though. When we get back to the hotel there will be a computer we can use to e-mail Cody. He can try again with the police, using the Abbott name," she said. "I never knew he was Abbott. I never heard Marisol use that name."

The next morning we left the frozen zone without regret while Marisol stayed behind to spend a few days with the Crosses. I wondered how often she would see them again after she returned to México. Maya and I were both depressed. It was another gray day when we got on the plane, but as it climbed above the clouds we left something behind. The sun emerged and stayed with us, first on one side, then the other, all the way to the Houston stopover and then to Leon. Maya began to flirt with the man next to her on the aisle and I knew she was feeling better. I just wanted to have a brush in my hand again. We had been gone only two days, but it seemed like the right antidote to funerals and wind-chill. Maybe some of my paintings would still be intact when we got back to San Miguel.

We pulled up before our house on Quebrada and while Maya settled the cab bill I pulled out our luggage and set it on the eighteen-inch wide sidewalk and threw the coats on top. Thankfully, our door was still locked. Inside I went up the two worn steps and reached for the light switch a little further on. My hand missed it when I tripped over something bulky lying in my path. It was too dark to see the stone floor, even when it hit me in the face.

I didn't quite lose consciousness. Then the light

was on and Maya was screaming in the way that normally would have awakened the dead, but it didn't work this time; the man whose body my legs were laying across was still dead. I got to my hands and knees and put two fingers to the man's neck, but there was no question of a pulse. His skin was cold but yielding. The air was thick with an unfamiliar but distinctive smell that I hadn't noticed at first. There was an exit wound on the back of his head with dried blood mixed with other material I didn't want to try to identify.

"This man has been dead for a while," I said. "The rigor is gone." I had read somewhere that it lasted less than a day.

He was lying face down with one arm outstretched and the other beneath him. One knee was bent and he did not seem like a large man. He had thick black hair caked with blood, and medium dark skin. Even before I turned his head to see his face I thought I knew who he was, although I had only seen his photograph on one recent occasion, far away in the Yucatan.

CHAPTER ELEVEN

Maya was kneeling beside the dead man, her hands working uselessly as if she thought she should be doing something for him. "It is Ramon Xoc," she said. I turned his face. His nose was flattened to one side from pressing on the stone but the resemblance to the picture in Izamal was unmistakable. One eye was gone from the entry of the bullet, the eyelids puckered and blackened. The other was open. Blood had streamed around his face in a narrow band and dried in his ear. His mouth was slightly open and on the floor was a bright coin. I picked it up. "Twenty centavos," I said, not surprised. I put it back on the floor, knowing I shouldn't have touched it. My forehead was still throbbing.

"How did you know it was Ramon?" I asked her.

"Who else could it be?" I put my arms around her and we sat on the floor for a while, away from the body. She wouldn't look at it but I couldn't stop myself, as if it were about to speak to me.

"I guess we should call *Licenciado* Delgado," I said after a while, "the one who's been working with Marisol."

In México murder investigations are typically handled by the Judicial Police, who are much like assistant district attorneys in the U.S. They are often found working the same scene with the aid of uniform police, but their rank is higher and their chain of command goes up through the court system. They are part of the Agencia del Ministerio Publico. Training for this position includes a law degree as well as forensic and investigative studies. Most Mexicans don't trust them any more than they trust the uniform police.

Still dizzy, I got up and phoned the Policia Judicial and reached Delgado. While we waited for his arrival I brought in the luggage, then thought of something and ran upstairs to check the studio. My pictures were all undamaged.

A white unmarked car arrived in ten minutes with an ambulance immediately behind. It was Licenciado Delgado with two uniformed cops, plus the ambulance driver, a medical tech, and a forensic tech.

Diego Delgado was a slightly bulky man of about forty with pouches under his eyes. Delgado means thin, but the only thing truly thin about him was his mustache, which reminded me of a 1950s Mexican movie star. His neck bulged comfortably over his collar and his suit was brown with shiny spots at the knees and elbows as if his job required him to crawl around now and then. As we introduced ourselves he gave us a neutral look.

The tech confirmed that the man was dead. "I'll have to make a test to determine how long," he said.

Delgado pulled on a pair of latex gloves and looked at the bruise on my forehead. "You had a fight with him, *Señor* Zacher?"

"No. I tripped over the body when I came in."

"Do you know him?"

"No." Maya looked at me but said nothing. We were still so shocked we hadn't decided how to play this.

"*Señorita* Sanchez, do you know him?"

"No. I never saw him before."

One of the other police began to photograph the scene while Delgado made a careful inspection of the room. "You did not move him?" he said over his shoulder.

"Only his head a little, to see his face."

"Normally a man who is shot in the face does not fall forward like this when he dies. Did you clean up the blood?"

"No. Everything is as it was, except that I picked up the coin to look at it. I'm sure my fingerprints are on it."

Delgado continued to search the walls and ceiling with a flashlight. He scanned the surfaces of my two Diego Rivera copies that hung flanking the entry to the garden and moved his hands over the wood of the street door, showing no reaction. When the photographer had finished the ambulance driver and one of the uniformed cops turned the body onto a stretcher. Delgado went through the pockets and placed the contents on the hall table beneath one of my fake Riveras. There was a hotel key with a plastic oval tag that read "12," seven coins, and a small comb.

"No identification," said Delgado. "Why would he come to your house? You had business with him, yes?"

"As I said, I have never seen him before."

"So you did. Was the entry door locked when you returned?"

"Yes."

"Did you find that odd?"

"Not until I saw the body."

The forensic tech began to dust the door and the

lock for prints.

"I would like to have your fingerprints," said Delgado, "both of you, so we know which to ignore." One of the men got out a kit from a small satchel.

"You each have a key?" I pulled mine out and Maya searched in her purse and produced hers.

"Is there an extra key?"

"Yes, in the kitchen." I went to find it. It was in its usual place, the drawer below the phone. Back in the *zaguan* I said to Delgado, "I don't understand how they got in; the key is where I left it."

He merely nodded. "You have been traveling today?"

"Yes, we were in Minneapolis for the funeral of Tobey Cross."

"Deep in Gringolandia."

"Very. Too deep, in fact."

"So you came in at Leon?"

"Yes, Continental and Immigration will confirm that."

"What time did you leave this morning from Minneapolis?"

"About nine o'clock." Delgado made some notes in a spiral notebook.

"Is anything missing from the house?"

"We haven't looked at the other rooms except for the studio. We called you as soon as we found him and we waited right here."

Delgado walked with us as we went through the rest of the house. I turned on lights in the garden and in each room as we went. Again I had the sense of violation.

In the studio Delgado paused before Barbara's

painting. "This is you?" he said to Maya with his eyebrows raised.

"No," she said. "It is another."

"So there is another woman who takes her clothes off for you?" He looked at Maya instead of me as he said this. She didn't react.

"It's a living," I said.

"It must be difficult for you," he said to Maya.

"Sometimes."

"And that is not her husband downstairs?"

"No, I know the husband of this woman. He is a collector. He will buy the picture."

"How much does he pay you?" I didn't see the relevance of this, but with a dead body laying in my entry hall I didn't want to antagonize him.

"Four thousand dollars."

Delgado whistled. "Forty-four thousand pesos!"

"Yes." Of course he knew the exact exchange rate.

"You are a famous painter then?"

"Not famous enough."

He moved toward the door. "*Señor* Zacher, I will wish to speak with you tomorrow in my office when we have had more time to think about this. Shall we say at ten o'clock?"

"I'll be there."

"You know the place? It is the police office on the *jardín*, not the one on the Querétaro Road."

"Yes."

When we went downstairs the body was gone and the ambulance had driven away. The other police were waiting outside for Delgado.

He turned to me in the entry. "You seem to have much trouble, *Señor,* I hope it does not continue."

"Thank you," I said, wondering as I closed the door behind him what other trouble I was having that he might know about.

There was not much blood on the floor, just a dry flakey mark where Ramon's ear had touched the stone. I cleaned it up and washed my hands. The odor still lingered, and probably would for a while. Welcome home, travelers. My head was throbbing. We went to bed, but it was a long time before either of us fell asleep. When I finally did, I dreamed of snow, arranged in neat rows of mounds, with bodies beneath.

CHAPTER TWELVE

Three sides of the *jardín* are graced with elegant seventeenth or early eighteenth century arcaded buildings. On the fourth side stands the *Parroquia*, a nineteenth century fantasy of what a European cathedral might look like if the builders had put down a little too much *grappa* at lunch and it blurred their vision. Or perhaps the architect had been looking at picture postcards and couldn't quite make out the detail. Nonetheless it is a sentimental favorite in San Miguel. At night the detail is lit and can be seen from rooftop gardens all over town, including mine.

A few years ago I was greatly startled to see Salma Hayek hanging by one hand from a second story window of one of these arcaded buildings, her skirt fluttering enticingly in the breeze and a look of stark panic on her face. *Once Upon a Time in México* was being shot in San Miguel. I never did see Johnny Depp or Antonio Banderas. It seems like the movies come to this town a couple of times a year, and not only in the theaters. Naturally the cooler residents try to ignore this, but it's hard to ignore Salma Hayek. In my dreams I had painted her a dozen times. Each version got better. The detail was better than on the Parroquia.

It was a bright and cool morning as I headed for the police station, which occupies two floors of one of these grand colonial buildings on the square. The flower and balloon vendors were out already working the tourists and the newspaper boy was just arriving. Ten-year old girls were selling chewing gum by the piece. I bought one and stuck it in my pocket. I could have painted them all. And maybe that's what I should have been doing. I had no special desire to sit down with *Licenciado* Delgado, and parts of the investigation were now piling up around me in ways I didn't like. Our meager progress on the case didn't justify the risk. I couldn't help but ask myself if one of us was next. I'm sure this was what I was supposed to be thinking.

Delgado's office was on the second floor occupying the entire front of one of the buildings facing the *jardín*. The architecture of the interior was all early eighteenth century colonial, but the furniture and fixtures were late twentieth century K-Mart. If the look was meant to be eclectic, it was, but it didn't work. Fluorescent lights marched across the ceiling in two rows. Several of them buzzed like captive flies. The furniture was mostly particle board covered with wood-grained vinyl. As I sat down at Delgado's desk a fan was turning slowly on the twenty-foot ceiling. No air reached me from that distance. I didn't need any; it was cool enough without it.

Licenciado Delgado came in with a sheaf of papers in his hand and sat across from me. He didn't rate an individual office of his own. He reminded me of the kind of Mexican that American film directors like to use in supporting roles. They have the occasional good one-liner. Their teeth are excellent and their mustaches well trimmed, but they never get the girl, even though they grin a lot. She's reserved for the gringos. I liked the way this plot line ended; it reflected my life in San Miguel.

"I wish to thank you for coming in," he said. "We are very busy here today. We have had no murder in San Miguel for two years and now we have two within the space of two weeks."

I nodded sympathetically.

"You will understand that, normally, when a murder victim is found in the home of someone we look to that person for the main suspect. That would be you." He paused and looked at me expectantly. Was I supposed to confess now? Mexican criminal procedure was a mystery to me. I settled for a general statement designed to cast me in a benevolent light.

"As you know, I am a painter. Painters are by nature nonviolent. If I wanted revenge on someone I would paint a true picture of him. That would usually be enough."

"I see. We are still trying to identify this man who was dead in your house. As you saw last night, his pockets had no wallet. We are checking on his fingerprints but that will take some time. You are certain you did not know him?"

"I have never seen him before. I can't think why he was in the entry of my house."

"We believe he was brought to your house already dead. There was very little blood at the scene. The bullet that killed him entered through the right eye and exited from the back of his head, but there was no bullet in the room. As nearly as we can determine, he has been dead about three days, perhaps somewhat less.

"At about that time I was waiting to get on a plane for Minneapolis."

"Yes, we know this. And then on your return you were changing planes in Houston, Texas, and you came into Leon at 4:35. We have your record from the Immigration. When you arrived at home at six o'clock you found the body."

"Yes, and I called you."

"Thank you."

"Least I could do."

"Of course. Do you know why someone would leave a body in your *zaguan*?" He leaned back in his chair and pressed his fingers together. Was he suggesting he could squeeze the truth out of me?

"No. But it is possible that I am being a thorn in someone's side."

"Mine, most certainly. But I think you are right. There is no doubt to me that these two recent murders are related, and I know that you and *Señor* Williams have been, shall I say, interested in the crime of *Señor* Cross's murder. And you have seen much of the widow lately, yes?"

I didn't think it prudent to ask how he knew this, not that he would have told me. "She is a close friend of my girlfriend Maya. She asked me to help. I meant no disrespect to the police. By that time she had already spoken to you."

"Maya...you mean Maria Sanchez, the woman who lives with you, who poses with no clothes for many of your pictures?"

"Yes. I only call her Maya, because of the series of pictures I am doing. They mostly use backgrounds from the Yucatán."

"She does not mind?"

"No. She likes the name of Maya."

"I mean with no clothes. So anyone may see her in that way."

I paused for a moment, not certain of where he was going.

"They do not see her. They see only the painting. When she is nude I alone see her. She does not take her clothes off in the *jardín*, for example." I felt like we were now going around in circles.

"That is a good thing."

"Yes. But posing nude is an old tradition, going back many hundreds of years. Think of the Renaissance."

"I will. But some would object. Most Mexican women are more modest than that."

"True, but Maya has a good body and she is proud of it. Besides, only one person needs to like a painting, besides me and Maya."

"And that would be?" He leaned forward over the desk expectantly, as if we had now reached some important piece of evidence.

"The buyer."

"Of course, but to return to the dead body. I think someone is trying to warn you off. Perhaps we of the police are being persuaded to think you are the killer, but we are a little too smart for this."

"Right. I'm sure you didn't fall off the turnip truck yesterday."

"The turnip truck?" Vegetables, particularly broccoli, were the backbone of the rural economy here, and they did raise turnips, but even so...

"*Una camioneta esta llena de los nabos*. Just a phrase among the gringos. *Una idioma*. It means you cannot easily be fooled." I admit this was a stretch.

"You are correct, but nonetheless a warning might be a good thing here, except for the unfortunate victim, of course. Anyway, these are things you have no experience with. They are best left to the police."

"I am beginning to think you might be right."

"We have made some progress with this crime. We think the killer is a foreigner because having the gun is not very common here for Mexicans. If we had the bullet from this murder we would expect to find it came from the same gun that killed *Señor* Cross. And we have found the office of *Señor* Cross in Dolores Hidalgo and it has been broken into. Do you know why?"

"Perhaps he had other antiques there. I'm only guessing."

"No. There was nothing but empty packages and a few pictures, although there was a computer and other records. We now have much information on his business. But what I wonder is why he would have an office in Dolores Hidalgo? So inconvenient, yes? Every day to travel back and forth."

Empty packages in Tobey's office? I thought. Had Ramon returned to clean the ceramics out of the office before his death? If so, where were they now?

"Maybe the office rents are too high here in San Miguel?" I said.

"Well, that may be. Certainly real estate here has become very high with all the gringos. Just like the States perhaps. For someone like me it is hard to afford even a small house now."

"But surely when you sell you get gringo prices."

"True, but that is one time only. Then we have

to move out of town. Some of us must live in Atotonilco or Santa Teresita. And all the other prices are higher as well. You see, here in México we work very hard. You may already know this. I don't mean only long hours and difficult work. We need to use any opportunity we can find. If I drive a tourist bus around the town and the visitors wish to stop for an ice cream, then, for example, I will also know to have my cousin Luis with his ice cream truck just at a certain place and time. Because otherwise it would be the ice cream truck of someone else who would get the business, do you see? Then at the end of the week Luis would not give me my percentage for bringing by the tourists and I would not do as well, nor would his family. This is what I mean by working hard. Here in México we watch for every opportunity."

"I see."

"I have another question for you, and then I think soon we are finished. Before you went to Minneapolis you went also to Mérida, I believe?"

"Yes, I have a show coming up in June at the Galería Mundo Maya there."

"And you show your paintings here as well?" From his look I felt he already knew all this.

"Yes, at Galería Uno, but it is hard to sell enough from just one gallery. Two is good, three would be better."

"And you are quite certain that no one hit you, leaving that mark on your face? You did not, for example, discover someone leaving a body at your house and have a little disagreement about it?"

"No. I tripped and fell over the body, as I said. The mark is from hitting the floor."

"Then only one more thing. From the shipping

boxes at the Dolores Hidalgo office we have obtained the name of Ramon Xoc, with an address in Izamal. It is a small town of no importance. Do you know him?"

"No."

"You did not see him in the Yucatán?"

"No." I really didn't want to help the police and I wondered if Marisol would want me to. Clearly they didn't want me involved anyway.

"I am finished then with my questions. Please stay away from this. There is a very bad gringo out there with a gun. Make more pictures."

Indeed. Maybe I should call Barbara. Mix a little more *azo* red and *terre verte*. I felt relieved. At least I wasn't a suspect. I went down the worn marble staircase to the main floor and stopped in a little shop under the arcade across the *jardín* and bought an overpriced Cuban cigar. Time to celebrate; but then what? I paused under the drum-shaped treetops and watched the crowd. Poor Ramon Xoc. It was getting risky to be an artist here. My usual belief is that most risk is good, but it doesn't always pay off. I was certainly feeling less out of place investigating this case, but making some progress would have been better.

Cody came by for dinner that night. I suspected he had worked up something on the Abbott Cross angle. Maya had been chained to her laptop all day, recasting her notes in readable form. I had marinated some pounded chicken breasts in a tequila-orange-chipotle mixture and made mango salsa. No one came by to drop off any more bodies and none of my pictures was slashed to pieces. I had not yet been charged with murder, and I hadn't done any spying on my friends. I had taken in no money, but still, a successful day. Too bad they weren't all like that.

Maya had sprayed on a pair of jeans and had her hair up in a way that made you notice again the great curve of her neck. She wore one of her heavy Mexican silver necklaces and a silver ring with an oval turquoise stone. Her rose-colored top was sleeveless and nicely scooped. I had on an old pair of chinos and a dark blue tee shirt that said, "STAFF."

"Expecting someone special tonight?" I asked.

Someone pounded on the door. "Open up! Peoria Police!"

"That's him," she said. "It's my big sweetie."

I guess there are a lot of fifty-eight-year-old guys that would enjoy having Maya wrapped around them. I couldn't blame Cody, but I do think she liked to torture him. Next he'd be buying one of her nudes for his bedroom.

I mixed a couple of margaritas for Maya and me, and a planter's punch for Cody and we settled in the *loggia*. It had been a warm day for early February and it felt like the temperature was still in the mid-sixties. Perhaps it only seemed as warm as that after Minnesota. The stars were bright and I turned on the ground lights in the garden. The only other light was from the candles Maya had lit as I started the charcoal.

Cody took a long pull from his planter's punch, a drink he favored over any other, except possibly cold beer, and said, "And why didn't we know his name was Abbott?" Cody likes to get right to the point.

"Never thought to ask," I said. "A man calls himself something, you tend to accept it. Next you'll be saying that your own name is really Bernard, and why didn't I know it." He ignored this.

"Marisol never said Abbott to me; I think Tobey never used it. Of course she knew it," said Maya.

"Well, here's what they found in Chicago. Abbott Cross graduated from Princeton, no less, double major in economics and art history, *magna cum laude*. That was in 1983."

"He must have had a practical turn of mind," I said. "Art history can be a tough way to make a living unless you're teaching. The economics major would certainly help out."

"Exactly. He spent a graduate year in New York afterward at the Parsons School of Design. That's part of the New School now. Records show that in 1985 he received a Series Seven securities license, an insurance license, and an investment advisor's license while on the staff of Laine & Needleman, St. Paul, Minnesota. In June, 1989, the securities license and the advisor's license were revoked on the basis of churning and factual misrepresentation."

"What is churning?" asked Maya.

"Too many transactions in an account. Makes good commissions for the broker but results in high costs for the client. The insurance license was not revoked, but lapsed at the end of 1990."

"So by then he had been forced to leave the industry?" I asked.

"Yes, and my guess would be that his employers had to pay out some kind of settlement to a few of his clients. Maybe more than a few. That's the way they make it go away. Most brokerage houses have a reserve fund just for that. They're not hesitant to settle if the amount is at all reasonable because they don't want the publicity. These settlements are always confidential."

"What then?" asked Maya.

"After that, nothing. No other activities hit the official records."

"But he married Marisol in 1994, I think," she said. "She became an American citizen some time after that. I don't think he was living in Austin any more. That's all I know about that part."

I was thinking. "Do we have an ethical problem here with regard to Marisol? I mean, how much of this do we want or need to tell her? For example, the securities business problem might be much more painful than enlightening for her. And it's clear that Tobey never talked much about business with her."

Cody leaned back in his chair and folded his hands over his stomach. It wasn't hard to find. "Well, she asked you to help solve Tobey's murder. It seems like anything that might have led up to it is mainly relevant to us in answering that question. I don't think she needs all the detail. Maya?"

"I agree. She would not want to know this. I already feel bad for her. Let's start the chicken."

I spread the flattened pieces on the grill and glanced at my watch. Since they were thin it would be ten minutes total, flipped once half way through. I freshened Cody's punch, made two more margaritas, and opened a bottle of Chilean wine. We always drank red, even with chicken. "I had a long talk with *Licenciado* Delgado this morning," I said as I worked. "He wasn't overtly leaning on me, but it was clear he thinks we should keep our distance from this case. And he thinks you should keep your clothes on, Maya."

"I don't believe that. Everyone likes my pictures. Why would he say that?"

"I told him you don't undress in the *jardín.*"

"Maybe I will." It was never difficult to bring up her contrary side.

"He gave himself a lot of credit for finding Tobey's office in Dolores Hidalgo. Interestingly, he said the place had been broken into and there was nothing there but a few pictures, some records, a computer, and empty packing boxes. So now he's looking to find Ramon Xoc."

Cody smiled. "So the boxes are empty now. Did you tell him to check in his own morgue for Ramon?"

"I figured if he's that smart he can figure it out for himself. It didn't seem like he was looking for any help, in fact, he told me in so many words to stay out of it. He's got the fingerprints."

"But he doesn't think you did it?" asked Maya.

I shrugged. "There was no bullet in our entry and too little blood. He knows the body was moved. Anyway, why would I kill Ramon somewhere else and plant the body in my own *zaguan*? Not even a gringo would do that. He's right about one thing, though. He said it was a warning." I flipped the chicken over and shuffled the vegetables. "Five minutes." Maya pulled the tortilla warmer out of the oven and set the table. I poured wine all around.

"I wonder if you've noticed that Delgado's been following you," Cody said. "I saw him tonight on the way over, parked just down the block. A white Chrysler."

"I hadn't noticed but I'm not surprised." I sliced the chicken into strips and served the vegetables.

"So we know Tobey was ethically challenged,"

Cody continued. "If he'd sell penny stocks to little old ladies and churn them into poverty he surely wouldn't mind selling pricey fakes to rich expatriate collectors."

"You read the complaint?"

"Yes. He specialized in elderly clients." He rolled up a tortilla full of chicken and vegetables and looked at me. "Do we think that all the pictures we saw in Dolores were genuine? You would know."

"That stuff is too expensive to fake for what it would bring," I said. "You saw on the sales records that none of them went for more than $3,000 or so. I wouldn't do it for those prices. It's tough to find blank canvas and stretchers that old and some of those pigments aren't made anymore. The technology of paint is different now. There was no Chinese or titanium white back then. Ultraviolet light would show up the newer paint instantly. I think his business has to be a blend of old and new. Maybe the pictures were an effective cover, like there was one or more parts of his trade that were completely genuine and they lent credence to the rest. I imagine the jewelry and silver coins are the real deal as well."

"And so now *Licenciado* Delgado is a major collector of Mayan ceramics?" said Cody. "Or some of his people? Or did our friend Ramon just clean out the office himself?"

"I think the *Policia Judicial*," said Maya, chewing. "They are not well paid. Some would explain that it's a fringe benefit. Is that the right term?"

"Yes, and Delgado told me a little bit about Mexican business practices today. It involves keeping an eye out for the main chance."

"I could have told you that," said Maya.

"Besides," I went on, "I don't think Ramon would have left the packing materials behind and just pulled out the pots. He would have had too much respect for his own work. It shows a great deal of care and expertise."

Maya served a flan she had made that afternoon. I poured three brandies and lit the Cuban cigar.

"You are celebrating?" asked Maya.

"I know. Now my breath will stink."

"You'll sleep with the guests, and you will snore."

"We have no guests."

"Lucky for you."

"You know," I said, "we've never really figured out the coin in the mouth aspect, and now we have it twice."

"That's easy," said Cody. "I guess we all went to college. It's for the ferry."

"Tinker Bell?" suggested Maya.

"No, she was a pixie. I'm thinking of Charon, in Greek legend the boatman who ferried the souls of the dead across to Hades. His fee was a coin left in the mouth of the deceased. If there was no coin the dead had to wander the riverbank for a hundred years."

"But what does this tell us?" said Maya.

"That the killer is mythologically sophisticated?" said Cody.

"That's very obscure," I said, taking a pull at the Cohiba. "I don't know what to do with it. How do you know this? You didn't really study Greek mythology in college?"

"I was a psychology major. Anyway, cops know things. You'd be surprised what you come across in thirty years, even in Peoria. Plus, I read a book now and then when there's no football on. I don't think the ferryman's fee was twenty centavos, though. More like a drachma. But I don't know how it fits in except that it ties the two murders together."

"So the killer is an antiquarian? Or he's Greek? Or he just had too much pocket change?" I asked.

"Whatever it is, he's making a statement."

"OK. Twenty centavos is less than two cents American," I said. "Is the statement that life is cheap? Because when it appeared in Tobey's murder I thought it was there to say he was of no significance."

Cody laughed. "Life is cheap to any killer. Look, there are two ways to view this. Either we have a serial killer, in which case there may be similarities but no personal link between the victims. Or the second murder stems from the first, like it's an unintended consequence. The killer is getting pulled further in. In this case we know from the packaging that Ramon Xoc knew Tobey, so there's the link, and we can eliminate the serial aspect. Did Ramon know who killed Tobey, in which case maybe the motive for killing Ramon is that he was blackmailing the killer? Or did he even know that Tobey had been killed?"

"Interesting that Ramon didn't show up at Galería Cruz, he showed up at the office in Dolores Hidalgo because that's where he shipped the ceramics," I said. "Wait, didn't Marisol say someone had called for Tobey right after his death, someone who didn't identify himself?"

"Right," said Maya, "probably it was Marisol who told Ramon that night that Tobey was dead. Ramon panicked and came up here to see what was going on, maybe to recover his pieces. So he breaks into the office."

"But we still have no link between Ramon and

the killer," said Cody.

"Ramon probably took the sales ledger and the Rolodex from the office." I said. "The Rolodex has the customer list. The killer's name is in the Rolodex." Flawless logic.

"And then either the Rolodex is in Ramon's hotel room with his luggage, or the killer got it from the gallery and most likely destroyed it."

"The hotel room is somewhere in Dolores Hidalgo. We may be able to find the hotel, but how do we get into his room?" said Maya.

"You're right there," said Cody. "We have no standing in this investigation. No hotel will let us into a guest's room."

"Maybe the police will have it quickly anyway, as soon as they get a match on the fingerprints. It won't take them long to figure out that Ramon went to Dolores Hidalgo. His mother would tell them. Then all they have to do is start with the hotels near the bus station. I'm guessing Ramon did not fly in if he was keeping a low profile. So why not stay near the bus that brought him? He would have had luggage to carry and he had no reason to think anyone knew he was there. Delgado got the room key from his pocket in our *zaguan*. So most likely the police have the Rolodex by now and if they don't, they have the computer from the office and we know the list is on the computer. It's the same thing. The only thing that would be useful is if the killer still had the Rolodex.

"My head hurts," said Maya.

"What do we do next? Wait for another murder?" It didn't occur to me that it might be mine.

CHAPTER THIRTEEN
DIEGO DELGADO

Licenciado Delgado had long been aware of the dealing activities of Tobey Cross. The commerce in Mayan ceramics was not a problem to him as long as all the pieces stayed in México, and he had no evidence of any export activities by Galeria Cruz. It was not against the law to merely own them. Indeed, he watched all the gringos of San Miguel, not because their ranks were flush with criminals; on the contrary, their good deeds in the city were legend. They ran more than thirty different volunteer groups in San Miguel. Delgado watched them because in his view the American community with all its wealth represented a business opportunity not to be ignored. In fact, one of his cousins who maintained a booth in the Tuesday market made a good living just dealing in their castoff clothing.

When the call from Marisol Cross alerted him to the possibility that Dolores Hidalgo might be the site of Tobey's office, he was in his white Chrysler and on the road to that historic city within five minutes, pausing only at Galería Cruz to pick up the key. There was no need for subtlety on the way and he turned on his flashing lights and laid on his horn as he flew past the traffic in his own lane. Once in Dolores Hidalgo he unknowingly repeated

Maya's plan of starting from the plaza and searching each street for a 132 address. After a few wrong streets it did not take him long to find the apple green building. He waited for a crowd of schoolboys to disperse and then tried the key.

"*Beengo*," he said.

Once inside he made a rapid search of everything there. He noticed the break-in almost immediately and was relieved to find most of the packing cases were still full. He pulled out one of the pictures and wrinkled his nose. A withered old saint with a dim halo, eyes lifted heavenward; hardly as interesting as the nudes by Paul Zacher, which Delgado had only pretended offended him. It was an excuse to talk about Maya nude and visualize them again. He unpacked the ceramics, practically groaning with joy, and laid them on the worktable. Then one by one he carried them to his police car and wrapped them all in a couple of blankets he kept in the trunk for accident victims. He would drive more slowly on the way back, without the siren.

Inside the office he dusted and lifted the fingerprints wherever he could find them and then packed up the computer and the contents of the desk. He eyed the stereo system longingly but decided to leave it in place. He searched further for any sign of a Rolodex, but there was none.

Back in San Miguel, he stopped first at home and hid the ceramics in a garden shed at the back of his lot. An obvious place, perhaps, but they wouldn't be there long. Back at the station he had one of the uniformed officers unload the rest of the office contents from his car. With the aid of one of the bilingual officers—Delgado had no aptitude for languages and so made it a point of pride to know almost no English—he scanned the contents of the computer, printed the customer and supplier lists and saw that Ramon Xoc's name and address were there too. He had already copied it from the packing materials at 132.

Looking over the customer list in detail first, he found he knew many of the names. One that particularly rang a bell was John Schleicher. In the files of the San Miguel Police the name of Schleicher had a special mark after it; one that meant "Do not approach." Any question involving Schleicher was to be referred to the highest level of the state police in Guanajuato. *Licenciado* Delgado knew this could mean only one thing: that Schleicher was paying for protection and had influence both with the state police and the court system, the latter being Delgado's own superiors. He was unsure how to read this. The sales records told him that Tobey Cross's biggest customer over the years had been Perry Watt. He knew Perry Watt was probably the richest gringo in San Miguel, even richer than Schleicher. Might as well start at the top.

Licenciado Delgado was going to be an antiques dealer. He had always felt that new skills came easily to him, and as a cop, he was no stranger to risk.

When he came to the station the next morning the information had come in on the fingerprints. The dead man in Paul Zacher's house was Ramon Xoc. Delgado was not surprised, but what link there could be with Zacher was not clear to him. That afternoon Delgado was back in Dolores Hidalgo looking for Ramon's hotel. He knew from his calls to the airlines that Ramon had not flown from Mérida, so he began his search near the bus station. In the third hotel he visited he showed his

ID and was told that, yes, Ramon Xoc had been registered there but he had not paid his bill after the second day and his belongings had been removed from the room and stored in the back office. Xoc had not reappeared. The desk clerk identified the key and showed Delgado the room, which he searched without result, and with a little persuasion the clerk released Ramon's suitcase. He could not remember if Ramon had brought in anything else. Delgado gave him a receipt and sat in the car outside and went through the contents.

It contained routine things that anyone would travel with, as well as a rotting mango in a plastic bag, and there was no sign of any secret compartments. Nor was there a Rolodex or anything else of interest. Xoc must have encountered the murderer soon after his arrival in Dolores Hidalgo. Yet there had been no sign of a shooting at *Señor* Cross' office. The key had to be the customer list on the computer. Since he was going to contact Perry Watt anyway, he might as well start his search there.

CHAPTER FOURTEEN
PERRY WATT

In Casa Watt, his great neocolonial mansion in Los Balcones, Perry was seated at his desk in the paneled study he thought of as his "cabinet" in the Renaissance sense of the word—an intimate paneled private office. From the second floor this elegant room framed a view across the city, and downward its western exposure overlooked his own garden below, and beyond the wall, the rooftops of San Miguel punctuated by the twin towers of the *Parroquia*, a double exclamation point emphasizing the city's continuing religious tradition.

Beyond, on the adjacent hills and on those across the city, the lesser ex-pats held court in their lesser neocolonial mansions. Later in the day they would be serving cocktails in their neocolonial gardens. On winter afternoons, when the sun came in low and harsh, he could close the paneled shutters on the two eight-foot windows and rely on the mellow light from numerous wrought iron lamps with their parchment shades. From over the broad mantel a pair of seventeenth century descendants of the Conquistadores looked benignly, if somewhat soberly, down upon him. These were the ancestors he didn't have; his own family had arrived in Texas from Tennessee in the 1920s, poor as the dirt clinging to their shoes. But there was no dirt under Perry's feet now; his Florentine calfskin slippers rested on an antique walnut floor in a herringbone pattern that had been removed from a castle in Spain. Two huge Aubusson carpets in old rose and pale green covered most of it. He didn't mind that it creaked sometimes when he walked over it; it was an echo of the history he didn't have. Perry Watt was his own gated community.

Before him on the desk rested a tray of crudely struck colonial coins from the rosewood cabinet. These were silver with crosses on their faces; seventeenth and eighteenth century pieces from the mint in Lima. Their edges were irregular and the strikes uneven. Most had been recovered from hurricane-wrecked galleons of the silver fleet in the Gulf or the Caribbean. From time to time he picked one up, wondering whose dead fingers had gripped it in the past, whose clothing was weighed down by these coins as they were swallowed by the waves.

Mostly he was deep in thought. He wore a plum colored velvet jacket with black lapels, the kind some people might call a smoking jacket, except nobody smoked anymore but for the occasional Havana cigar. His hair was immaculately brushed back and his camel slacks went perfectly with the jacket.

In the corridor, Barbara paused by the door.

"Barbara!" he said, looking up. "I just got the damnedest phone call."

She came into the room and stood by his desk.

"Cop by the name of Delgado called me a little while ago; I heard he's the one looking into how Tobey Cross got himself killed. Anyway, he says he's got some Mayan ceramics that might interest me. Says they're from an old family collection. He described them and they sound like what I was getting from Tobey. I can't think how Delgado got hold of them. He's got eleven pieces. That's an awful lot. Feels dicey to me. I can't think what to do."

"Perry darlin', you always know what to do." She moved behind the desk and put her hands on his shoulders and kissed the top of his carefully groomed head. His left hand traveled absently down her leg and stopped behind her knee, a favorite spot of his; one of several.

"Yes I do. But just today I don't for some reason." The manicured fingers of his right hand moved aimlessly again over the coins. "If they're like the others, they're probably worth nearly two hundred thousand."

"Are we sniffing out a bargain here?"

"There's no bargain if they're stolen. I mean, he was talking a good price but he wouldn't say how much. I'm wondering if he got hold of some of Tobey's inventory. But Paul said there was nothing missing at the gallery." He adjusted his cuffs. "I'm going to think on this a little. Were you going out?"

"Just a little shopping in *centro*."

"You're not going to Paul's to pose again? Don't you do anything I wouldn't do. I trust you, but you never know about those artist types. Course he's got his own lil' brown gal, but I'm still not used to you being naked over there."

"She's not very brown, Perry. I don't think she's got but a little Indian blood. Anyway, I haven't called Paul yet for another session. We don't have anything set up."

He went across the landing to their paneled bedroom. This room faced the front of the mansion and had a view over the scruffy plateau toward the reservoir, which he could now barely make out. Here others had built homes in pale imitation of Casa Watt, wishing, no doubt, that they were him. The view was not inspiring, but in the bedroom he mostly looked at Barbara anyway. He could imagine her picture now over the bed. Wouldn't do to have it down in the living room. One nude there was enough, and he didn't care to have every guy in San Miguel ogling Barbara's naked body, even on a painting. It was bad enough that Paul had seen it, but that couldn't be helped. Besides, he liked the Maya picture just where it was. He put the thought aside for a while and rearranged his coin collection, then called Houston and worked until mid afternoon on a deal for a new drilling technology he wanted to acquire, when he closed the upper shutters. He stood for a while before the ceramics case with a sour look on his face. Reaching a decision, back at the desk he used one of his three lines to call the national anthropological museum in México City and got the number for the agency that was charged with overseeing the commerce in and export of antiquities. He explained the situation and they gave him the number of a special investigator at the national police, the *federales*.

CHAPTER FIFTEEN

Barbara Watt called me for a second sitting and Maya had almost graciously packed up her laptop and gone to Dolores Hidalgo so as not to be tortured by the thought of the *güera* lying nude before me. Or perhaps she still was. But she seemed especially affectionate when she left. Maybe just to remind me of what I already had. There were times when the politics of painting nudes made me want to go back to still lifes.

Barbara had brought her own robe this time, knowing the routine, and she emerged from behind the screen in a deep blue brocaded silk number, slit to the hip, with white piping and a mandarin collar.

"That's great," I said, and it was. It caught my eye immediately. "Some other time I'll paint you in that." She tossed it over a chair and rubbed the skin beneath her breasts where a line remained pressed into the skin from her bra.

"Let me see, how was I again?"

"On your back, face toward me, left knee up higher than the right. Welcoming look, but not too welcoming. Hands one on top of the other over your navel. There it is. Your knee could be just a bit higher. Good. Wait, we need the choker." I went to the prop cabinet and pulled out the drawer I use for small items, but the choker was not there.

There were not many places where it might be. Maybe Maya had washed it when she washed her own robe after Barbara's first visit. I scanned the tops of the cabinets, the bar and looked on the floor behind the screen. There was no choker.

"OK," I said, "we'll go ahead without it. I know what it looks like and in the picture I have the edges of it marked on your neck." The light was even and unchanging since it was early February and the sun was well to the south; I was able to get her skin tones just right. They matched what I had done on her left leg during the first session. This was not a difficult pose for her to maintain so we took breaks only every forty minutes instead of every twenty.

On the second break she put the robe back on and I made coffee for us.

"You look great today," I said. "Your color is right and you're relaxed. I like your expression. Can we go on a bit more? I'd like to do your ear. They usually take a while."

"Sure. It feels good just lying there. I really don't have to do much. Can I ask you something?"

"Go ahead."

"How are you doing with the Tobey murder? And with the other one too, I guess. They're related, aren't they?"

"They do seem to be related. We have Tobey's customer list and the next thing will be to contact everyone and have a quiet conversation."

"There must have been lots of customers."

"Just thirteen here in San Miguel for the ceramics, because they were pricey. Quite a few more for pictures and silver. It won't be hard, assuming they'll talk to us. I don't know what we're going to do about the others. There are some in Acapulco, three or four in Manzanillo. And there's a bunch in Guadalajara. It could take a while, but it makes the most sense to start here."

"Perry always likes to talk about his collections, but mostly about the things themselves. He's not always so open about how he got them. I mean, the public auction things he'll talk about. But you saw those Navajo rugs in his study. I know he got them from a man who owed him money in Dallas, but he'll never talk about the circumstances because I think he forced the man to give them up. It's owning things that's very intense for him. He buys a whole aura with each piece he gets. If it's a religious painting, it becomes sort of surrounded by the church and congregation. You can smell the incense and hear the chant."

Later she slipped off the robe after one of our breaks and handed it to me. Then she walked back to the day bed, glancing back over her shoulder. "Do you like my butt?"

"Very much. Don't ever change it. It's among the finest I've ever seen." Might as well tell the truth.

"But not the finest?" I didn't answer this immediately. She apparently had the same view that Perry did about her place in the hierarchy of things. Barbara resumed the pose and I worked on her ear for a while.

"It could be. I guess I'd have to see all of them in the same room to be sure. Like a line-up, you know?"

"You're so sweet. That would be a big room, wouldn't it? But do you really think the killer is one of Tobey's customers?"

"Can't be certain yet, but most likely it's a

gringo. Delgado says that guns are not impossible to get, but usually uncommon among the local people, plus it's hard to think what else the motive would be. There was no robbery that we can see. I think this looks most like some kind of business dispute. We'll know more after we talk to the customers."

I began working up her hair around the ear. Blond hair is not difficult to do if you avoid yellow. For the most part it has to be a dynamic blend of different light tones, with deeper shadows glimpsed below the surfaces. A bit of ginger here and there. Some burnt umber further down near the scalp.

I didn't have any reason to distrust Barbara, but I didn't feel like letting her know about Ramon's role in this, or about the virtual certainty that most of the Mayan ceramics gracing the shelves of collectors in this town were well-crafted fakes. I suspected that this included her husband's group.

"You don't think Perry did it?"

"That's a startling thing to say, coming from you." I thought this was a nervy thing to say, but it also expressed her confidence in her husband.

"But really, I want to know what you think," she continued. "I mean, if it's one of Tobey's customers."

"Frankly, I think Perry's got too much to lose. He has a lot of standing in San Miguel. He's a big contributor to all kinds of causes. I'm not even sure he'd be capable of it."

She didn't address this.

"Here's something odd. *Licenciado* Delgado called him the other day. He offered Perry some more Mayan ceramics."

My brush stopped in mid stroke.

"This is confidential," she went on. "Perry didn't know what to make of it. He's usually so decisive. I said, 'But darlin', you always know what to do.' I've never seen him like that. Certainly not in his business affairs."

I came over to the day bed. "I just want to look at your hair more closely." The left side of it was behind her face as she looked toward the easel, but the right was swept back with the leading curve in full light. My eyes were searching the detail of it for the range of shadows under the surface, but my brain was still on Diego Delgado, now dealing Ramon's ceramics. He had to have been the one who cleaned out the office. So what was Delgado's game? Was it possible he had killed Tobey? But then why Ramon Xoc? He had said it was unusual for the local people to have guns, but surely Delgado himself had access to a variety of weapons in the evidence room. And when he seemed not to know the identity of the corpse in my entry hall he must have just been being disingenuous. Of course he would warn me off; it was only by tightly controlling the investigation that he could direct suspicion away from himself. He had as much as told me that I was being a pain in the ass by getting involved. Of course Delgado must have slashed my picture too; that was the first warning! Cops would have ways of getting through entry locks. And when Marisol tipped him off about the office in Dolores Hidalgo, the final chip fell into place.

The more I thought about it the more it fit. Ramon Xoc must have been a surprise for him. Marisol had told Ramon about Tobey's death, not knowing who she was speaking with, and then Ramon hopped the next bus for Dolores Hidalgo, using the address he had shipped his ceramics to. Of course no one was there to let him in, and he would have known that, so he had tools along to let himself in through the back. And he left the inventory in place because who else would disturb it, with Tobey dead? Galeria Cruz was a one-man operation. Ramon took the Rolodex and began to approach the customers; somehow Delgado found out and killed him too. He would have wanted to control Tobey's business himself. It was just another business opportunity, and as he had said, his antenna was always up.

In the twelve years I'd lived in San Miguel I never had a bad experience with the police. The relations with the ex-pat community were not always warm and fuzzy, but both sides sort of kept their distance and got along. I had heard stories of minor shakedowns from time to time, but basically I thought of the police as no better or worse than most. The idea that Delgado could be a murderer and a thief was shocking, but most of the facts seemed to fit.

"Paul darlin', what are you doing?"

I realized I was still kneeling motionless beside the day bed, my face inches away from hers, but only seeing the sudden rush of evidence that pointed directly to Delgado.

"Are you thinking about how to paint my nipples, Paul dear? Perhaps you could come a little closer. I know this isn't sculpture, but maybe touch could play a role in getting them right. Is it a thing where you might need *all* of your senses? Taste might even be important in this."

"Of course. Pink can be very tricky. You can't just plunge into it." But, instead of moving any closer, I moved away.

So, that bastard Delgado had Ramon's corpse lying on a slab somewhere and no one had notified his mother who was by now wondering what had happened. I needed to run this by Cody and Maya and see if they could find any holes in it. It certainly looked damning to me.

"I think we've gone as far as we can, today." I said. "I'm starting to get a little vague, and when I'm like that I don't do my best work."

"I can see that. It's OK, darlin', I'll come another day. I always want your best work." I expected her to add that she was worth it, but she left that out.

I held the robe for her. The deep blue was perfect with her coloring and I almost put my arms around her, but I didn't. There was something about her that made it hard to keep my hands to myself, but I'd had an unfortunate episode a few years earlier that had hardened my studio discipline, and it always came to mind when I had a subject like Barbara. Besides, I had Maya now.

⌘⌘⌘

After Barbara left I called Cody and set up lunch at the Villa Antigua Santa Monica. I didn't expect Maya for a while. Cody lived just up the hill from the restaurant in a condo with a lovely view of the *Parroquia* from his small balcony on the third floor. The Santa Monica is on Baeza on the west side of Juarez Park. It began life as a hacienda in the eighteenth century and in the thirties it was the home of Jose Mojica, a Mexican movie star and opera singer. There's a marker in the garden where Dolores del Rio was married there about seventy years ago. I don't know whether it lasted, but the appeal of the place certainly had.

Coming in from the street you enter a large reception area and lounge, and across the courtyard is the kitchen entrance and bar leading beyond to a great room with a cathedral ceiling. To the right of the fountain at the center of the courtyard is a tall birdcage, with two goofy parrots. When it rains the waiters move the cage back under the arches, which usually causes a mad scrambling among the birds. This is my favorite spot for lunch in San Miguel. Maya and I come here often when our schedules intersect. Over the arches bougainvillea and jasmine climb to the roof tiles, but only the bougainvillea was blooming in early February.

The parrots bickered constantly, like characters in a 1950s situation comedy. I wondered if one of them was named Ralph. Cody slipped into the seat opposite. "Back in the sweet spot," he said. "Dos Negras," this to the waiter.

"I had an interesting talk with Barbara Watt this morning."

"Do you talk to her much?"

"No, but I'm painting her now."

"Let me guess what she's wearing."

"Not much. A midnight blue velvet choker when we can find it."

"I see."

"As much fun as that might be to contemplate, something else came up in the conversation this morning. She said that Delgado had approached Perry Watt with some Mayan ceramics he wanted to sell. He's got eleven pieces. She wants this to stay confidential information."

"Just as we thought. He's going for a mid-life career change. Did Perry bite?"

"He's quite wary, she said, but she thinks he probably won't be able to let it go. He told her he didn't know what to do about it. Delgado hinted they could be had for a favorable price. Cody, I had a thought earlier while I was talking to her. What if the killer is Delgado? Just hear me out before you say anything, OK? I know you're going to resist the idea because he's a cop."

I laid out my thinking from the painting session this morning. "I hope you can poke a hole in this, because if it's true I'm not sure how we can bring him down. His judicial supervisors would most likely decide to protect him from the gringos. Maybe I'm not being fair. I hate it that I may be thinking in stereotypes here."

He studied his fingernails for a while. "It's possible, but it seems like an extreme way for Delgado to enter the antiques business. What about the twenty-centavo coin if it's him? How does that fit?"

I shook my head. "I couldn't make that part work. Can you?"

"I don't want to sell Delgado short, but I don't think he knows about Charon and the coin for the ferry operator's fee."

"What if the coin part has nothing to do with mythology and is a total red herring? Just designed to put us and the other police through hoops trying to figure it out?"

"I can't make that out either."

"So what do you think of the Delgado idea, aside from that?"

"I give it about a five for plausibility and a seven

for originality, but beyond that my gut doesn't like it much. I think he's just a guy who came across an opportunity at work and decided to go along with it. I could be wrong."

The waiter returned with the beer and we both ordered the *chiles en nogada*.

"But I do think," he went on, "that the next step is to split up the local customer list. Let's leave Perry Watt for later and you take the first six and I'll take the last seven. Let's use the position that we've been asked to help out Marisol and we're starting by trying to get a sense of Tobey's business. Get them to talk about their purchases, why they bought what they bought. Probe a little for any disagreements they may have had with Tobey. See if they know anything about his past. Are they proud of their things? Look for the tells, minor gestures or facial expressions that suggest they're hiding something. I want to ask you a question, though. Can you tell when someone is lying to you?"

"My old Cleveland girl friend used to try a few on me. I was able to read her most of the time, but I knew her pretty well by then, too. And I've been lied to by clients, I'm sure. People who say they're going to buy a picture but then they don't."

"How do they act?"

"Often they don't look at you when they say they're interested. They fumble around with their shirt buttons or something like that. Polish their glasses, maybe. Run a napkin over their teeth, you know. Scratch their ear as if something just landed in it."

"Grooming behavior. It's common when people lie."

"Were you lied to much?"

"It was a given. The trick was to figure out when people were telling the truth. It was much less common."

⌘⌘⌘

After we left the Santa Monica I called Bill Frost and set up a meeting for that afternoon at his home in the Ojo de Agua neighborhood, a walled enclave up the hill from Juarez Park. It was adjacent to, but much classier than, the development where Cody had his condo, just off Prolongacion Aldama. Casa Frost was a big house of recent vintage stuccoed in olive green with a triple garage designed to look like a carriage entrance, and the usual *cantera* stone trim to the doors and windows. The requisite ornate wrought iron lanterns flanked the entry. It was the home of someone who could afford more than one Mayan ceramic piece. Perhaps a couple of pictures as well, but I hadn't seen him on my own customer list, and unlike Tobey's, my records were always accessible.

Frost met me at the door and led me out to a *loggia* overlooking a large antique fountain in the midst of lush and ordered plantings. Sculptured boxwood bordered the paths. Several tall stands of bamboo climbed above the far wall. My place could look like this with a full time gardener, too.

"How about a gin and tonic?" he asked. "As the song says, it's cocktail hour somewhere, and I've got Bombay Sapphire."

It wasn't always easy to get here, and I would have saved it for martinis, but I didn't want to argue. I agreed and looked over the garden, trying to identify all the plants.

"What brings you up the hill?" he asked when he returned to set down the drinks.

"I've gotten involved in the Tobey Cross murder investigation," I began, implying that I was practically hand in hand with the police, "just to help out Marisol, his widow. Your name came up on the customer list." I gave him a cheerful look, as if it was no great matter.

There was no reaction. Bill Frost sat down and pulled his chair closer to the table. He wore a pearl gray, short sleeve, silk-printed shirt and black slacks. His hair was a startling white and it appeared to be all there except for a single strand on his collar. The fact that he could be considered a suspect did not ruffle him at all. He rolled his gin and tonic glass between his hands and pursed his lips. His attitude said he was confident, unworried, and willing to help.

"Well, you're running ahead of the police on this; they haven't contacted me yet. You may not know this, but Tobey and I actually went back a long way." He took a sip of his drink and stared off toward the fountain. "He used to be with a regional securities firm up in St. Paul called Laine and Needleman. They had just five or six offices in the Midwest. I was in the same business in Toronto, but on the underwriting side, and we used to do some placements with them for the American market." He leaned forward at this point with one elbow on the table, as if this were more confidential than what had come before. "Bert Laine had been kind of a stock selection guru when they started the firm, but he was already dead by the time Tobey came in, and Carl Needleman was the senior partner. He was mainly a PR guy and really didn't know shit from cinderblock about investments. He just brought clients in the door, and he did that well. The firm went on partly based on the strength of Laine's insights, like they were continuing his method of stock picking. I don't know if it was really that good a system, but they did a lot of business."

Frost looked out over the garden as if trying to remember something, then he shook his head.

"So anyway, Needleman did the schmoozing very well, but at that time a guy named Bob Ehrmann really ran the firm day to day. Tobey was just a kid when he came into it, but with strong educational credentials and very keen on the business. I used to have lunch with him now and then when I came down from Toronto. I think he mostly wanted to pick my brain; he was very interested in the underwriting side. I didn't mind. It's good to be looked up to; that all stops when you retire, of course. People forget you ever knew anything."

I said nothing because I didn't want to stop the flow.

"When we weren't talking securities he would get going on antiques. He was doing a little dealing on the side even then. At one time he had a line on an eighteenth century French paneled library from a chateau near Toulouse that he thought I should install in my house in Toronto. He could bring it in knocked down in sections and all I had to do was add a room to my house that had the right dimensions. I looked into it but the cost was so fierce I ended up not doing it. Besides, the contractor said he couldn't exactly match the brick on my house any more, which was built in the twenties, and that was worrisome. I guess in the end I couldn't see myself as a French marquis. Didn't have the outfits." He grinned and took a sip of his drink. "Besides, Toronto tends to favor the English style."

"Did you ever buy anything from him here?"

"I did. I came down here seven years ago and I ran into him working the crowd at one of the house tours. He had left the securities business by then. I guess antiques were his first love after all. I ended up buying a three-footed Mayan bowl from him. Beautiful little thing. It has a repair on one foot that was recent, but done by an expert. Most people couldn't find it. I'll show it to you on the way out. I know I can't ever take it out of here, but I'm hoping to never get out of here myself. As you get older you lose the ability to do the Toronto winters. This place grows on you, eh?"

I thought about winter in Minneapolis. "You didn't buy anything else?"

"No. I'm not really big on collecting. He had a couple of pictures he thought would work here, but they were too somber. I like something livelier on my walls. I should look at what you're doing. I like that one Perry Watt's got over his piano. Not sure my wife would, though. Too much skin for her taste. Not that I mind a little skin myself; I'm sure you don't either, judging from your work."

"Skin is good," I said, nodding slowly.

"But you should talk to Perry about this. You probably saw what he has in Mayan antiques at the party. Some of it, anyway."

"Perry's on my list. In fact, he was Tobey Cross's biggest single client in San Miguel." I wondered if I was volunteering too much.

"I'm not surprised. He'd be the biggest in a lot of categories. Any guy who can hook a wife who looks like that...top off your drink?"

"No thanks. So you were happy with the bowl?"

"Oh yes. Bit pricey but I didn't mind helping the guy out. He was just getting started then, and he had done me a few favors back in his Laine and Needleman days. You never bought anything from him yourself?"

"He had great things, but they were a bit out of my league, being a painter, you know."

"Well, let me show you that Mayan piece." We went back into the living room and Bill lifted a straight-sided vessel from the mantel. It was about eight inches high, glazed in black, with animal figures cut into the reddish clay beneath. He handed it to me. I compared the incised drawings with my recollection of Perry's pieces and I could see immediately that it wasn't by the same hand. Within the limits of what I knew, it certainly looked like the real thing and although I examined it closely, I couldn't see any difference among the legs. Whoever had done the repair was an artist, or had been. I gave it back to Frost.

"A lovely piece," I said. "Anyone would be proud to have it."

"Well, you come by again, Paul. If I think of anything that might help I'll call you."

We walked to the entry and I held out my hand. He shook it and said, "Be nice to see your house on the tour one of these days. Folks like that kind of thing; art studio, you know. Local color. Maybe have someone posing? Not nude, of course."

"Count on it," I said. "Glad to help out."

I got in the artmobile and drove through the gate. I could not see Bill Frost as a killer, nor had he played with his buttons once and he didn't wear any glasses to fiddle with. On the other hand, it did not escape me that he'd omitted any reference to Tobey's legal problems at Laine and Needleman. Was he only being discreet? Or perhaps it was ancient history and not worth bringing up, particularly now that Tobey was dead. Maybe it was something else. It didn't seem possible to me that he didn't know, being in the business.

As I drove down the hill I realized Cody would have asked him straight out.

CHAPTER SIXTEEN

The next day Cody came down from his condo on the hill above Juarez Park and sat down next to me in our loggia while Maya rubbed his shoulders and his neck. The neck was like the trunk of a small tree, but freckled. "OK, I talked with Anne Harris," he said with no preamble. Nice woman, late sixties."

"She would be the wife of the Dr. James Harris on the list?"

"Right. His widow, now. She lives here on your street, in fact, just two blocks farther down. Nice house, very substantial, with a well developed garden fronted by the old style arcades. She has a lot of antiques but no old paintings. I asked about that and she said they had done that Venetian plaster thing on the walls when they restored the house, and she didn't like to gouge it up with picture hangers. But she did have some good silver. Anyway, they moved here six years ago from Milwaukee. She ran the house tour for about two years before her husband died. He was a retired pediatrician.

"They had always traveled in Central and South America and they wanted to retire in a place that had an active ex-pat community. They had considered Costa Rica, but it was too far from their kids in the States. Plus, they wanted a town with a colonial feeling. Guadalajara has it, but it's too big, and they didn't care much for the beach communities. They thought San Miguel was perfect so they settled here, but then the doctor was killed a few years ago in a car accident on the edge of México City. They were on their way to Teotihuacan. Some guy in a pickup crossed the median into them. Anne Harris was hurt, but not badly. She buried him down here in the Panteón."

"I think I remember this, but we didn't know them, did we?" I asked. Maya shook her head.

"But I think we have been in her house," she said. "On the tour. I remember the candlesticks. I thought they were too big for the buffet."

"Anyway, she's got three of the ceramics. She loves them. To her they are the real México, the ancient culture. She's a little disdainful of the new house construction here, that's why she's got an old house in *el centro.* You should have seen the way she held them and moved her hands over them, like she could communicate with the distant past. Almost like rubbing a magic lamp. She wouldn't let me touch them; she just rotated each one in her hands as I looked, but they seemed like the things we saw in Dolores Hidalgo. I felt like they might be by Ramon Xoc, but then I don't have your eye."

"How about condition?"

"They were great, just a couple of tiny chips here and there to give them credibility. She may have been a bigger force behind the collecting than her husband was, just listening to the way she talks about it. She worshiped Tobey and was eager to help. The only way she'd be a killer is if you went after her stuff, or pounded a nail in her walls."

"So, that's two we can cross off." I had already

told him about my visit to Bill Frost, but mainly about his relationship to Tobey.

"What did you think about Frost's bowl?"

"I don't know. It might be real, but if it isn't, I don't think it could be by Ramon. Maybe Tobey had another forger in his source list. But if a forger had made it, would he be likely to break a leg off and flawlessly replace it? It seems like the point of doing a little damage is to suggest visible age, like some of the nicks I saw on Perry's things and on the ones in Dolores Hidalgo. Or like that figure Marisol gave us with hairline fractures on the arm. But I looked at this bowl closely and I couldn't see the repair. Maybe Tobey only told Frost the leg was replaced to give it a little history."

"But if it's real," said Cody, "then Ramon might have replaced the leg. It may have been a transitional piece between Ramon as excavator and Ramon as artist. It could be that replacing the leg suggested he might be capable of greater efforts."

"Well, in any case, Bill Frost's got no problem with it, and he has no plans to try to take it out of the country. That leaves us with eleven to go here in town."

"Then I've got the Alwyns, Tom and Abby," he continued. "You don't have a cold Negra Modelo do you, Maya? A man talks this much he gets thirsty. They live up on the Malanquin on Malaga, the main street. He's English and she came here from Winnipeg. They actually met here on the house tour fourteen years ago, corresponded for a few years, then came back and got married. Very romantic. She has a rather commanding presence and I got the sense that it's because she has the bulk of the money. Tom probably just likes to spend it."

"What's their place like?"

"Long and low and unlike a lot of the newer houses here. Aside from the facade, the style is more southwestern U.S. than Mexican colonial, but that's the Malanquin style. Other than some citrus and boxwood hedges, it's not much for gardens. The outdoors space is mainly a well-manicured grassy lot that just opens out toward the fairways below the hills. He had quite a few toys around; an expensive golf cart with a lot of money in clubs in the back. A Mercedes sport coupe in the triple garage. She drives an SUV, a Lexus, I think. He showed me around. There's an entire room off the garage full of exercise equipment. Separate his and hers bathrooms, with a lot of onyx fixtures. Gold plated faucets and towel bars."

"You really got the tour."

"I just kept oohing and aahing and he kept showing me more. Interesting gun rack in the den. Couple of high-end rifles and three Browning shotguns. No pistols in view. The man has to be comfortable with the hardware, though."

"How about art? Any Paul Zachers?"

"Nothing that classy. Actually, nothing that cheap. They've got a Botero over the mantel. At least, I think it's a Botero. They didn't seem to be the type to have copies."

Maya's eyebrows went up. "The kind with the *nalgas gordas*?"

"If you mean what I think you mean, yes. It's got the babes with the really generous proportions. Lots of padding."

"And the *Señora* Alwyn, she has them too?"

"Not at all. She's trim, very tailored. I'll bet she

shoots a better golf game than he does."

"Any ceramics in view?" I asked.

"Yes, but they're different." His forehead wrinkled. "Four pieces; all human, or maybe godlike, figures. No vessels. Tom Alwyn said they were either highland Guatemala or Jaina Island; I'm not sure where that is. Tobey told Tom he had bought them at auction from the estate of a professor in México City. I checked that against the vendor list and there's no record of such a purchase. I can't say whether they're real, but they look like nothing we think is from Ramon. That's not to say they couldn't be his, but it's a very different style. The surfaces are much rougher, the glazing is minimal, if it's there at all. I couldn't be sure because they didn't offer to open the case and let me handle them. Some of the Ramon purchase notes in Tobey's records included terms I don't understand, but as far as I could see, they don't mention figures."

"Jaina is the great royal burial island off the coast of Campeche in the Yucatán," said Maya. "It was used for many generations."

"Were the Alwyns knowledgeable? Could they talk about the pieces at all?" I asked.

"If they could, they didn't. They basically pointed and said, 'look what we have.' I had the feeling that owning the figures gave the Alwyns some credibility, like the Mercedes and the Botero. It's their ticket in. There was one odd thing, though. The case the pieces were in was obviously custom made. It matched their bookcases and a china cabinet in the dining room as well. Same light wood, same finish."

"Well, you would never find the right case in any store, would you?" asked Maya.

"No. But this case had room for five or six more pieces. It wasn't even half full. I asked if they planned to add to their collection and all I got was 'you never know.' It seemed like if they went to the trouble of having the case custom made they might have had more specific plans for filling it."

"What are you thinking?" said Maya.

"What if they had it full at one time and then discovered that some of them were fakes and put them away so they weren't tortured by the sight of them? Just seeing the way the figures were arranged in the case, evenly, with lots of space between them, I felt there had been more at one time and the remainder had been rearranged. That's all. Nothing conclusive."

"Or maybe they had a falling out with Tobey halfway through filling it?" I said.

"But they mentioned no trouble with him?" asked Maya.

"The way they talked I think he was someone who validated their good taste. I didn't detect any dissatisfaction. No tells."

"What a perfect position for him," I said. "What do the sales records say?"

"That's the first thing I checked. They're inconclusive; they list three pieces, all Jaina figures."

"But there are four?" asked Maya. "Maybe Tobey's records are faulty, but that doesn't seem much like him."

"There's one more thing. Tom said that about three or four days after Tobey was killed he got a call from a man asking whether he might want to purchase more Mayan ceramics."

"What did he say?"

"He said he was no longer in the market. The man thanked him and hung up."

"Spanish speaker?"

"Yes. Tom couldn't remember whether the man had a regional accent or not. He just didn't want to get involved with any ceramics that close to Tobey's murder. He seems like a conservative sort."

"So if that was Ramon Xoc, and I can't think who else it would be, and he was moving down the list alphabetically, wouldn't the Alwyns be his first call?" I asked.

⌘⌘⌘

The next name on my part of the list was Clare Mason. Clare had been at Perry and Barbara's party. I had known him for a few years, well enough to know that his first name was not Clare, but Clarence, and that he preferred not to use it. The gender ambiguity of calling himself Clare didn't bother him, and people who knew him quickly ceased to think about it.

The Masons were from Kansas City and had begun by coming to San Miguel so that Sally Mason could take a painting class at the Bellas Artes, one of the two big art schools. She could have taken the same courses in Kansas City, but she preferred the atmosphere of San Miguel. While she attended classes Clare would take the tours around the countryside provided by the ex-pats at the Instituto Allende. The town hooked them like it had so many others and they came down every year after that.

Clare had owned an insurance agency and

when it became clear that his only child preferred playing guitar in a rock band to selling term life, Clare sold out and they retired to San Miguel. At more than six foot one, he was taller than I am, with a spare, lean look and a bushy mustache that matched his salt and pepper hair, still thick and parted in the middle. He had the easy manner of one who has greeted a million strangers for business purposes. His handshake was always quick and vigorous, firm enough but not crippling.

The Masons had a large, unusual house in the Atascadero neighborhood, an area that continued along the ridge south of Los Balcones. Atascadero is an area both larger and more diverse than Los Balcones, edging farther down the slope toward *centro* and stretching onto the plateau behind as well. There are people of substantial means there who are perhaps a touch more bohemian in style than is quite right for Los Balcones, and there are also people who neither covet, nor could afford that area.

The Masons' house was not one of the newer ones and had the feeling of two houses joined at some point with less than complete success, an architectural fusion dictated by the need for more space, with coherence and planning coming in a distant second. The surfaces, interior and exterior, had all been well integrated, even expensively so, but the flow of things was wrong and there were odd duplications. The place was quirky enough to charm people who fancied their taste was a little different from most. It had two kitchens; one was explained as being more convenient to the garden, where the Masons ate many of their meals. Floor levels often changed from room to room. You walked three steps up to the diningroom, and then crossed a stairway landing and went down two steps to the living room. The garden itself was L-shaped, and in the far corner, tucked into the wall, was a free standing art studio with arches on two sides and a red tile roof with two skylights. This had been claimed by Sally. Unlike most San Miguel gardens, this one was entirely planted with grass. Maybe they played croquet, or bocce ball.

Also rare in San Miguel was the guest parking spot I found just outside the wall when I drove up in the artmobile. They both met me at the door. Clare wore a loose flower print shirt with shorts and sandals. Sally had on a smock with paint stains on the front. Establishing what she thought might be our common interest, I suppose. I had never owned a smock. That was for movies and wannabes.

"Too early for a drink," said Clare. "How about an iced tea? Sally?"

We both agreed to an iced tea and Sally went to make them. We settled in an outer corner of the *loggia* from which I believed I could see the Watt's house around the curve of the hillside about half a mile away.

"Nice party the other night at the Watts," said Clare.

"Beautiful," said Sally, pouring the tea. "I wish we could host a big group like that here, but we're just not laid out right. People would get lost." The way she said it made the house sound special in its eccentricity. I didn't care much for the layout but it helps to love what you have.

"I was amazed at some of Perry's new things, weren't you Clare?" I asked. He had been in Perry's study when he broke out the gold coins.

"Truly. But what I thought was even more interesting was when you asked him if he had ever wanted to be an artist himself. I really hadn't thought of that before. But it makes sense, if he was blocked from painting or whatever it was he wanted to do. He got a kind of wistful look on his face, I thought."

"Perhaps with a just a touch of steam coming out from his collar," I said.

"I'm sure you know very well, Paul, and you should know this too, Clare, that not everyone can be an artist. It takes a lot more than just wanting it, isn't that right?" She smoothed the smock down over her hips.

"Always, but wanting it helps too," I said.

"I'll bet you knew from a very early age, didn't you, Paul?"

"I was sixteen. I knew right away it was a good way to meet girls."

"And you probably drew constantly from a very early age." She was starting to sound like my mother, who liked to take credit for any painting success I had, although she'd never encouraged it.

"Actually, I hate drawing. When I'm dead and Maya's sorting out my stuff to go to the gallery for the estate sale, she won't find a single drawing to send. Even now, when I start a picture, I get through the sketching it on canvas phase as fast as possible. If you're ever offered a drawing of mine for sale, it's a fake. Call the police immediately."

"Well, we're not big collectors, anyway," said Clare. "You remember I bought that still life from you a couple of years ago, the one with all the squash and gourds in that basket. But we don't even hang it all the time. We bring it out in the fall and leave it up when we have some friends down here for Thanksgiving and then through Christmas until sometime in February. In fact, we just took it down. You wouldn't believe what we have to go through to get a fresh turkey down here. Or maybe you do know?"

"Well, we never do it. It's just Maya and me. Neither family has ever visited us. Anyway, you've probably heard that I've been looking into this Tobey thing. I saw you had bought some things from him. Some silver?" I knew there were ceramics too, but I wanted them to volunteer it.

"You know what we have?" Sally jumped up and disappeared into the house. She came back with a large solid silver bell in her hands. The wooden handle was black and worn to bare wood in places. She gave it to me. It had the mellow look and feel of thick old Mexican silver. "I'm not really sure whether this is an altar bell or not. It seems rather big for that. But we just love it."

"Any ceramics?" I decided not to wait.

Clare looked uncomfortable now. He slid his iced tea glass back and forth on the oilcloth. "We did get a couple of pieces and I used to show them all the time. We paid some pretty good money for them too. But then I started thinking that we'd never get them out of here. And where did they come from, anyway? They look so good they ought to be in a museum, so why aren't they? I called Tobey about it and he said they came from some excavators in the Yucatán and they could sell things to dealers if they were very close to other pieces the museums already had. I guess that makes sense, but I had them put in secure storage anyway. We don't take them out anymore. Now with him dead I feel even funnier than I did before."

"I think you did the right thing, Clare," Sally said, nodding.

"You didn't keep any pictures of them, did you?" I asked.

"Of course. I like to look at them now and then, and it's possible the insurance people might want to see them at some point. You can't ever forget that. I can't, anyway. I'll get them."

"Maybe you'd like to see some of the things I've been doing, Paul, when you and Clare are done here?"

"I'd like that. You do water color, don't you?"

"Only water color. I can't stand the smell of oils, and acrylics irritate my eyes."

She wrinkled her nose.

"It's possible to be too sensitive, I guess." I tried to keep my voice free of irony.

Clare returned with eight photographs, showing a one-quarter view of each piece. One was a cylinder vessel with a lid, three footed. Traces of multicolor glaze remained and the handle in the center of the lid was formed to resemble a human head. The other was nearly a cylinder that tapered in toward the top before flaring slightly outward. It lacked a lid and was deeply incised with figures I couldn't identify from the photos. I couldn't be certain they matched Ramon's work without holding them in my hands, but it was possible.

"Do you remember when you bought these?"

"A little more than three years ago. Both at the same time. It was kind of uncharacteristic of me."

I handed the photos back to him. "I've been trying to get a feel for his business, and seeing these things helps a lot. Were you a friend of Tobey's?"

"I wouldn't say that. We saw him around here and there. I first met him after a seminar he gave at the English Library. We talked for a while afterward. It got me kind of intrigued. He spoke with great authority about the design aspects, but he also stressed potential investment value. But I'm not sure now how I'd sell them if I decided to." He scratched his head at the edge of his hairline. I could see he didn't have much to add and I got up. "I really appreciate your taking time to talk with me about this," I said.

Sally was on me like a small dog. "Let's just take a peek down in my studio, OK?"

I was about to become an art critic.

CHAPTER SEVENTEEN
DIEGO DELGADO

Uncharacteristically, *Licenciado* Delgado had mostly forgotten about the murders of Tobey Cross and Ramon Xoc in the excitement of his new career move. He had other priorities. What was called for, he decided, was a new level of professionalism, so he retrieved the packaging material from the Calle Independencia 132 office in Dolores Hidalgo. It was too amateurish, as well as too risky, to be hauling around the eleven ceramic pieces wrapped in blankets. It made Delgado feel like a small time fence. If he was going to be dealing with the highest level of collectors, he needed to polish his presentation. When the ceramics were repacked in their original containers, with the name of Ramon Xoc covered by black magic marker, they would not all fit in the trunk of his police Chrysler so three of them rode in the back seat.

After their first phone conversation he waited an entire day for Perry Watt to get back to him and then Watt had insisted he quote a firm price for the entire lot before agreeing to a meeting. Delgado had tried to prepare for this and, with his stomach churning, he said, "One million pesos." (About $90,000.) This was an enormous amount of money and he had no idea if it was even in the ballpark, but he could always negotiate. He went over in his mind the things he could buy with the money. One possibility was a new house on a nice property in

Atotonilco. Or he could bank some of it and get a new Chevy Suburban with darkened windows to replace his aging Nissan. It was not at all unusual for police officials to drive new cars.

They had set the meeting for eight o'clock in the Jardín Botanico, after dark, the area that contains one of the two reservoirs for San Miguel's water system, surrounded by hundreds of acres of hiking trails. Its official name is not always used, and many of the locals refer to it as the Charco, for Charco del Ingenio, the Devil's water hole. At one end is a high dam of about fifteen meters, which often has some run-off coming over the center, even out of season. The park was easy to find, would distance their cars from the main road, and there would be no one around at that hour. Delgado had no idea, of course, that it was on this same road coming toward the parking lot that Ramon Xoc had been murdered.

Diego Delgado was no stranger to tense situations, and he prided himself on his ability to remain cool in the face of any threat. It was only the enormous amount of money at stake that had briefly rattled him. Fencing stolen Mayan ceramics was out of his normal range, but after all, what could go wrong? He didn't think that Perry Watt would turn whistle-blower. Why would he wish to alienate the local police, who could easily make life difficult for him, rich as he was? The worst thing that could happen was that he and Perry Watt would fail to agree on the price. Then Delgado would return home with the ceramics and think about who to approach next. There were many other potential customers on the list from Tobey Cross's computer. He would, of course, stay away from John Schleicher.

He had borrowed one of the street cops' small police pickups that had been sidelined for routine service, and drove it home after his shift. As dusk came on about 6:45, he loaded the back of the pickup with the eleven packages and pulled a tarp over them. When the evening deepened into darkness, clouds covered the moon. It would be a good night to do business.

At twenty minutes to eight Delgado checked his penlight and pulled away from his house. He came down Ancha de San Antonio toward *centro*, where he picked up Tecolote going steeply up the hill to Cuesta de San Jose. He passed within 200 meters of Perry Watt's house. Even going out of town like this, the road was still cobblestone, but Licenciado Delgado's ears had tuned out the noise years before.

He was now on the plateau above San Miguel, about a half a mile from the entrance to the Charco. In his rear view mirror he could see headlights in the distance. Hopefully that would be Perry Watt. He took the left turn onto Paloma slowly, knowing that although there were no more speed bumps at fifty-meter intervals, the road itself was worse than primitive. No sense jostling a million pesos worth of antiques.

At the end of the parking lot a nightlight illuminated the gate, which had been locked at six. The gatehouse and gift shop were both dark. The fence going both ways from the gate was cactus, upright and thick, like a file of spiny soldiers ranked shoulder to shoulder. Delgado routinely checked the layout of any place he worked, looking for ways his prey might escape. Tonight he saw just one; a small void in the cactus next to a recently installed electric meter. Not that Perry Watt would want to escape from the best deal he'd ever been offered.

Far down Paloma, toward the point where the houses ended and it became a dirt track coming into the Jardín Botanico, Delgado saw the headlights moving toward him. When the lights reached the circular track into the parking lot he could see it was Perry Watt's silver Mercedes. Here we go, he thought, and felt his pulse rate inching up. Instead of slowing to park beside him, however, the Mercedes accelerated as it passed the police pickup and sped back out of the circular lot. Suddenly, as Delgado watched the Mercedes leave, a pair of high beams came on from an approaching vehicle and flooded him with blinding light as a black Suburban, typical of the *federales*, screeched to a halt directly behind the pickup. By the time it stopped he was already out the door and running toward the cactus fence.

Diego Delgado did not need to stop and think about his next move. Keeping within the shadow of his pickup he dove head first through the void in the cactus next to the electric meter. He had folded his arms and raised them to his face, but the spines still raked his forehead and his scalp. His right shoulder landed hard on the pathway as he heard the doors of the Suburban slam. He was instantly on his feet, trying to remember how the grounds were laid out. He recalled from a visit of eight or nine years ago that numerous paths crisscrossed the preserve, framing clumps of cactus and agave, lethal with spikes. It was too dark to see anything, and one misstep could result in blindness if his eyes were perforated by the clusters of thorns. He had the small penlight in his pocket but he didn't dare to turn it on because it might reveal his location.

Up the hill behind him at the fence, the two

federal officers, somewhat less desperate than Delgado, were stalled trying to find a more dignified way to get through the cactus. As Delgado inched forward his foot touched a stick that, when he picked it up, turned out to be about a meter and a half long. This would be his white cane. He began to move faster, holding the stick before him, seething with anger at the betrayal by Perry Watt. He would find a way to make him pay for this. The sounds behind him receded as he distanced himself from the fence; they were not through it yet.

He kept moving downward toward the reservoir; he could tell that he was still on a path from the bare dirt beneath his feet. There was a crash above him at the fence and flashlights appeared up the hill. Then there was a pause and the two flashlights moved apart.

After a while Licenciado Delgado could smell water and hear the gentle lapping of the reservoir. He tried hard to recall the configuration of the dam. He remembered it was possible to walk out along the top edge, but he couldn't recall whether he could get all the way across. Last time he had visited the Charco, a large rusted steel pipe had rested with one end at the opposite end of the dam, the far end pointing downward into the gorge and the near end just above a projection where the slope back up to the plateau was gentler. This was the remnant of an old spillway system that hadn't been in use for many years. If he could cross the dam without being seen, he could crawl through the pipe and drop to the ground and freedom.

One of the flashlights was approaching closer; the other had gone off toward the far end of the reservoir.

Delgado located the end of the dam by the sound

of water lapping against it, and felt concrete beneath his feet. There was a rail on the drop-off side and he moved along the dam until the concrete stopped. Sticking out his right foot he determined that the surface only dropped about ten centimeters, but had the additional complication of about three centimeters of water flowing over it. Fortunately there was a chain at hand height supported by uprights, but the concrete under his shoes was slick and covered with a growth of moss that made the footing treacherous. As he moved over it, water flowed over his shoes. The chill moved into his ankles and up his legs.

The flashlight was approaching the edge of the dam now, and he was faced with a difficult choice. He could attempt to outrun the federal officer, and risk being shot, or he could allow himself to slide over the edge and hang on to one of the uprights that supported the chain. If he went over and lost his grip, he would be smashed on the rocks at the bottom of the dam. But if he could hold on, and keep his hands below the water line, he would not be seen because of the lip at the edge of the overflow. His body would hang between the falling water and the wall of the dam itself.

He sat at the watery edge, gripped the steel upright with both hands, and allowed himself to slide over. Diego Delgado was a strong man, and his years on the streets had put him in many physically demanding situations. When he became a detective he still worked out regularly, so hanging from his hands was not a grave risk as long as the post held. After two or three minutes he could see through the water the flashlight playing along the dam. He waited a while after it passed and then pulled himself high enough over the edge to look around. The flashlight now moved away from him along the edge of the reservoir. He pulled himself into a sitting position on the top of the dam and then continued his flight. In another ten meters the overflow portion of the dam ended and he emerged onto the wider concrete walkway.

The next part was chancy. He was approaching the old pipe, but he would soon have to use his penlight to see just how far it was from the dam. He quickly moved toward the far end, and using his body to shield the penlight from the others, he located the pipe against the wall of the canyon. It opened almost at the edge of the concrete. He was surprised that it was more than two meters in diameter, larger than he remembered, but he had never been this close to it before. In the dim light he could see a bar welded across the center of the interior, and dimmer yet, another bar about two meters further in, set at a right angle to the first. His light reached no further, but there were probably more at the same interval beyond.

Delgado leaped lightly across the empty space and landed just inside the pipe. He almost whistled with relief.

What he had not seen, because the penlight did not reach that far in front of him, was that the section of pipe he was now entering was no longer a continuous run perhaps a hundred meters long, but a much smaller section of twenty-five meters that had broken away some time ago. This shorter piece now rested with support at its approximate center from a narrow rock formation thrusting out into the gorge, and at the dam end, on a concrete abutment that helped to tie the dam into the rock wall.

The steel walls of the pipe had once been about a centimeter thick, with each six-meter section bolted with a collar to the one next to it. Decades of rusting had left the steel layered and spongy, and as he worked his way through the pipe, the braces occasionally came loose in his hands and papery flakes of rust rained down on him. He was hoping there were no rusted-through places below his feet.

About fifteen meters along he unknowingly passed over the rock support near the center, and shortly after he heard the first groan. Perhaps it was only the wind. Three meters further there was a distinct movement in the pipe and a louder groan, accompanied by a scraping sound. He went on more slowly, telling himself that it was, after all, not unnatural that the pipe might shift a bit after so many years, the main thing was to get to the other end and drop to the ground before it moved too much. One meter more and the floor of the pipe suddenly dropped away beneath him, then stopped. His feet came down hard on the rusted metal, which made him feel queasy, but it held.

Steadying himself with one of the bars, he paused to consider for a moment whether or not he should go on, and at that instant, the end of the pipe he was facing dropped quickly away as the entire twenty-five-meter section turned end over end into the ravine, passed the first cataract and looped again into the second, cracked in half, and then into three more sections, which all fell like a train wreck into the stream at the bottom of the third cataract.

Licenciado Delgado had managed to hold on to the interior bars through the entire fall. The bar held almost all the way down, breaking free only on the final shock, but the impact in the shallows at the gorge bottom flattened the section of pipe and punctured it in several places from rocks in the streambed. If it had been daylight, the two federal officers would have seen the immense cloud of rusty red dust hovering over the canyon.

Even though the fall had broken three ribs, his left ankle, and his collarbone, as well as given him a dandy concussion, Licenciado Delgado experienced no discomfort as he lay in the streambed below the third cataract. His section of the pipe had been reduced to about five meters long and had a distinctly oval profile. Flakes of rust thickly covered his black clothes. The discomfort would begin in an hour or so when he regained consciousness. He was more fortunate than he knew, since it was only the lower half of his body that was under water.

⌘⌘⌘

When Licenciado Delgado awakened he didn't realize in the dense darkness that his vision was blurred, but he knew from the intense pain that wracked his body that he was no longer trying to escape the federal officers. They had become his only hope of getting out of the stream alive. He tried to yell, but the fractured ribs limited his breathing to shallow gasps and the only sound that came from his mouth was a muted wheeze. It didn't escape the ends of the pipe.

Nearly two hours later he heard one officer calling to another and abruptly a powerful flashlight swept over his body. It was not until dawn that the medical team was able to reach him and strap him to a stretcher. Another hour and a half was required to muscle the stretcher out of the gorge and into the waiting ambulance.

Diego Delgado's career as an antiques dealer had come to an end, as had his career as an officer of the judicial police.

Having done his duty, Perry Watt had been home sleeping peacefully for hours.

CHAPTER EIGHTEEN

The home of Julian Soames was on Loreto, only two long blocks from our place on Quebrada, with a faded reddish-brown facade and two tall grilled windows on the first floor and three on the second. The windows were framed in old *cantera* stone, blurred from centuries of weather and fractured in places. The double doors of the entry looked like mesquite and possibly eighteenth century; relatively recent additions, judging from the look of the rest of the house. As I stood there I began to wonder again what my standing in this investigation was, not sure whether I myself would talk to someone like me in these circumstances. The best official title I could muster was friend of a friend of the spouse of the deceased.

After a couple of rings he answered the door. Soames was a short, thick-chested man in his mid-fifties, bearded and wearing steel-framed glasses that may once have been fashionable and perhaps were about to be again. He had coarse, sandy hair, just touched with gray here and there. The beard was mostly gray, and he had no mustache, giving him a farmer look. I had met him a few times at various gatherings, and he was friendly enough, although he hadn't seemed comfortable in a large group. His wife Laura, taller than Soames and with short auburn hair, was not in evidence this afternoon. I remembered her as looking as if she had once been very attractive but hadn't held up well. Maybe the air here was too dry.

"Come in," he said. We shook hands. He had a firm grip, but his fingers were thick and stubby. He would never play the piano.

We went up the two deeply worn stone steps into a living room that ran across the width of the house. The ceiling was probably eighteen feet high, with an ornate stone fireplace at the side opposite the entry. The ceiling beams bore traces of decorative painting that I could not quite make out at that distance. Bookshelves lined the walls up to eight feet and the deep leather chairs and two matching sofas seemed not quite to the scale of the room. Probably not much would be. The coffee table was an ancient door four inches thick, still bearing its iron strap-work, thickly varnished over.

"You haven't been here before, have you?"

"Never. It looks like a very old house."

"It is. That's what appeals to me. I can't quite say for certain that Cortés slept here, but he could have. I'll give you the tour."

I wondered whether the realtor had told him this. Cortés died in 1547, five years after the town was founded. Although it was an old street, Calle Loreto wouldn't have been thought of yet at that point. Was Soames a little gullible and had it influenced his purchase of ceramics?

On the far end the living room led directly to the narrow end of the dining room, which was twice as long as it was wide, with walls that had been taken down to the bare stone. Or it was possible they had never been plastered. Two tall stories up, the ceiling was barrel vaulted in the same stone. It almost felt like it should be part of a monastery, and maybe it had been. A small sixteenth-century abbey serving the needs of the mule drivers bringing silver down from Guanajuato on the way to the fleet at Veracruz.

On the long outside wall a massive sideboard ran from one end of the room to the other. I couldn't place the style of the figures carved in deep relief on the doors, but it had obviously been made for this room and could easily have held four pair of the tall silver altar candlesticks that Maya thought were too large for Mrs. Harris's dining room. Soames had chosen hammered copper vessels instead. On the opposite wall an arched doorway led to the small tiled kitchen, which was lit by a tall shaft leading to a skylight. Other than this there were no windows in the room.

Many people in San Miguel leave their stone or tile floors bare, but Julian Soames had covered almost every inch with a large number of old Persian rugs, most of them worn and almost threadbare. They gave the house the feeling of having been lived in for generations with the same furnishings. You could walk from room to room without making a sound and you almost expected to see hunting dogs on the furniture.

In two corners of the dining room circular balconies projected from halfway up the wall. But the dominant feature was a tall pine carving of the Mayan God of Maize, bracketed with iron fasteners into the stone. It did not look very old, but it certainly fit the feeling of the house. He looked like an old friend.

Soames saw my look. "I got that from a Mayan carver in Campeche in 1996. He's dead now."

"Have you traveled in the Yucatán much?" I asked.

"I did years ago. My wife liked it a great deal, but

I found after a while that the climate bothered my asthma. I stopped going down. I guess I was tired of the people too. Seems easier now to just hang out with the Americans up here. My Spanish was never that good. Too many verb tenses, don't you think? Doesn't always make sense to have that many ways to say something."

I didn't know how to respond to this. Maybe if blunt were a verb tense he could have gotten by with just that one. The subtleties of Spanish verbs can be difficult, but it seemed to me they were just part of the richness of the culture. Mexicans had a lot of ways to say what might happen under certain circumstances, few to say what absolutely would. None that were take it or leave it blunt.

Beyond the dining room a hallway led to a bathroom and a large bedroom. The bed was held by a black metal frame with mosquito netting over the top and tied back like draperies at the four corners. A sleekly modern glass wall with French doors in black steel frames led to a small garden area with sheer stone walls on three sides. It probably caught the sun for an hour a day. I preferred a garden to be more spread out, so it didn't seem like I was lying at the bottom of a shaft. But my house was about 150 years later than this one, from a time when the conquistadores were feeling more secure, able to stretch out a bit and relax without worrying about the Otomi coming through the windows at them with hatchets.

"This is the guest room," said Soames. "I haven't had many guests since Laura left. In fact, I can't think of any."

"I'm sorry, I didn't know."

"She went off with a German tourist she met at the house tour. Sent me a postcard from Guadalajara. His name was Wolf."

"Sounds appropriate." I was trying to sound sympathetic but I didn't know what else to say. His manner was matter-of-fact, not looking for sympathy. We went up a stairway next to the bathroom to a sunlit landing roofed with glass. One bedroom over the living room faced the street and had a glass door opening onto one of the balconies halfway up the dining room wall. The other was evidently the master bedroom. It also had a Juliet balcony to the dining room and a glass wall with another balcony overlooking the small garden I had seen below. On the back wall of the house was a bathroom and dressing room, and on the inside wall a display case with several old swords and daggers and two Mayan ceramic pieces.

"I think these are what you mentioned on the phone," he said. "I got these from Tobey Cross a couple of years ago. They're probably the best things I have."

The ceramics had the look of Ramon Xoc. I didn't exactly feel like an expert in the Mayan style yet but I was definitely developing a feel for Ramon's work. Even though they both lacked the loopy incised figures I had seen on many of the other pieces, hand made things do have the look of the person who made them. It's a subtle thing, and difficult to define. Maybe it was just the concept that I was seeing, since the ceramics bore no tool marks. There was nothing like, say, a particular brush stroke that would help identify a painter, like Van Gogh or Monet.

"Let me take them out for you," he said. "I'm sure you've handled things like this before." I guess that was his way of telling me not to drop them.

He opened the case and placed a three-legged bowl in my hands. It was lidless and the edge was ragged for a couple of inches along the top where chipped clay was visible through the paint and glaze. The bottoms of the feet were worn a bit, too uniformly, I thought, as if they had been rubbed over with an abrasive. Other than that, nothing about it specially suggested Ramon Xoc, yet I still felt they were from his hand. I gave it back to Soames.

"What was Tobey able to tell you about these?"

"Well, he felt they were both northern Mayan, probably from the State of Tabasco. Sixth to eighth century, so not early, in fact, past the classic period. He got them from a collector in Mérida and they've never been recorded. The one in the case has two legs replaced. I don't handle it much. That's always the vulnerable spot, of course."

"Yes. And you weren't ever moved to buy anything more from him?"

"I had bought these weapons from him earlier, and I thought I might add to that part of my collection, but then he couldn't come up with any more pieces I really liked. He had a spur that I considered for a while, but then I decided I wanted more arms."

"How was he to deal with?"

"Knowledgeable but rather cold, I thought."

"Did that bother you?"

"I didn't think so at first, but it may have as time went on. He had a take-it-or-leave-it sort of attitude. I guess people may have said that of me as well, when I was in business. I didn't mind. I can decide things pretty well for myself. I don't need anyone to stroke me a lot just to make a purchase. If I like a thing I buy it. I always have. And I don't like to quibble about price the way everybody does down here."

"They must have been expensive." I already knew what he had paid for them from the office records.

"They were. But my bias is for the very old things. It's the same appeal as this house. Some of these walls, maybe all of them, go back to the earliest days of San Miguel." Here it was again. Was it that he absorbed some of the pedigree of the house? We came back downstairs and sat in the living room. Soames was wearing faded gold corduroys, worn and baggy at the knees, and oddly, a crisp white shirt. I couldn't think when I had last seen a white shirt in San Miguel, except on a waiter. It didn't seem like he was about to leave for work at Tio Lucas or the Santa Monica. I'd always heard he was well off.

"He tried to interest me in some pictures as well, but they were mostly eighteenth century and they would have seemed too modern for this place. Anyway, I had already owned a large number of eighteenth century paintings in a Georgian house I restored in Baltimore. I wanted to live in a different period here."

"You had no disagreements with him?"

"Why, do you think I killed him?" He spoke without hesitation, looking me in the eye, but his face held no expression and his tone of voice did not change. It was as if what I might think was not that important to him.

"No, I don't think that, but I am trying to get a feel for his business. When Marisol asked me to look into this I found that his dealing activities were veiled and she knew practically nothing about it. I'm wondering why."

"I can't tell you that. Maybe he just liked his privacy. Maybe his clients did too, and that certainly included me. But I will say that I've pretty much always been able to do the business I wanted to do without killing anyone. Seems excessive. There's usually a less complicated way. Besides, murder can have unintended consequences. I prefer that all my consequences be intended."

There seemed no reason to not believe him, especially the last part. "What sort of business were you in, if you don't mind me asking?"

"Residential property, mainly. When I first came to Baltimore in the seventies there was a wave of house restoration just beginning, and there were many properties for sale in terrible condition. You couldn't get a mortgage on anything like that, of course. The real estate business was being done on a contract for deed basis, at least in that neighborhood. The sellers all carried their own paper. It was hard to get insurance. The blacks often thought they were being gentrified out of their own turf. I suppose the locals think the same thing here, not that it matters. People without means always move on to cheaper properties. I certainly did before I had any money and I never resented it.

"But there was money to be made by fixing them up and turning them around quickly to people with more money than time or ability, who wanted to be seen as on the cutting edge of a trend. I had a great fondness for Georgian buildings then and I kept the best of the restorations for myself. Laura and I had a lovely mansion with formal gardens, lots of boxwood hedges and a summer kitchen at the back of the lot. Brick pathways. It was built in 1730. Only middle-aged by San Miguel standards. We entertained a great deal then." He gazed into the cold fireplace.

"Don't you ever miss it?"

"Not really. I got tired of surrounding myself

with other people's ancestors. I do miss the entertaining, though. This was a good house for it." He began to stroke one of the leather pillows at his elbow. "If it weren't for that Wolf..."

"I suppose he said it like a V."

"Never really saw him, but yes, it would have been Volf. So where are you in this? Any ideas?"

"I have Tobey's customer list. The killer's name must be on it. But they're not all in San Miguel. Could be anywhere in México, practically. I'm hoping he's here."

"How about the wife?"

"Not likely. She's devastated. My girlfriend Maya has known her for a long time. She can't see her doing it. Besides, if she's guilty, why would she invite me in on it?"

"Muddy the waters?" He grinned. "But I suppose the police are already doing that. Who's on the case, Rodriguez?"

"No, Delgado. Do you know them?"

"I try to follow the local politics. That includes the Policia Judicial in this town. Delgado's ambitious, he might try to solve it. He's got his finger in a lot of pies. Can't say that I'd trust him, though."

"Why not?"

"I don't trust any of them. It's just my policy."

"Is it a gringo thing?"

"Not really. It's that they don't make enough to get by so they're inclined to supplement their income any way they can. People have to live. There are a lot of oportunities when you're an investigator."

"Well, it's hard to tell what he's doing. At any rate, the police aren't telling me anything much except to mind my own business."

"Maybe that's a good idea." He was watching me carefully with his cool blue eyes behind the steel rims. "What I mean is, you don't know who might be coming after you if you start getting too close. And you're not likely to know it until you are too close. Might be too late then."

"A lose-lose situation."

"Potentially. What do you have to gain, after all, Paul? You identify the killer, you get the eternal gratitude of the widow. So what? You aggravate the killer without knowing it, quite possibly you're eternally dead."

"Either way, it lasts a long time."

"Exactly. A little cost/benefit analysis might be in order here. Give it some thought."

"What would you do?" I thought I knew. He would sit and admire all his stuff in its sixteenth century showcase house, and wonder about the appeal of Wolf. It could have been more about what Julian didn't have than what Wolf did.

"Just as I always have done," he said. "I pick my battles. The trick in business is not to know how to win every one; it's to know which ones you can win and then to ignore the rest. People think the great determining factor for success is power, but it isn't. It's restraint—the ability to just walk away. Not many people realize that. You may have picked the wrong battle here. It's not going to sell any paintings for you, so why does it matter?"

"But this situation has a personal dimension. It doesn't boil down exactly in the way you describe."

"Only because you allowed it to develop that way." Again the steely look.

"So what would you have said to the widow?"

"Sorry, Mrs. Cross, but I'm a painter. That's all I do. I'm not that smart and it's too hard to be good at more than one thing." Maybe this was why Laura Soames was now tripping down the primrose path with Wolf. I tried to see Soames with brush in hand, with Maya or Barbara posing. It didn't fly.

"Julian, suppose for a moment that you actually were a painter. Would you paint only the pictures that you knew would turn out?"

"Of course. Only those. I'd want to know in advance."

"Then you would never paint any pictures because you can't know that, especially in the beginning. And later, let's say here that you had somehow painted your first fifty pictures anyway, you could never grow from there because you would be eliminating the element of serendipity, and without that, your pictures would be dead and lifeless. Every painter who's any good is a gambler. The farther you reach out of your comfort zone, the greater the likelihood that you'll fall on your face. But out there on that same tricky edge is the possibility of doing something great. Being slightly off-balance is good. I'm off-balance now, going around sticking my nose into this. Maybe if I do aggravate someone I might be quick enough to see the blow coming. And then the killer will be off-balance."

Soames looked at me in silence for a moment. "I don't fall on my face," he said finally. I think this was the only part of what I said that registered with him.

"That's why your shirt is so crisp."

"Exactly."

We shook hands again on the worn steps. How many footsteps did it take to wear through an inch or two of stone? And how much shoe leather would that be? And what would it take to wear Julian Soames down? I couldn't imagine. It would not be anything I could come up with.

"Come on by some evening for a drink, Paul, and we'll have another look at this idea of comfort zone."

I shook his hand and as I moved down Loreto I reentered the world of risk and possibility. However, one possibility I hadn't factored in was the bullet hole through the windshield of the artmobile.

CHAPTER NINETEEN

Had I been sitting in the driver's seat the bullet would have gone right into my forehead. Toward the rear of the van was another hole, ragged and somewhat larger, in the headliner short of the rear door. I got out and ran my hand over the top outside, but there was no hole there, only a tiny bulge; the bullet had not exited. Just another souvenir of this case, and as far as I was concerned, it could stay where it was. I considered calling Delgado, but all I'd get from him would be another lecture on minding my own business. Driving home, the hole in the glass made a low whistling noise. I chewed the single piece of gum I'd bought from the girl in the *jardín* and plugged it.

When I pulled up to the house Maya and Cody were standing outside talking. As I stopped at the curb Cody saw the bullet hole at once and came over to the artmobile. He leaned his arms on my door and looked in.

"Well, I can see from the freckles that the bullet missed you."

"I wasn't in the car at the time. What freckles?"

"In this kind of attack you get freckles on your face from the molten glass powder blown off by the bullet. That plus the hole in your head."

"I don't have any freckles."

"Exactly. We'll check for the hole later."

Maya slid in beside me from the passenger door. She put her arms around me.

"Are you all right? You scare me sometimes. Who shot at you?"

Cody had taken a pen from his shirt pocket and was poking out the gum to get a closer look at the hole.

"I don't know," I said. "But it wasn't Julian Soames because I was with him when it happened, inside his house."

"Good alibi," said Cody. "Looks like another small caliber. Mind if I dig it out in back? I always wanted to get into the forensic side. I assume you didn't call Delgado."

"No. Go ahead and dig it out."

"How could anyone shoot like this in the middle of the day?" asked Maya.

Cody's voice came from the back now, as he probed the headliner. "With all the firecrackers around, people don't notice the noise. If the shooter was not directly in view of anyone, like down between the cars, it wouldn't be that hard. Here we go." He withdrew his fingers from the fabric to show us a flattened and curved slug. In the palm of his hand, it was only the back end of the bullet that wasn't totally distorted from the impact of the glass and then the brace of the steel top of the van.

"Twenty-five caliber, I'd say. Not a common gun, but I'll bet if the police shared with us what they know about the gun that killed Tobey, it's probably a match."

"Paul, maybe you should back out." This from Maya.

"Back off?"

"OK. Whatever. You know what I mean. I am very worried here. I could be screaming soon."

"Then do you tell Marisol or do I?"

"You are not fair. This is a gringo thing. You always try to make us have choices that we don't want to have. You and I have to go on and Marisol is already ruined. We can't bring back Tobey." She slid back out onto the sidewalk, distancing herself from me. I felt like she was about to blow up.

"Now wait a minute." Cody's ham-like paws descended on Maya's shoulders. His thick fingers found the taut cords in her neck and her whole upper body relaxed in less than a minute. Her head began to wobble slightly like one of those plastic figures people mount on their dashboard. The tension faded as traffic moved past us in a steady rumble; water trucks, ice cream trucks, pickups full of workers in from the farms, cars full of kids coming back from school, taxis with tourists, seven Benedictine nuns in a van. Cody pressed his face into her hair from behind. I had never seen him like this. "Don't discount me," he said. "I love you guys. If I have any say in it, nothing else bad will happen here."

She turned around and pulled him down to her face and kissed him on the mouth. These Mexican girls. Everybody's family. I guess if someone had to be family, it ought to be Cody, but I just don't kiss guys that big. I locked the van and we went inside the house.

⌘⌘⌘

The next name on the customer list was John

Schleicher. It was familiar because he was said to rival Perry in wealth (or at least, in expenditure) and although he never attended the normal gringo gatherings, he was spoken of with respect in the expat community because of his heavy contributions to their charities. The only thing I knew about him other than that was that he owned a great historic house in town which had not, during my time here, ever appeared on the house tour list. Nor did I know anyone who acknowledged having been inside. The house was said to have belonged at one time to General, and later eleven-term President, Santa Anna, the butcher of the Alamo. Of course, this ownership had been claimed for other houses in San Miguel as well, usually those on the market with spectacular price tags.

In my early years in San Miguel, Schleicher's house on Cuadrante had sat empty and unloved with a perpetual for sale sign affixed to the second floor, even though its potential was obvious. At one of the house tours I had heard that it was owned by a newly rich dot com couple from New York, who had bought it impulsively on a visit to San Miguel, but then sadly walked away from it when they realized how daunting a project it would be. Another case of more money than sense, I thought at the time. When the dot.com boom folded, nothing further happened, other than the sign going up.

Its architectural style was the high classical of the eighteenth century, with pedimented windows and a grand entry. Brass knockers with lion's heads on the tall double doors challenged your approach. The elaborate stonework of the facade had taken a series of hits from what must have been revolutionary gunfire. No shortage of that over the years.

It didn't sell again until two or three years after I arrived; the potential was there to bring it back as the great mansion it had once been, but it was too much beyond the means and ambitions of most people I knew. Folks like Perry and Barbara Watt, who had enough money to do it without breaking a sweat, often preferred new construction. They wanted their fiber optic wiring in the walls under the reproduction finishes, the larger sewer pipes, the grounded outlets, the purified water systems. Now pristine, the Schleicher house sits in disdainful isolation; there is nothing on the street remotely like it because Cuadrante is a street of mixed uses. Farther down to the west its name changes to Pila Seca and the first block there holds, among other things, a bed and breakfast, a laundry and two art galleries. Neither of these galleries has ever exhibited a single painting by Paul Zacher, which suggests, I fear, just how mixed it becomes.

On the morning after the Diego Delgado debacle at the Charco, news of which had traveled rapidly through town, I dialed the number from Tobey's customer list for John Schleicher. After three rings it picked up. The man who answered had a refined voice but an abrupt manner.

"Schleicher," he said, without saying "hello." He sounded like he was in a hurry. I introduced myself and said I was sorry to bother him.

"I wonder how you could have gotten this number? I'm not in the book."

I explained I was a friend hoping to get some information about Tobey Cross and his name was on the customer list.

"I didn't know him."

"Tobey Cross was the antique dealer who was

murdered three weeks ago," I said, noticing he had said, "didn't know him," as if he knew Tobey was no longer around. "Perhaps you'll remember making some purchases from him. He specialized in Mayan ceramics and colonial paintings and silver and gold."

"I don't have any of that. Not a collector, sorry."

"Tobey Cross's records indicate you purchased four ceramic pieces and two paintings from him over the last six years. The latest was five months ago."

"Must be a mistake; don't believe everything you read. Anything else?"

Without waiting for my response, he hung up. We were a long way from the courtesy of Bill Frost and Clare Mason.

I wrote down the conversation as closely as I could get to word for word and then dialed Cody.

"Williams," he said.

They both must have gone to the same finishing school. "I'm trying to reach a moth-eaten old cop who's got more bullet holes in him than a roadside yield sign in Montana."

"That'd be me. What have you got?"

"Schleicher, John." I gave the address on Cuadrante. "The eager purchaser of six pieces from Galería Cruz over the last six years and now has never heard of Tobey Cross in his life."

"Alzheimer's. It's a killer. Turns your brain to jelly. I suppose it goes without saying that he also doesn't want to see you."

I read off the conversation from my notebook.

"He's terse and pithy. What do you say I call the boys in Chicago and see if they can get a line on him?

That name sounds like I ought to know it. I thought that before, when I looked at the customer list, and I should have done it then. It'll probably take until tomorrow. I'll get back to you."

I put down the phone and sat for a while in the living room. The chair creaked as I leaned back. I had naively hoped I might talk to Schleicher this morning and now I had a void. Maya was at the market and I had finished the foliage on the replacement for the ruined picture and Barbara had not called about another session. There was probably not going to be any painting today. I locked the door, double checked it, and left.

Walking south on Quebrada, the morning light was clear and beautiful. That crap the local painters always say about the quality of light here is probably true. A woman realtor from Texas drove by and waved at me from her Acura SUV. The passenger side was badly scraped. There are some tight corners in this town. There have been times when I considered buying a motorcycle.

After two blocks I turned left on Pila Seca and walked past the two galleries. One of them was showing pictures with what looked like sequins all over them. Maybe paint was in short supply now. I could understand their role on evening gowns, but I wondered how you would render skin tones in sequins. I've done too much painting to be trendy.

Three blocks down, where Pila Seca becomes Cuadrante, the Schleicher house stood as if reborn. Suddenly it was 1740. A great thing about San Miguel is that there are craftsmen here who can do anything. As in Europe, the old skills live, the ones that, back in the States, everyone thinks are dead and forgotten. The pockmarks and bullet holes in the skin of the old mansion were gone. The mashed and eroded stonework at the windows and the front door was now freshly reproduced in exactly the same patterns, no shortcuts, carved the same way as the originals. The rusted ironwork of the window grills and balconies had been sandblasted and repainted. The entry doors gleamed with new varnish and the freshly polished lion-head knockers flashed in the sun. The old stucco was smoothly patched. Whatever else this grump Schleicher might be, he knew how to restore a house to the last level of detail, or at least he could afford the most expert help and didn't hesitate to sign them up.

The house stood on a corner lot, and I left Cuadrante and walked down the side street. Seventy or eighty feet down the street, the house wall became a garden wall about twelve feet high. There was a single gate in it that filled the opening and gave no view inside. At the far end of the property a roof line appeared eight feet higher than the wall, with a row of square mullioned windows below it. Staff quarters, I thought; no slaves here.

I hung about for half an hour, pretending to look in the shop windows, watching the traffic. The casual American tourist taking in the sights, nothing much on his mind. From a doorway, an old woman in a shawl thrust a cup at me; I added a few brass coins to the others in it. I gave her more than twenty centavos. Could have been forty, even.

During the time I was there no one entered or left the house. The windows were shuttered on the inside and gave away nothing. Walking past I heard no sounds from within or from the garden. Friendly, outgoing John Schleicher. His life was an open book, but on inspection the individual pages were oddly blank.

On the Cuadrante side of the house, at the left edge of the property, was a double carriage gate with an open grill near the top. Over the gates was a stone arch with a lantern above. By standing on my toes I could see through the ironwork down a drive that ran past more windows, but they were smaller than on the other two sides on the street. Evidently this was the service side of the house. The gates were padlocked. I picked up a pebble from the cobblestones of the street and threw it as far down the drive as I could. In about four seconds a large Doberman came screaming toward me, legs flying, and hit the carriage gate, fangs bared, and barking with everything he had. This answered my second question: Schleicher had security.

With my hands in my pockets I slipped quickly down Cuadrante. A couple of neighbors looked out their doors, but I saw no movement from the mansion.

⌘⌘⌘

Much later that day I was in bed with my favorite Mexican artist's model when the phone rang. I was starting to hate these 10:30 calls. But it was not Marisol; it was Cody. Maya started to sweet talk him until I pinched her bare butt and she gave me the phone.

"Zacher," I said.

"This one is what I think you guys call *beengo*. We didn't use that word in Peoria, but I understand it now."

"It's bingo," I said. "I know this."

"Well, our boy John Schleicher has got what we used to call in the trade a checkered past. Twenty-one arrests going back thirty years. He's fifty-one now. Starts with cocaine possession, which he pled to and got a suspended sentence for first offense. There's some minor stuff, but later also possession with intent to distribute, illegal firearms, assault with a deadly, and sex with a fourteen-year-old girl. He walked on most of it, usually from witnesses becoming suddenly unavailable. He came to trial only three times, with one acquittal and one hung jury, after which the charges were dropped. The only conviction was at the last trial, consensual sex with a minor, and he got off with a suspended sentence and probation because she supported his argument that she was a hooker who claimed she was eighteen."

"One sweet guy. So why is he down here?"

"This is good. He walked into a narcotics buy that was a set up out of Trenton, New Jersey. Something like three or four kilos of coke. Not really big time, but a great stash for your own parties. He figured it out somehow and dropped the cop on the ground before he could get his gun out or call in back up. Then he ran. That was the last they saw of him."

"But why aren't they all over him? He's down here under his own name, right?"

"The Mexican authorities have never allowed him to be extradited. Our guys have been trying for years. He's connected, or his family is. I think that's how he walked all those times. It probably wasn't muscle on the witnesses, more likely it was cash. His last address in the States was in Short Hills, New Jersey, a pricey suburb of New York."

"So you don't think he's Mafia? Or do you?"

"I think he's most likely a very spoiled bad boy with a gun. Or several guns. And good taste, and enough money to live the way he likes. He's chosen our little backwater to do it in."

"Jesus."

"Exactly."

"Why didn't we know about him?"

"Because I think he's behaving himself down here, or at least he was until he had a serious disagreement with Tobey Cross. I mean, if the authorities were holding extradition at bay for you, you'd want to keep your head down, right, and not embarrass them? I'm sure he's paying someone off, but he doesn't want the heat to fall on them, either. Because if it does the price of protection goes way up."

"So you like him for Tobey?"

"Think on it. Why else would Schleicher deny knowing him?"

"A deeply rooted tendency toward discretion. After all, it was a murder. Look at his background; why would he want more attention, or any?"

"OK, he's discreet. But he's also a habitual felon hiding here in the tall grass of San Miguel. Have we turned up anyone else with more than a traffic ticket? Put him next to Anne Harris and Bill Frost in the line up. Even the Alwyns or Julian Soames. See how he looks."

"So let me get this straight. What you're telling me is that this morning I called up this guy, gave him everything but my social security number, told him I was investigating a murder which he probably did, and then went and stood outside his house for half an hour so he could practice getting the cross hairs of his rifle correctly placed in the middle of my forehead?"

"Pretty much. Plus, if it is him, he already knows

how to get into your house and leave a body there. You know what? You two get dressed now, throw together an overnighter, and get on over here, OK? Have Maya pack up that Liga Mexicana *futbol* jersey she always wears. Bring that bottle of brandy. I've got pictures of him being faxed down. We'll pick them up in the morning."

"*No hay problema.*"

Maya learned years ago that I don't panic. It simply doesn't work for me. In a crisis a great calm washes over my mind and I think, "What should I do next?" She had understood most of the conversation from what I said to Cody, and I felt her punches landing all around my bare back.

"And now we are dead next, right?" She was not yelling, but I sensed she was searching for the Spanish word for pencil neck, or perhaps simply idiot. Sometimes being a good painter was not enough, especially in the last few weeks.

"OK, let's pack it up. The house is not safe, we are staying tonight with Cody." Normally she would have made a crack about how that gave her a choice of boyfriends, but now she flew through the bathroom, gathering toothbrushes, makeup kits, and dental floss. We were in the artmobile in less than four minutes. She had dressed in thirty seconds, normally what it took her to undress. No bodies were in the *zaguan* when we left. Not quite a first, but I was OK with it.

It is good being the friend of an oversized ex-cop with multiple guns who has killed people in the past. Cody had the guns out on a table when we arrived. I was trying to look brave for Maya, who despite her high-pitched tone was probably braver than I was. I had never seen her falter.

There were two .38 revolvers with a full box of bullets.

"You have never seen these," he said. "It took major stealth to get them down across the border, but after all those years as a cop I find I can't be without them. I won't be able to explain it if we have to use them, but it will be better than being dead. I prefer revolvers because they don't jamb. Ever. Are we straight on this? I am giving you one, and the cylinder is full. Six shots. If it takes you more than that, you don't deserve to live."

That was clear enough.

"Shoot in the upper center of the chest. The head shot is usually lethal, but it's harder to hit if it's in motion, and in these situations, it often is. OK?"

"Yes," I said. "What happens now? Are we safe here?"

"I don't think he knows about me, unless you told him that too on the phone. You didn't give him my address?"

"Only the first two numbers. And I didn't tell him which unit."

"That's my boy."

"So we just wait until he comes after us?" asked Maya, with an expression she must have meant to be a grin, but wasn't.

"We're much better than that, sweetheart." He put his arm around her narrow waist. "In the morning we take the battle to him. I think until then we'll be OK here. But I want one of us to be up all night. The sofa folds out, so you two can sleep there. And no funny business. I'll stay up first."

"We already did the funny business," said Maya, poking me in the ribs.

"Good. You two get some rest."

Right. This was going to be sweet dreams.

"I don't think he can get through the front door because no one is likely to buzz him in this late, so I'll be on the balcony looking both inside and out. I'll wake one of you in three hours." He opened the sofa and unfolded the mattress. "If anyone taps on the door, I'll hear it. Don't answer, and don't stand in front of it."

At this point I preferred the part where a dollar's worth of sweat gave you only a dime's worth of information. I had more information than I could handle. Cody went out to the balcony and put the chair near the rail so he could see below. I put my arms around Maya but I knew sleep was not likely.

When Cody's hand touched my shoulder three hours later I knew I had slept, but I wasn't sure why. Maya shook her head. Her hair was a mess. I sat up and Cody put the gun in my hand. It was colder and heavier than I expected and it brought me instantly awake. It was 2:45.

"This is the safety." He slid a button on the side back and forth. "We'll leave it off. Keep it in your hand. Anyone climbs up toward the balcony, just pull the trigger. We'll figure it out later. Maybe put the body in your entry. That seems to work as a cover." He left for the bedroom.

Cody did the command part well, but I was not so sure about him being asleep. Maya rolled over and faced the wall. I went out to the balcony and sat in the chair. There were small covered lights lining the paths in the garden. No one could approach the balcony without being seen. There was no way I was going to fall asleep because my heart rate was approaching its upper limit. I wondered whether Schleicher was now machine-gunning our bed at Quebrada. We hadn't thought to put pillows under the blankets. Nice guy. A skilled house restorer. A staff to lean on for young girls. I thought General Santa Anna might be happy at who was occupying his house. I know I wasn't.

At 5:45 I shook Maya's shoulder. She sat up quickly with her fists out and a snarl on her lips. "It's only the *pintor*," I said.

"It's a good thing."

I showed her the action of the safety. There was no sun yet; it was about an hour and a half off. She pulled a blanket over her shoulders and went out to the balcony and I laid down again in my clothes. As a painter the only time I usually spend questioning what I am doing is when a picture fails. But now I had dragged everyone into this. Cody could probably take care of himself, but he hadn't been tested for a while. Maya, I knew, was resourceful and tough, but Schleicher was a real low life. Perhaps as Julian Soames had suggested, I just should have told Marisol no thank you, it's not my thing. Maybe my stock would have gone down with Maya, but we never would have taken all this risk. You can probably second guess yourself to death. Or to sleep.

Because at about eight o'clock the next morning the smell of bacon and pancakes on the griddle pulled me back to the smallish condo hanging on the hill above the Santa Monica. Maya was at the table sipping a cup of coffee, the .38 lying within easy reach. She had never put on the *futbol* jersey, and was still wearing her jeans and a white tee shirt that said, "GODDESS" across her chest, a gift from me in a sentimental moment. Cody was in a wife-beater tee shirt with a shoulder holster under his left arm, turning the bacon. How could anyone replace friends like these? I hoped I wouldn't have to try before this mess was over.

We sat down to eat. "He didn't come for us," I said.

"Only because he didn't know where you were. You won't be surprised to learn that I have a plan," said Cody. "We hit the house on Cuadrante today, as soon as we know he's gone."

"Hit it?" asked Maya.

"Yes. We get inside and scope it out. I want to see that collection and whatever else is of interest. Mostly, I want to see his gun, if he has one, and I don't doubt for a minute that he has. Can you rent a car? Because the artmobile is too well known."

"I can rent a car," she said. "Any special kind?"

"Anonymous. A small Chevy or Ford with the tinted windows. Something you can park across the street and watch the house from. Paul and I are going to need my Escort for getaway, but we'll need someone outside."

I tried to recall whether I had committed a felony before. It seemed like I would have remembered.

"And then the police will come after you?" Maya.

"He won't call them. I don't think Mr. Schleicher wants them in his house. It'll be just between him and us."

"Oh, this is good," she said, rolling her eyes. I knew she was wishing she had stayed in México City with its low crime rate and clean air. Where kidnapping is unknown.

"Well, it could hardly get any worse than it is

now," he said.

We dropped Maya off at the Hola RentaCar agency on San Francisco and went on to Caravan, which is a business on the same block as the post office. Many people in San Miguel, and not just the ex-pats, don't use the local post office for international mail. Sometimes it can be fast, but most often it's not, and you never know which it's going to be. Caravan collects mail in Laredo, Texas for all its clients, so we all have a US address. Once a day a courier from Caravan picks up the accumulated mail and drives it down to San Miguel, and at the same time sends off all the mailings from us. It's a good system, although it adds to the cost of mailings, but at least you know pretty closely when your mail is going to arrive. Caravan also sends and receives faxes and supplies Internet service for anyone who doesn't have it at home.

We stood out on the sidewalk and studied the two faxed photos that had come down from Chicago. They were apparently late mug shots from the time of Schleicher's last arrest, which made them about ten years old. They showed a square-headed jowly man with thick dark hair and eyebrows. The description indicated he was five feet ten inches tall and weighed one hundred ninety pounds. He had no tattoos, but there was a three-quarter-inch scar at the left corner of his mouth. He did not resemble my image of a connoisseur.

After checking my house for intrusions and finding none, we alternated with Maya watching the house on Cuadrante, parked so we could see down the garden side as well as the front, and switching every two hours. We did not want the same car parked there all day. "Too bad there's no place to get donuts here," Cody said. "It's so hard to do surveillance without donuts."

Nothing moved all day. Then around six o'clock, a man who had to be Schleicher came out the front door and opened the carriage gates. A moment later a blue Mercedes sedan emerged. He locked the gates again and drove off, turning left on Cuadrante. When he reached the end of the block, we pulled out after him. I called Maya on my cell phone.

"We're leaving with him now," I said. "We'll keep you posted."

The streets are too narrow in San Miguel for a wild car chase, and the traffic is often too thick, so it was easy to stay a block or so behind Schleicher and be invisible, I hoped. He threaded his way toward the edge of town and turned onto the road for Querétaro. This was a break. There is nothing much between here and Querétaro, and it's an hour's drive away. That would give us some time. Once he cleared the outlying businesses, we turned around and went back to Cuadrante. Maya was still in place across the street and we parked a bit down from her. She opened the window as we came up.

"Dial Paul's cell phone number and both of you keep your phones on and we can chat as this goes down. If Schleicher comes back let us know immediately," said Cody.

"Roger," She said. The girl knew her slang. I kissed her on the cheek, trying not to show how nervous I was, but I bumped my head on the doorframe. We walked down the side street as the sun was going below the mountains. When we came to the garden gate Cody pulled a clear plastic bag out of his pocket. It held what looked like a ball of hamburger.

"I ground up three heavy duty sleeping pills in this," he said. "They were past their expiration date, but I don't think it matters in this case. We're going to give that dog a rest." He wadded the end of a piece of string into the ball, repacked it, and slid it with his foot under the two inch gap at the bottom of the gate. Most of the string stayed on our side.

"You've done this before," I said.

"Something like it. Dogs are easy." He tapped softly on the gate and there was the patter of four leather feet on gravel and the string abruptly disappeared.

We waited for half an hour and then went to the carriage gate and tossed a pebble over it. Then another. Nothing happened. Cody went back to his car and returned with a bolt cutter and broke the padlock. We were in. "Can't be helped about the lock," he said. "It's first class and we don't have another twenty minutes to work on it. Schleicher will just have to know we've been here."

"How's the dog?" asked Maya on the cell phone.

"He nodded off," I said. Behind the house along the back wall was a garage for the Mercedes and the servants' quarters I had seen from the side street. No light came from either building, but we still moved as quietly as we could. Between them and the house was a serene garden where we could make out a fountain in the center with benches around it. We took out our flashlights and went up three steps to the back entry. The dog snored softly below, eight inches of string hanging out of his mouth. He was lying on his side, with his feet stretched out in front of him. Suddenly he twitched and started making that funny whining noise dogs make when they chase rabbits in their dreams.

The rear door was eight feet high with two of the vertical wooden panels replaced with glass. Cody scanned the sides of the doorway for an alarm keypad and found none. Then he pulled out a small packet of tools and began to work the lock. It was antique in style and opened easily. No alarm went off as we went in. I aimed my flashlight around the room. The shutters on the windows were closed and there was no chance the light could be seen from the street.

It was another gentleman collector's room, but unlike Perry's, the furniture was all eighteenth century. There was nothing eclectic here. The pictures were correct for the period and in perfect condition. The frames were also of the period. Mercier again, I thought, the restorer whose name we had seen in Tobey's office in Dolores Hidalgo. Between the small windows on the side of the carriage drive, rows of cabinets displayed more than a dozen superb Mayan pieces including two of the Jaina figures similar to what the Alwyns had. Above them were trays of carved jade and rows of gold jewelry. It was two or maybe three times what Perry had on display. It seemed like Schleicher must have bought from other dealers as well, because the office records showed Perry as Tobey's largest customer.

I opened the cabinets and looked at each of the ceramics. Under my flashlight I could see that some of them were almost unmistakably by Ramon Xoc; the incised drawing had the same loopy quality of the pieces I had seen at Perry's party. Others were unlike Xoc's work. The Jaina figures might well have been genuine, but that was a harder call to make, and I wasn't the one to make it.

Cody was seated at a mahogany desk with an inlaid-leather writing surface. His flashlight picked out the gold tracery on the leather. He pulled out the center drawer and then beckoned me over. It held a large automatic.

"It's a Glock Nine. Definitely not the weapon that did Tobey and Ramon. This one would have taken most of their heads off."

The other drawers contained a small local phone book, a pair of scissors, pens and pencils, an engraved letter opener with an antique look, and an address book. Cody turned to the C page and there was Tobey's name and the Galería Cruz phone number. In the last drawer was a medium size manila envelope with the name "Sandy" written in pencil in the lower left corner. Inside were four photographs of an obviously underage blond girl with no clothes on. She was not in an art pose, at least not one I would have used.

"At least we know his tastes haven't changed. Now I'm wondering why he didn't use this gun on Ramon and Tobey."

"Is it too noisy?" I asked.

"They're all too noisy. And there's no silencer on this. Doesn't mean he hasn't got one though. I just don't see it."

"I can't reconcile this rude, perverted, drug-addicted child molester with everything I'm seeing in this house. This is the home and furnishings of someone who buys opera tickets."

"Paul, the Mafia dudes buy opera tickets. They love it. You can't make any assumptions about people based on the fact that they commit crimes. It can be nothing more than a business. They come home at the end of the day, they eat dinner, they talk to their kids about their geography assignment. Next morning they go off to work again and put somebody down. Think of *The Sopranos*. Schleicher just happens to have better taste than most. He probably grew up that way."

"You're saying there's no link between virtue and culture."

"Exactly. None that I've ever been able to find."

"Damn." I was getting restless. We had waited half an hour for the dog to drop off. I didn't want to see headlights moving along the carriage drive since that was our escape route. Schleicher would be instantly alerted as soon as he went to open the gates and saw the ruined lock.

"Nothing moving out here," said Maya's voice on the phone. "But it's getting late. I missed some of that about the Mafia dudes." There was a nervous edge to her voice.

"I'll fill you in later," I said.

We moved silently through the rest of the house. Between the back sitting room and a large formal reception room in front was a dining room with quantities of old silver and more of the same kind of pictures, and a library with tall floor to ceiling bookshelves and a ladder that moved along a rail. The books were of the same period as everything else and didn't appear to have had much use. Mostly heavy leather-ribbed bindings, all in sets. Beyond that was the kitchen, definitely not of the period, with state-of-the-art stainless steel appliances and sleek cabinetry. Schleicher was probably a gourmet chef too.

Up the grand staircase, all limestone and marble, we found a central atrium with a leaded glass skylight and bedrooms all around. Two were suites with sitting room and bath, three more single bedrooms but also with bath, and four more were not furnished. There had been some remodeling here, but the eighteenth century style had been mostly retained. Only the bathrooms were modern. Who wants a chamber pot now or a zinc tub to bathe in? In the largest bedroom facing the street was a Spanish colonial armoire adapted to hold a television set and a sound system.

We went through the nightstands, closets and medicine cabinets but the only things of interest were two canisters of cocaine in the main bathroom. No surprise there. There were no other guns. Judging from the contents of the closets there were no other inhabitants besides John Schleicher. End of story.

We went out the back entry. The dog had not moved. It was a lovely house, possibly the finest I had ever seen in San Miguel. Aside from the gun and the cocaine and the pictures of the unfortunate young blonde, it reminded me of the weekly house tours, only less crowded and not as nicely lit.

We turned in the rental car and the three of us returned to Quebrada in Cody's Escort. The pistols were hidden under the front seat. Once we got inside the house there were no signs that Schleicher had invaded in our absence; maybe he was classier than we were after all. As I looked around I also had a sense that we could pick up a few decorating tips from him.

I made a pot of coffee; we had forgotten the brandy bottle at Cody's. We stretched out in the *loggia* and I left the lights off in the garden.

"One thing bothers me about Schleicher," he said. "With the record he has, he ought to be good for it, but why are all the ceramics still displayed like that? If he had found out they were fakes, or at least some of them, why not get them off the shelves? Why did he still want to look at them? It would have been humiliating for him. I still think that's what happened with the Alwyns and their half-empty cabinet."

"What if getting rid of them would reveal that he knew it?" I said. "Maybe keeping them in view would be a kind of cover. After all, the police have got the customer list too. They'll be coming to call on him at a certain point, unless he's too well positioned for them to attempt it. Or, if he didn't kill Tobey and Ramon, then he doesn't know they're fakes, so of course he's still displaying them. Either way it proves nothing."

Maya pushed her half full coffee cup aside. "I'm going to bed. I shouldn't have had this coffee. That was hard work. You two will figure it out." She kissed us both and went through the great room to the stairs.

"I don't want to keep you from sleeping tonight," said Cody, "but the one thing I really don't get is why he isn't coming after you. There's a time element here. The longer he waits the more likely you are to talk about him to someone. All the same, though, you better hang on to that pistol I gave you. Keep it by the bed."

"I left it in the car. Don't let me forget it before you go. One thing I don't understand is why we found only the Glock Nine. I mean, doesn't it make sense to have weapons stashed all over the house? So let's say for a moment that it's not Schleicher. Then we go back to the customer list and do more interviews, hoping something will pop out. When we've covered the rest of the local customers, we go to Guadalajara and all the rest of the towns where customers live? This could drag on."

"But I always found that talking to people can stir up trouble, maybe hit a nerve," said Cody. "Then they make mistakes. That's what a lot of this business is. You just get in people's faces. Mostly that's all you can do, besides processing the physical evidence, and the police have collected all of that. I've never been able to read a person's whole life from just a glance the way Sherlock Holmes did, or maybe you do when you're painting a portrait."

"So where are we now? We've seen six people out of thirteen on the list, if you count Schleicher."

"If he doesn't come after us, we've probably seen as much of him as we're going to."

"Maybe Perry knows something about him that would help," I said. "I have the sense that he keeps his ear to the ground. I think I'll go see him tomorrow. If nothing else, I can get a better look at his ceramics. I had the strong feeling before that they were all from the same hand. How would you feel about staying with Maya while I do that? Just in case Schleicher tries something. Maybe you two could play whist."

"That needs four people, or at least three. But we'll think of something. Go ahead and set it up. I've got no problem spending time with her, especially with you gone. We could do some tango dancing. My tango could use some work."

I had the image of Cody wearing a sash and Maya in a slit skirt with a rose stem in her teeth, sweeping across the *loggia*. *Puede ser,* as they say here, it could be.

⌘⌘⌘

On the morning after our visit to John Schleicher's

house I dialed the Watts' number and reached Barbara. She sounded busy and thought I wanted to schedule another sitting.

"I'm not going to be able to do it for a few days, darlin'. I've got to go up to Houston. I don't know if I ever told you, but I've got a sister there. She married one of those engineers at the Space Center. I'm just packing now."

"Actually, I wanted to talk to Perry." As I said this I couldn't help wondering what a sister of Barbara's might be like.

"Perry?" Like she couldn't quite place the name, or maybe she was just disappointed.

"I'm still working on this Tobey Cross thing and I wanted to ask him some questions about John Schleicher."

"I don't think I know him. Does he live here?"

"Over on Cuadrante. Quite a nice house, in fact."

"I think I might know it. Is it a gorgeous restoration in the middle of routine stuff?"

"That's the one."

"I'll let you talk to him, then. I've got to finish packing. I'll call you when I get back." She made a kissing sound into the phone.

I spoke to Perry briefly and we arranged a meeting for that evening at eight o'clock. He said we could certainly have a close look at the ceramics, but he didn't know how much he could tell me about John Schleicher. It wasn't clear from the way he said it, but I thought that what he might have meant was how much he *would* tell me.

CHAPTER TWENTY
VALENTIN GUZMAN

Valentín Guzman was not a happy man. The Boss had made some nasty and quite unfounded references to his mother's employment history when he discovered that Valentín had abandoned Ramon Xoc's sample case on the street. Valentín had been sent back under protest to find it, but there had been no trace of it on the sidewalk where he had forced Xoc into his van. He was not surprised. It was obviously a thing of value and would not have gone unnoticed. He wondered whether the Boss thought he had kept it himself. It was too late now, and the Boss had paid him the 5,000 pesos anyway. That was when he said the other disturbing thing; that there might be more work for him of the same kind. Valentín didn't feel he could object.

Sighing deeply, Valentín kept his mind on the next fistful of pesos as he parked near the intersection of Quebrada and Callejon Blanco. The house of the painter, where he had left the body of Ramon Xoc, was a few numbers down. Directly ahead of him was the white Chevy van the Boss had described to him.

It was 6:30 in the evening and there were few people on the street. Darkness had fallen quickly when the sun went behind the western hills. Valentín eased his substantial frame out of his own dusty van and moved along the sidewalk to the passenger door of the Chevy. No one was within half a block of him. From his belt he extracted a flat piece of metal about three inches wide and eighteen inches long. The Boss had called it a Slim Jim. At the top, the edge was curled over to form a grip, and at the bottom the profile of a hook had been cut into the metal.

The Boss had explained in detail how to slide the hooked edge downward into the door between the glass and the rubber gasket and then to move it back and forth until he caught the lever of the lock and it slipped open. He made Valentín Guzman practice on his own van until he could do it in less than thirty seconds. The Boss wouldn't let him try it on his car.

The lock on the Chevy was somewhat different, but he was still able to get the door open in under thirty seconds. He slid inside and felt for the small silvery gun in his pocket. He didn't like to touch it, even less now that he had used it on Ramon Xoc. He locked the door again and moved awkwardly between the seats. Unlike his own van, the Chevy had windows all the way back, but of course, being a Mexican van, they were all darkened. He settled onto the bench seat behind the driver's and stretched out, his knees in the air. There was no reason to watch for the painter because Valentín had no plans to move until Zacher was in the van and had put the keys in the ignition. At that point he would place the gun to the back of the painter's head and order him to drive out of town. Somewhere out in the country he would fire a bullet into his head, dump the body in a secluded spot, and then return the van to Quebrada and switch to his own van. He examined the radium dial of his nearly gold watch and waited, thinking mainly of the next new inflow into his family budget. Maybe he could now afford a new rooftop water tank, a *tinaco*. The current one had a slow leak that he couldn't find and his family ran out of water frequently. The time was 7:15.

Up the street in front of Casa Zacher, the artmobile pulled up and parked, easing into a space better suited to a smaller vehicle. Maya got out of the driver's side and Cody Williams joined her on the sidewalk. They went inside and the door closed behind them. From his prone position on the middle seat of a different Chevy, Valentín had seen none of this.

It would be soon, now, he thought, his heart beating too fast.

At 7:28 he heard voices near the van and pulled his knees down. A key was inserted into the passenger door and when it opened a hand lifted the lock tab and Valentín heard all the locks on the van open. The sliding door at his feet suddenly opened and a small form slid into the space between him and the front seat, and then another. Suddenly he was surrounded by the piercing screams of little girls as they trampled each other, struggling to back out of the van. A woman's face appeared in the door opening and she began to scream.

Valentín had only six bullets, and his instructions did not include gunning down half a dozen shrieking 8-year-old girls, as well as several of their mothers. Improvisation was not his best skill. He struggled to his feet, not bothering to reach for the gun, and wrestled the street side door open and landed unsteadily on his feet. Losing his balance on the cobblestones he stumbled backward into the path of a pizza delivery motorbike. The impact threw him against the van where he slammed his head into the doorframe and fell unconscious into the street. The motorbike threw its driver and careened across the narrow street and up onto the opposite sidewalk, where it tipped over and spilled three pizzas to the pavement from the fractured box over the rear wheel. But for Valentín's rash interference, the pizzas would have been on time.

CHAPTER TWENTY-ONE

Maya had taken the artmobile to run some errands around 5:30. She thought she could pick up Cody so he could stay with her and still be back in plenty of time for me to head up the hill to meet with Perry. They came in at about 7:15.

"Where's the tango outfit?" I asked.

"It's at the dry cleaner."

"Tango?" said Maya, her eyebrows going up.

"I thought you could give Cody a tango lesson while I'm gone."

"It's been a long time, but I do know some good slow dances."

She moved off through the dining room with her hips swaying and one hand in the air as if on someone's shoulder.

"Any special questions for Perry?" I asked Cody.

"Get any background he has on the ceramics. Even if it's some baloney from Tobey, I'd like to have a sense of whether he has any misgivings about them."

"He may not be that easy to read. He's probably played a fair amount of poker in his time."

"And when you ask him in detail about Schleicher, remember our conversation about lying. Watch his grooming."

"He's always well groomed. It may not tell us anything." Hearing myself, I realized I wasn't expecting much from this meeting.

As I stuffed a small notebook in my pocket and left, Maya was sorting through some CDs and holding them up to Cody for his approval. I hoped she'd stay away from Ravel's *Bolero*, which someone had given us as a joke after seeing the movie *10*.

Out on the street, down closer to the corner, there were two ambulances and a police pickup, all with flashing lights. Six or seven little girls, all dressed in the same kind of uniform, were running through the crowd shouting at each other. A police officer was speaking with a woman who leaned against a white Chevy van even older than mine. The other adults were merely chatting, many with their arms folded. It looked like the situation was under control so I got in the artmobile and headed up the hill to Los Balcones.

As I drove up through the arches on Santo Domingo I was remembering the ceramics, mainly the incised tooling on the figures. When I first saw them at the Watts' gathering right after Tobey's death, the clear similarity didn't have nearly the significance that it had now, after I had seen so many others. There was no traffic to speak of and I pulled into their drive at two minutes before eight. Oddly the floodlights directed over the facade were not lit, only the pair of carriage lamps flanking the door. Maybe the grand lighting was only for parties.

I rang the bell and waited. Nothing happened for a moment and then the door opened and Perry appeared with a startled look that quickly changed to one of welcome.

"Perry, did you forget about our meeting? I don't think I'm early, am I?"

"No, no, Paul, please come in. I guess I did forget about it. I've been working on some business things upstairs. That's mainly what I do when Barbara's gone. Come on up, we can take a look at the ceramics and have a chat. Join me for a drink?"

The lights downstairs were all off except for the ceiling fixture in the foyer that also lit the stairs.

"I'll take a cognac if you have it."

"Of course."

At the small bar in the corner of the room he pulled down an ancient looking bottle and poured an inch or so into a snifter.

"You won't want any ice with this," he said, gesturing to one of the wing chairs near his desk as he handed me the glass. "Have a seat."

There was a glass already on the desk, centered on a gold-stamped leather coaster. There was nothing else but a telephone and a Rolodex. I didn't see any business. It reminded me of my visit to Galeria Cruz on the evening of Tobey's death. Business could be elusive here, but somehow I doubted that Perry also had a little office hideaway in Dolores Hidalgo.

He seemed edgy, although he made an elaborate show of settling into the desk chair and crossing one leg over the other, adjusting the crease of his pants on his knee.

"So you've been talking to John Schleicher," he said, taking a sip from his glass.

"Trying to is more accurate." I shrugged. "He

wouldn't say more than a few words to me, and only that on the phone. He denied being a collector of anything, said he didn't know Tobey Cross and that Tobey's records showing recent purchases were an error. He's a man of few words. I thought you might be able to give me more information about him. What am I drinking, by the way? It's phenomenal."

"It's just a blend of old cognacs, most of them over a hundred years old. Glad you enjoy it. As for John Schleicher, I've been debating how much I should say about him, since not much of it is good. But I can tell you a few items. For one thing, what he said about not being a collector is bunk. He approached me last year about buying some of his collection. He seemed to know I had an interest in Mayan ceramics and said he had--I can't remember the exact number--maybe a dozen or so pieces. I asked him to fax me a list with the prices and he did that. I've never had much contact with him here and I ran a few checks on him with some people I know in Houston and the word came back that he's a pretty iffy character. Had some legal problems back east and my sources in Guanajuato say he has a protected status here. The authorities back home don't seem to be able to break him loose."

"I take it you didn't go any further with the antiques." I looked around the room as we talked, trying to see whether anything was different since the party.

"I sent him a note saying there was nothing on his list that I thought would greatly enhance my holdings. I thanked him for thinking of me and that was it. It never went any further. But I assume some of it, at least, came from Tobey. Maybe all of it. No question that he was the best source for ceramics in this part of México."

"I wonder why Schleicher didn't offer it back to Tobey?'

"He may have thought he'd get a better price from me, since I'm a collector too, rather than a dealer."

"This information you came up with on him, particularly the legal issues, is it widely known here?"

"No, definitely not. He keeps a low profile, donates to the right causes. Some people profess to have a lot of respect for him, although no one admits to knowing him very well. It's crossed my mind that he might be worth a hard look in this Tobey thing. What with his background, you know? You look like this might not be new information to you. Am I right?" He took a long sip from his glass, holding it in his mouth before he swallowed it.

"We came up with some things, but they were mostly drug-related. And one morals charge."

"I saw that too. The morals thing resulted in a conviction, as I recall. Can't imagine why you'd want to mess around with kids. But as for the other thing with Tobey Cross, you do come across murder fairly often in the drug trade. Texas being a border state, we see it all the time up there. I've been thinking about this since you called this morning. My first reaction was to dismiss Schleicher and I was hesitant to pass on to you the background information I'd received. But what if drugs are somehow linked to Tobey's death? I don't know whether the police have looked at that. Maybe they haven't looked at much. They haven't called me, and I'm sure I was his biggest customer."

"They wouldn't say even if they had. But are you suggesting that Tobey was financing his antiques business with drugs, or that it was merely a cover?"

He looked at me for a moment. It was the same look he had given me at the party when he thought about the possibility that I might see things differently. "I'm not entirely certain what I'm suggesting, Paul. Could it be possible that the shipments of antiques going back and forth might include the means to conceal drugs? I'm just thinking out loud here. I happen to know that the house and gallery he had on Umaran cost him more than $600,000. And as you know, there are no mortgages here."

Very well indeed. I remembered my shock at finding out that the $90,000 I needed to buy my Quebrada house nine years before was all coming out of Grandma's bequest money, none of it from the bank. I ended up with just $5,000 left after I redid the roof. At least real estate prices had ballooned since then.

"I thought it would have to be something like that," I said. "Prices were already taking off when he bought there. But his trade was focused on high-end items. Isn't it possible there was a good living in that? Plus, some of my inquiries into his background suggest he may have brought in some capital from his years in the brokerage business."

"I was told he left under a cloud," Perry said, tilting the last of his drink into his mouth. He also subtly glanced at his watch at the same instant.

"Doesn't mean the cloud didn't have a silver lining. Perhaps he was making too much money from his clients, rather than not enough."

"Another round?"

I nodded, and Perry went back to the bar. When he poured his own drink I could see it was a small batch boutique bourbon. When he came back to the desk he pulled the chair up closer and leaned his elbows on the leather top.

"So you don't think it was drugs," he said.

"Tobey had an office away from the gallery. We found it in Dolores Hidalgo. It was the place where he received and reshipped his inventory. He kept his records there. We examined it carefully and if he had any involvement in drugs we saw no sign of it. It was nothing but antiques, and it was separated from the public part of his business here. Even his wife didn't know it existed. If he was trafficking in narcotics, that office and warehouse would have been perfect for it."

"But there was no sign of it," he repeated.

"None. So why have *two* carefully concealed places? Because that's what you would have to believe if he was dealing, and there was nothing like that in Dolores Hidalgo, believe me. And if you think that his connection with John Schleicher was a drug partnership, then you'd have to also think that Schleicher was the one running the warehouse and shipping end of things if Tobey wasn't. And that doesn't square well with a man trying to avoid extradition. A man who wouldn't risk embarrassing the people in high places who are protecting him."

Perry leaned back in his chair and briefly drummed his fingers on the desk. "Well, I can't figure it then. I admit you make a good case. Maybe there's some other angle."

"I wish I had one. Do you mind if we look at the ceramics?

Perry got up and crossed to the display case near the powder room door. He brought the pieces out one by one and placed them on the desk. When he finished they were in a line facing me and he sat down, pulling the chair closer to the desk.

"The way I've placed these are in order of age, from your left to your right."

The one on the left was the squat cylinder vessel with the two small rim fractures.

"This one," he said, his fingers moving over the damaged edge, "was found near Landeros in southern Chiapas. It's attributed to the first century AD, or current era, as they like to say now. The darker clay is characteristic of that area."

"Do you mind if I touch it?"

"Go ahead. You're used to handling art works."

I picked it up and moved my fingers over the bottom. It had three stubby legs, all with the same abraded surface on the bottom I had noticed on other vessels among the San Miguel collectors. Above, the surface was rough to the touch, and the glaze thin and uneven.

"What would something like this have been used for?"

"That's rather speculative. Most experts think the vessels that were decorated and survived were used in religious ritual. Possibly it held the blood of sacrificial victims. There are always a great deal of shards on these sites and they're mostly undecorated. People's everyday crockery. This next piece," he pointed to a godlike figure, "is from Bonampak, just north of Landeros, so it's the same general area. It's probably third century, obviously a cult figure, but just which one it is now I've forgotten. I'd have to look it up." He chuckled uneasily.

How unlike you, I thought. Was he distancing

himself now from these pieces? This figure had no incised drawings on it, but the feel of it when I picked it up seemed subtly similar to the first one. Maybe it was just the same thickness of the sides.

The next was a deep plate, crowded with figures and with more coloring in the glaze than the others. The figures were the typical loopy style. I realized it would have been a big help to have seen Ramon Xoc's signature at some point. I could imagine the same loops in his Os and the top of his Rs.

"This one is from near Yaxchilan, but over on the Guatemala side of the border. Probably an offering bowl for maize or other foods. Same period as the second one. I think it's my favorite." "A very handsome piece."

"Now this one is from Zac Pol in the Yucatán." It was a deeper bowl, with human figures inside and out. Again the three blunt feet with smooth bottoms. "This town was just on the coast opposite Jaina Island. It's Campeche State there."

"The great burial island."

"You know a little about this?"

"Just a few things Maya has told me. I've also seen some of their human figures in another collection."

"I know Tobey had some of those, but I didn't like them as well as the vessels."

"And these two?" I asked, indicating another bowl with animal figures and a tall cylinder vessel.

"From Sayil and Labna, respectively, neighboring towns in Yucatan state, down in the southwestern corner. Fifth or sixth century, both of them. Toward the end of the great period of Mayan culture. Still very collectable, though. I myself don't see any deterioration in skills. If I had, I would have passed on them. It's possible that as the tradition deteriorated, some individual artisans still maintained a higher standard."

I didn't see any deterioration either. Ramon was always skillful, no matter what period he worked in. "Have these been published?" I asked. "I mean, isn't it customary when high quality items come to light that they get some journal attention?"

"Now it is, but not always from the older collections. Digging was less supervised years ago and Tobey said that all of these had come from holdings that were originally dispersed in the sixties and seventies. He had never seen any publication data on them, and he said he had all the journals. It's even possible, I suppose, that some of these were found in the nineteenth century. There would have been no supervision at all then. It was a free-for-all for anyone with a shovel."

I didn't comment on this. I knew I hadn't seen any scholarly journals in Galeria Cruz or in the Dolores Hidalgo office.

I surveyed the group for a while as Perry searched for an elusive speck of lint on his sleeve. The coherence of these six had nothing to do with being at the heart of Mayan culture and ritual for the 600 years they purported to represent. The coherence was entirely in coming from the hand of Ramon Xoc, I had not the slightest doubt. I compared them with my visual memory from the party and I was pleased at how accurate my recollection was. That's a skill you never want to let go of. My eyes ranged back and forth over the group, and settled finally on the Rolodex next to the newest bowl. It was a discordant note, and not just because it was late twentieth century and not

Mayan.

I immediately recalled the desktop as it had appeared at the party. There had been the leather-covered notepad, the impressive fountain pen, the silver framed picture of the newlywed couple. I thought of how Barbara's hair had been up the day of their wedding, her "sophisticated" look she had called it. Then there was the phone with buttons for three lines. Other than the phone, none of these items were present today from that grouping, except the Rolodex. I had flipped through it. It was the tray form, not the ferris wheel, with a semi-transparent top and an opaque brown tray below. What I was looking at now was a black tray below. I was not mistaken. When I see colors I often automatically mix them in my mind. It's an exercise. I remembered thinking that the base of the Rolodex would be mostly burnt umber, with a touch of cadmium red, and then maybe a dash of ultramarine to dull it down. Not anyone's recipe for black.

I'm not sure what my face was showing, but when I looked up Perry was regarding me with that same careful look. I decided to say nothing. Maybe he owned twelve Rolodexes and rotated them monthly on his desktop. It was an uncomfortable moment, for reasons that were not obvious. He rose and began replacing the figures in the cabinet. His motions seemed a little unsteady; I didn't know how many whiskeys he'd had before I came. I finished my cognac. It was nearly nine o'clock.

"I appreciate your taking the time to show me these," I said.

"Any time, Paul. I know you're a connoisseur yourself in many ways. By the way, what's Marisol Cross going to do with the gallery? Have you heard?"

"She told Maya she's going to close it and liquidate everything. She doesn't have the expertise or the time to run it herself. It sounded like she's going to move the furniture out of the great room and collect everything there on display and hold an auction. There'd still be enough room for seating for bidders. Imagine folding chairs in Galería Cruz! Tobey would split."

As he turned back to me his mouth was rather slack, and his face unreadable. Maybe he did play poker. I hadn't detected any dishonesty in his statements, and he didn't seem terribly surprised about the auction. I set the brandy snifter on the bar and we went downstairs. Something unspoken seemed to hang in the air between us at the door.

"Good night," he said. "I hope to see you soon." He did not offer to shake hands. I wondered now if he had held back something about Schleicher.

As I drove back through the arches and down to *centro*, I tried to sort things out. I wasn't sure whether I had something, or just more antiques road show. I had sounded to Perry more certain than I really felt about his drug theory and John Schleicher, and I suspected that Cody might be prepared to take it up. For cops, a record like Schleicher's is irresistible proof of guilt. Cody didn't lack imagination, but he still tended to think as he had always thought as a cop because it had served him well—he had solved a lot of cases and he was still alive.

Back on Quebrada the crowd had cleared and the street was quiet. The moon was cheerfully hanging over the lit spire of the *Parroquia*, but I felt deflated. I had hoped that Perry, as the biggest customer of Tobey's gallery, would be able to provide more helpful information.

Inside, instead of wild dancing and merriment I found Cody alone reading in the *loggia*. On the table beside him was a bottle of wine with two glasses. The one farthest from him was still half full, as was the bottle.

"Did you wear her out?"

"Actually we had just gotten started when Marisol called and said she was ready to start packing up Tobey's clothes and would Maya come over and help her. She left about 20 minutes after you did. She didn't feel like she could refuse."

"Poor you. So Marisol's moving on. The clothes part is probably the hardest thing to do. I'm glad Maya's helping her. Do you feel like some coffee, or do you want to stay with the wine?"

"Coffee sounds good."

I didn't really feel like drinking anything more either so I put on a pot of coffee and sat down with him. Cody had apparently taken off his gun for the dancing, because now it lay on the seat of a bench against the kitchen wall.

"So what do we know now?" he asked.

"It just confirmed my original impressions, Perry's ceramics were all by the same person, most likely Ramon Xoc."

"Does he know that?"

"I couldn't tell, and I didn't feel like I could ask him. He gave me the history of each one, the dating and so on, with a straight face. It didn't seem to bother him that none of them had ever been published in the journals."

"And there are how many?" asked Cody.

"Six." Something occurred to me. "Just a minute. I want to check our files."

I went into the dining room and pulled out the box of printouts from Tobey's office computer disks. On the pages of sales records I found what I wanted and took it out to the loggia, and set it down between us.

"Look at this. Perry bought seven pieces from Tobey. One is missing."

"Maybe," said Cody. "Remember how the Alwyns had four Jaina figures and the sales records for them said three? How many were there at his party?"

"Just the six. So it's not the first discrepancy. Perhaps the Alwyns bought one somewhere else. They may not have been Xoc's work. And remember, the quantity we found at Schleicher's was way off."

"This doesn't really prove anything," said Cody. I poured us both a cup of coffee. "Was he friendly?"

"Basically, but I think he'd had couple drinks before I got there. He claimed he was working on some business things, but I didn't see anything."

"What about Schleicher? Did you talk about him?"

"Well, that's an interesting part. Perry thinks that Tobey and Schleicher may have been involved in a drug deal, or more than one. He mostly has the same information we have on Schleicher, and he thinks that the antiques traveling in and out of Tobey's hands may have provided a way to conceal drugs. I was thinking about that on the way back. What if you could make plastic peanuts for packing, but it was really puffed heroin, or something like that?"

"Wouldn't the drug dogs still be able to smell it?

Even puffed?" He gave me a skeptical look. "I don't think that flies, but even so I keep going back and forth on this in my own mind, and I just can't let go of his record. No, we did not find the murder gun. But we did find a gun. And we found cocaine, a fair amount of it, and he has a lot of money, as well as his Mayan pots."

"But we know there's also family money," I said. "Here's something else, and I've been struggling with how much weight to give this. When I was at the party and taking a private look at Perry's study, I made one of those visual records for myself of the ceramics and the desk."

"As if you were going to paint them later from memory?"

"Pretty much. You'll probably think this is nothing, but the Rolodex on the desk top is different from the one that was there during the party." He looked at me as if to say, "So?"

"Wait, hear me out," I went on. "That one had a brown base and tonight's Rolodex had a black base. I looked casually through the earlier one and there was no listing for Galería Cruz or Tobey Cross. Yet Perry acknowledges buying six pieces, the record says seven, from Tobey. Also, the listing for Maya said, 'Maria Sanchez,' which is not what Perry and Barbara call her. Do you see what this means?"

"I think I know where you're going," said Cody.

"I wasn't able to scan the black Rolodex tonight with Perry sitting across the desk from me. But there's only one reason I can think of why the brown Rolodex didn't have a listing for Tobey, and that's that you don't put your own name and number in your own Rolodex. Also, the Crosses would know Maya as Maria because Maya and

Marisol go way back, but Perry and Barbara never did because I was already calling her Maya when we met them. I think that it's possible Perry took Tobey's Rolodex when he killed him and two days later at the party, he was still scanning it to get a feel for the gallery's business. It would look completely harmless on his desk, wouldn't it? I'm thinking out loud here."

"I just don't know. They could have heard the name Maria a long time back. You've known them a couple of years. Maybe she was still Maria occasionally then?" He sighed and rubbed his hands together. "I think this might be worth looking at, but that basically it's thin. It's the kind of thinking you fall back on when all the good leads peter out and you have to go back to your notes, wondering what each little thing means. What if Perry just decided not to buy anything more from Tobey and pulled his card out of the Rolodex? Or maybe they had a falling out, who knows? He could have just torn it up because Tobey was dead. He doesn't sound like the kind who would call Marisol and offer condolences. If you could get back in there and check the black Rolodex, that's the only way we could settle this. You said Barbara has gone back to Houston now, but what about when she gets back?"

"OK," I said, "there's probably a way to do that. I did think that Perry looked at me strangely when he saw I was studying the Rolodex."

"But he'd had a few drinks, you said. And you probably had a couple too, right? Maybe that wasn't the only strange look of the evening. Alcohol will not only make you miss a few details, it can also cause you to make up a few that aren't really there. This is why cops don't drink on duty. If that's what it's coming down too, there's not much more we can do until Barbara gets back. But I still think it's thin. A man like Schleicher would commit murder far more quickly than Perry Watt. This is just based on my experience and my knowledge of human nature. There's something we're still missing here."

"Maybe we would have seen it if Schleicher had been willing to talk face to face, but I can't think how to force him to do it without police authority."

"Any way to persuade *Licenciado* Rodriguez to pull him in, since Delgado is off the case now?"

"That would never happen. His dream is that we just go away."

I had just refilled our coffee cups when my cell phone rang. I looked at my watch; ten o'clock. It was Maya, her voice low and edged with panic.

"Paul, there's someone in the house! Marisol thinks it might be John Schleicher. Can you come now? Fast, and bring Cody if he's still there."

"We're leaving now. Call the police and tell them we're coming. We'll probably get there first and I don't want to get shot."

CHAPTER TWENTY-TWO

We were running the two long blocks down Quebrada to Galeria Cruz. It was a toss-up; the artmobile was faster, but then we'd have to park, and there was no guarantee how close we would get. Cody was keeping up admirably for someone of his weight and age. Especially considering that the sidewalk was eighteen inches wide and made up of stones the size of eggs. I could hear his shoulder bouncing off door-jambs as we passed and I was wondering whether we were about to encounter the Glock Nine we had seen in John Schleicher's desk. We had stopped to collect our own guns in the car on the way.

"Why did she think it was Schleicher?" he gasped.

"Maya told me that Marisol let him into the gallery once, months ago. She thought he was scary."

"Shrewd judge of character."

We flew around the corner and stopped at the entry. The lamp over the door was not lit. Cody pulled out his penlight and examined the lock after he tried the knob. It was locked.

"It's a good one," he said. "Fairly new."

"I don't think this house is more than eight years old. I remember when it was a ruin behind a half-fallen wall. An American couple built this place on spec."

"Hold the light for me. It may take a minute." He was still wheezing from the run and his hands were unsteady.

"How would Schleicher get through it?" I asked.

"He must have the same tools I have."

As he fiddled with the lock the seconds ticked by and I wondered what was going on inside.

"What's it like in there?" he asked, sliding slender shafts into the lock one after the other.

"This whole street wall is not part of the house itself. You come into an entry that opens immediately into the garden, which is roughly square. Several paths cross it, one on the right follows the other street wall, where there's a fountain. There's a ring of ficus trees in the center. On the left the path goes toward the kitchen. The main path in the center, looping around the trees, leads right up to the *loggia*, which is as long as the great room behind it. From there you can go into one of three sets of French doors or you can go left into the kitchen, which has its own entrance. Behind the kitchen is the dining room, which also gives access to the great room."

"Staircase?"

"Behind the great room fireplace. One up and one down."

"Marisol has a basement? I never heard of that in San Miguel."

"Like I said, this house is not old. I don't know what's down there."

"OK. I'll go through the kitchen and you go along the fountain wall and then through the French doors and maybe we can come at Mr. Schleicher from two sides. Have your gun ready. If you see me having to pick the door lock at the kitchen, wait for me to get through it before you go in."

The lock yielded quietly and we opened the door a crack. I pushed it open a bit further and when there was no response we went in. I closed the door quickly and hugged the wall of the entry. In the garden, low-wattage ground lights dimly lit the paths. The kitchen was dark, as was the *loggia*, but through the open French doors I could see dim light in the great room, possibly coming from the openings at the bedroom level above. Cody moved off to the left. The evening was comfortable, not especially warm, but my hand was sweating on the grip of the .38. No sound came from the house, or any sign of movement.

There was going to be a problem at the wall fountain, because the lighting at that point rose from the ground and bathed the upper structure in light, a bronze figure of vaguely hermaphroditic tendencies pouring water from an elegant urn into a half circular base. No water came from the urn now. Approaching it I dropped to my knees and crawled twenty feet under the cover of gigantic elephant ears until I was comfortably in semidarkness again. When I reached the *loggia* Cody was already at the kitchen door. He didn't have to pause going in.

As I threaded my way through the outdoor furniture and moved toward the French doors I picked up the murmur of conversation, not nearby, but where it was I couldn't tell. I flattened myself against the wall next to the center pair of doors, pulling the gun out of my belt.

"Tobey always said you were a fool with more money than sense. What can you prove now?" It was Marisol's voice. "It was for this that you killed him?"

"Well, darlin,' he made the same comment to me,

and that's what cost him his life. Do you think I cared about the money?" It was Perry Watt's voice! "I would have killed him for a tenth as much. Everybody thinks I'm all about money, but that's not it. It's only a means to own what I don't have time to create myself. Not that I couldn't. And then to have Tobey laugh at me. I didn't plan to kill him; any man with money in México needs to carry a gun when he goes about, but he was so goddamned condescending!"

"I think you must be crazy. Those pieces are not fakes. You have done all this for nothing. Now you think you need to kill me too."

I had no idea where Cody might be at this point, but I knew if I didn't act soon Perry would probably kill her. And where was Maya? Surely not standing there silently with Marisol. That would have been beyond her. The thought crossed my mind that Perry had already killed her, and I forcibly put it aside. Marisol wouldn't have been as composed if he had. I slipped out of my shoes and began moving into the great room in the direction of the voices. There was lamplight coming through the portals on the second floor. Within the vaults of the ceiling I could make out the frescoed angels. Silently I moved across the front of the fireplace. Suddenly I could see the back of Marisol's shoulder. They were standing at the base of the stairs that ran upward behind the fireplace on the left.

I dropped to a crouch and moved quickly into view.

"Drop the gun, Perry!"

Before I could fire he spun Marisol around and got behind her.

"I think it's your turn," he said.

There was no way I could fire past Marisol. Perry was not that big and she screened him easily. I let the gun fall to the floor. Now, as he focused on me, Cody would have a chance to come at him.

"In fact, I'm glad you came. Let's get out here a bit so we can talk." We moved toward the front of the fireplace. "This gives me a chance to bring this whole thing to an end. You've been messing in my business too long, Paul. I just can't have that. When I saw how you looked at the Rolodex I knew you had seen the other one at the party. It was my damn fool mistake. And it must have been you in the powder room when I came back upstairs the night of the party. You must know by now that I had Xoc killed too. When were you going to spring that on me? I tried so hard to sell you Schleicher. Why couldn't you see that? He makes so much more sense than I do." He was shaking his head. "It's just character."

"And you cut my picture too, then?"

"Oh no, Paul, you misjudge me. I'm a collector. I respect your painting. I'd never damage a work of art. It goes against everything I believe in." The argument from principle. Where the hell was Cody? Of course. Then it was Delgado. He would have been able to get into my house. DO MORE PICTURES. He had said it again when I talked to him at the police station and I hadn't caught it.

"How did you know the ceramics were fakes?" I asked. If I was going to die I might as well die well informed.

"I dropped one downstairs the week before the party. We were moving them up to the study to get them out of harm's way. Can you believe it? I dropped it myself. The great collector. Marble floors. I looked at the fragments. I guess I was hoping it could be glued back together. There was a coin in the debris. Twenty centavos. I saw it right away. Xoc had put a coin in every one, it gave him deniability. He admitted it to me later when he came to sell me more. I don't think he ever realized Tobey was selling them as the real thing. Xoc could never be accused of making fakes. All you had to do was put them in front of an X-ray machine. But Tobey had to have known. I went to see him. He denied it all. Said if they were fakes it was not his doing. I made him an offer. He could give me back the nearly three hundred grand and I'd return the fakes and not say anything. He could go on with business as usual. He laughed in that damned elegant way he had. Then he said I was just a businessman.

"After I killed Tobey I thought it was finished. But Xoc called me two days later and said he had more of the ceramics for sale. He said he knew I had bought many in the past, and he could make a much better price than I had been paying Tobey. He only wanted to continue the business. I just couldn't let him. I asked him not to call the others because I wanted the first choice. He said he'd already called Tom Alwyn but that he didn't want to buy any more. I really thought by dumping his body at your house you'd get the message to leave it alone."

"You were only a victim, Perry," I said. "Just like the others. Can't you end this now? Take a plane back to Houston?" Where was Cody? I hoped to God he was hearing this.

"I don't do victim very well, Paul. You have to realize that. No one makes a fool of Perry Watt. I just can't allow it." He cocked his head and listened for a moment. "Are you alone tonight?" He spoke slowly, as if listening through his own words.

"Of course. I was just coming to give Marisol a progress report."

"I don't want you to think I'm a bad guy, Paul."

"Of course not." His personal ethics were legendary. Was Cody wandering around lost? Marisol was eyeing me with an unhopeful look, like why didn't I do something?

"I'm just in this too far," Perry went on. "I've taken care of Delgado. He'll be lucky if they let him be a garbage collector when he gets out of prison. But I'll tell you what I'll do. I'll buy one of the Maya pictures from your estate once you're gone. Hell, I might even look in on that lil' brown gal of yours; you know, see if she needs anything." He smiled now, for the first time.

"She might be a little too sassy for you, Perry." Marisol said nothing, but her eyebrows went up at the brown gal comment.

"I'm used to sassy. I've even gotten to like it."

"What brought you back tonight?"

He pushed Marisol in my direction so he could cover both of us and reached into his pocket.

"I left something behind that night," he said. In his palm were a spent bullet casing and a bright brass coin.

"The shell casing."

"Exactly. I won't say I was rattled that day, but I was just a bit upset and I had to leave sooner than I intended. I have a young friend in the police who kept me posted on the investigation. A few pesos go a long way here. I knew they didn't have the shell, but when you told me about the upcoming auction, and moving all the furniture, I knew they'd find it."

"And the coin?"

"That was going to be for Marisol, if she caught me searching. But now it can be for you."

His hand rose and the coin sailed through the air toward me. I caught it. I didn't have to look at it to know it was twenty centavos.

"Should I put it in my mouth?" I asked, trying to sound much calmer than I felt.

There was a loud pounding on the entry door and the bell began to ring. Perry whirled toward the *loggia*, and took a step forward. Cody moved rapidly out of the dining room in our direction, but Perry saw him too, from the corner of his eye, and fired off a shot before Cody could get into a position to shoot past Marisol. Cody went down on a side table that held a large onyx lamp with a fringed shade, taking it with him, then slid thrashing to the floor. Suddenly, before the sound of the gunshot had died away, Maya emerged from the basement stairs at the right of the fireplace and in her raised arms was one of the Mayan figures from the wall niches. There was a mighty look of concentration on her face as she brought the statue down on the side of Perry's head. Perry was still looking over the settling rubble of Cody and the lamp table, trying to decide whether to fire again. It was the last thing he saw on earth.

"Lil brown gal?" she said. Perry now lay at the same spot on the floor where Marisol had said that Tobey died.

With my toe I moved his gun away, then knelt

beside him. His eyes were still open but he wasn't moving. My fingers found no pulse in his neck, but I was no expert. His head was misshapen from the impact. As I looked at him for a moment, a rush of contradictory feelings went through me, and I knew I'd have to sort them out later. I leaned over Perry's body and sifted through the ceramic fragments on the tile. There it was, the newly minted coin. I picked it up and put it in my pocket with the one that had been meant for my mouth. Now I had forty centavos. This didn't even pay as well as painting. Then I remembered Cody. The door was still pounding, now with more urgency.

"Let them in," I said to Marisol. "It's the police."

Cody was trying to get to his feet but the best he could do was sit up.

"Damn it to hell," he said. "And I thought I was done getting shot. This must be three; or is it four? Is Perry down?"

"Very down," I said. "Maya got him. I think he said something she didn't like, even more than announcing he was going to shoot me."

Blood flowed through his fingers over a hole in his pants leg. I pulled the table and the lamp away. I could hear the police coming through the garden.

"Are you hurt very much?" Maya asked.

"I've had worse. At least it's a small caliber, I think, if it's the same gun that did the others. It didn't go through." He was holding his thigh with both hands, applying pressure. "So it was all Perry. Not Schleicher."

A lanky man in a suit and tie came running in with two uniformed cops. His gun wavered as if he wasn't sure who to point it at.

"It's over," I said. "That's the shooter on the floor by the fireplace." The only blood was a trickle from Perry's ear. The cop knelt beside him, examining the massive head injury and placing two fingers on his neck. "This man is dead," he said.

"We've got another man shot here," I said, pointing to Cody. The cop pulled out his cell phone and called for two ambulances and the forensics man.

"I am Licenciado Rodriguez. And you are Paul Zacher?"

"Yes."

"Can you tell me how this happened?" Maya appeared at my side. "Please wait in the dining room," Rodriguez said to her. The other cop led her off. My heart rate was coming down a bit. Closer to 150 than 200. I gave him a brief account of what had happened. One of the other cops took Marisol into the kitchen to take a statement.

When the ambulances arrived it took both medical techs and two policemen to lift Cody onto a stretcher and get him out to the ambulance. Fortunately they had one of those carts to roll it on most of the way. The forensics tech arrived on their heels and began recording the scene.

"I will need both you and *Señora* Zacher to come with me to the station. We will ride separately," said Rodriguez.

"Sanchez," I said. "S*eñorita* Maria Sanchez."

"But just now you called her Maya, I think?"

"Yes. I only call her that."

"But she does not look Mayan?"

"No. She is from México City."

Licenciado Rodriguez knelt on the floor and lifted

up Perry's pistol and the two expended shells—one from Tobey's murder and the other from Cody's wound—with a pencil from his shirt pocket.

"This is most interesting," he said. "This gun is much the same size as one found earlier tonight on the next block, however, that was a revolver. I begin to understand now why Licenciado Delgado called your house a 'hot spot.'"

"I don't think I follow you."

"You are not aware of the accident tonight near that corner? It was somewhat before eight o'clock."

"I did see two ambulances, now that you mention it."

"A man was hit on Quebrada tonight by a pizza delivery motorcycle. At the hospital he was found to also be carrying a small caliber pistol. He had broken into a white Chevy van similar, I believe, to yours. He was hiding inside when the owner came. When he fled he was hit in the street."

"So he was hiding in a Chevy van like mine with a gun?" I wondered how he knew about my van, but maybe he'd been briefed on the case by Delgado as he was led away in chains. Unless Perry had sent him after me. That would explain why Perry was surprised to see me.

"Exactly, and so from his wallet we found his vehicle nearby, also a van, and in the rear was a large piece of carpet stained with blood and other materials yet to be identified. So now we are remembering the two deaths recently, excluding of course, the one you have just caused here, and how the victims died from small caliber guns much like these. Also in the pocket with the gun was a twenty-centavo coin. You will see that we have much to think on from this."

They had us sit in separate rooms while the police worked up the scene. They would not let me speak to Maya. It took more than an hour. When we entered the police station it was after eleven o'clock. The fan still turned lazily over Delgado's former desk, which was piled high with files. I guess they hadn't replaced him, only given Jésus Rodriguez his workload. Some people are just impossible to replace. We sat at *Licenciado* Rodriguez's desk in the corner of the room and I told the story again, this time with all the detail.

"So *Señor* Watt admitted to you that he killed *Señor* Cross and Ramon Xoc?"

"Yes."

"And was it not Ramon Xoc who was the man found last week in your house? You will excuse that I am new on this case, but I must be certain of the details and Licenciado Delgado is not available at this time."

"Yes, but I didn't know Ramon Xoc before that."

"Do you know why he was killed?"

"Perry said it was a business disagreement. I don't know what." I was protecting Marisol now. I didn't want all the gringo collectors in town descending on her for a refund. From what I had heard, they were generally happy with their purchases. I tried briefly to analyze the ethics of this, but it was not the time; Rodriguez was already moving on.

"In a different room now we are speaking with Maria Sanchez. Do you know why she would kill *Señor* Watt?"

"Of course. As I said, Watt had just shot Cody Williams and he was about to kill me. She had no choice.

When I was dead, he would have killed *Señora* Cross next."

"But he did not know then that *Señorita* Sanchez was there?"

"No, I told him I was alone."

"He did not see her approach?"

"No. He had just fired the gun at *Señor* Williams, who pulled down the lamp table as he fell, and the sound was still ringing in the air. Maria Sanchez ran from the staircase nearby. She had been in the house when Perry Watt came in."

"She was there already when you came?

"Yes, assisting *Señora* Cross with the packing of the clothes."

"And she hit him with a valuable antique?"

"Yes, she must have pulled it earlier from one of the display niches in the great room." I still had the coins in my pocket. If I had had them from all the victims it would almost be bus fare home. Assuming I was going home.

"When *Señor* Williams is finished with the doctors we will speak with him too. I hope we find that you all tell the same story."

"I am sure you will. I think you will also find that testing Perry Watt's hand will show he fired the gun. *Señor* Williams had a gun with him, but as you know, or soon will, it was not fired. As for the gun that Perry Watt used, you may be able to trace it. It wouldn't surprise me if there was more ammunition in his house. Maya Sanchez and Cody Williams both heard what he said. That's three witnesses."

"Why would he want to kill you?" he asked for the third time.

"As I said, I had been talking to others who had business with Tobey Cross. I was trying to find one who had had a disagreement with him, perhaps over the antiquities. I hadn't found any problems, but Perry said he felt I was getting too close. That I was messing in his business. When I spoke to him earlier this evening he tried to convince me that the killer was John Schleicher." I watched his reaction at the name. Perhaps his eyebrows twitched a millimeter, but nothing more. His was a cooler temperament than Delgado's. "I don't know whether you have talked to John Schleicher yet," I couldn't resist adding. "If you haven't, maybe you should."

There may have been a slight shake of his head as I said this.

"I think we are finished talking for this evening. Please wait here for a while and I will see what *Señorita* Sanchez has told the others. Interestingly, there was also one twenty-centavo coin in the pocket of *Señor* Watt." I thought immediately of the other coins. Perry probably kept rolls of them in his desk. "It is possible that it was merely pocket change. We will probably never know."

I sat at the desk for half an hour thinking about the marathon of death we had been through over the past few weeks. No one could have predicted that Maya would kill Perry, but she's a nervy person and it was a close thing. I surely would have killed Perry myself in the same situation. Cody would have as well, probably with even less hesitation. He's a nervy guy and it wouldn't have been the first time he killed someone.

And what would become of Barbara, the ever delectable, ever available, and now, Widow, Watt? Would she be crushed by all this? She and Perry always seemed great together in public but I knew from my experience painting her that she had her own life, one that didn't entirely overlap with his. I couldn't imagine her not coming out of this in good shape. She was too much of a survivor.

I thought of Maya and wondered how badly they were grilling her. She was tough enough to take it. She probably knew enough about Mexican police to keep her cool. I wanted to go home with her. Maybe we needed a lawyer. I was not up on the nuances of Mexican criminal law. There should be a course in it for the ex-pats here.

Maya came into the outer office with Licenciado Rodriguez in tow a little after midnight. She was smiling.

"You are able to go now," said Rodriguez, "but like they say in the western movies, do not leave the town." I tried to think what he meant. Was it like 'Get out of Dodge'? Not exactly, but things can get lost in translation.

The night was very black in San Miguel as we walked back to Quebrada. No one had offered us a ride and it was a good time for thinking anyway. I held Maya's hand and her fingers intertwined with mine.

"You are holding the hand of a killer," she said.

"Are you all right? Really?"

"No, not really. I will have some things to think about. Right now, I wonder if there was another way to save you and Marisol, without killing him. Perhaps I could have hit him less hard. Maybe if the police had come running in they would have done it instead of me."

"They wouldn't have known who to shoot, and besides, he could have just gone ahead and shot us. But in hitting him more lightly you wouldn't have been sure he'd go down. How hard is just enough? It was all going too fast. In another ten seconds I would have been dead. No more sixty years of life with you."

"No. I was strong with the police, but now I am not." She looked at me with an expression that invited support.

"You're still strong. You will always be strong. Sometimes we question whether we did the right thing, but as you think about it you will find there was no other way. If you had not hit Perry with the statue, how could you have stopped him? And if you had just hidden in the house, then he would have found you and killed you too. We would all be dead. Just ask yourself what other way there could have been. I can't think of one."

"So now I am stronger?"

"You must be. Think of what the gringos say, 'What doesn't kill you makes you stronger.'"

She thought about this for a moment. "It fits," she said. "I'll remember that."

We were both lost in our own thoughts for a while. I held onto her tightly, except where a power pole in the middle of the sidewalk made me step off into the street. Perry and I were opposite in some respects. His business expertise was something I could only imagine; yet what he valued most was his connoisseurship. When Tobey cheated Perry and then mocked him over it, he sealed his own fate and Perry's as well. My own expertise in art was much deeper than Perry's, but not as wide. And I didn't take it as seriously. How strange that Maya, who often informed my life, ended his. Once things settled out for her, and I knew that would be a while, we'd have a few probing conversations about these ironies.

We stopped on the narrow sidewalk and I hugged her closely. My fingers touched her neck beneath her hair.

I could feel her heart beating against my chest. Over her shoulder, the tile on the house facade said 132. In the dim light I could barely make it out. I knew it was one where I had tried the key. She put her head on my shoulder for a moment and then we moved along.

CHAPTER 23
MARISOL CROSS

Two days after the death of Perry Watt a uniformed San Miguel cop delivered Tobey Cross's Dolores Hidalgo computer to Marisol, together with the other records the police had taken from Calle Independencia 132. He also returned the key. It was a quick turn around for México. Within five minutes Marisol had set it up on the huge mahogany desk in the great room and was poring over Tobey's financial records.

In addition to sales lists for the entire time he had been in business, she found a bank account in Austin, Texas that held more than $200,000 and an investment account at Fidelity with almost one and a half million dollars in mutual funds. She spent considerable time composing a note to all the customers of Mayan ceramics offering a full refund on any purchases that were x-rayed and showed the presence of a coin in the clay, twenty-centavos or not. She also offered to reimburse each client for the cost of the procedure no matter what the outcome. Primarily for ethical reasons, but also with an eye to protecting her own business, she didn't wish to be associated with anything fraudulent.

Later she called Paul Zacher and offered to exchange the clay figure she had given him for other antiquities of his choice that were legitimate.

He laughed politely, thanked her, and replied that he was proud to have a piece from the hand of Ramon Xoc, a man he respected as an artist. It would be payment enough for his efforts.

Three days later she received a call from Barbara Watt, saying she had no need of a refund, and she hoped that Marisol would keep the money in view of Perry's terrible violence against her husband. She would be happy to keep the six Mayan pieces as a reminder of Perry's enormous ego. Grieving can sometimes include an anger component.

CHAPTER TWENTY-FOUR

Galería Mundo Maya occupies a venerable colonial building on Calle 60 just around the corner from the Plaza in Mérida, the capital of the state of Yucatán. Along the street an arcade runs across the front providing valuable shade for those who wish to stop and look through the gallery window to take in the sight of the nude Maya seated before one of the stony Mayan gods. That painting summed up the show. Maybe someday I would paint her clothed. From a third floor windowsill a long red banner hung limply in the afternoon sun. It said, PAUL ZACHER: GODS AND GODDESSES. It was Friday, June 17 and it was five o'clock. Showtime had been a long time in coming.

The gallery had been closed all day and we had spent most of the afternoon hanging the last of the pictures, straightening edges, mounting titles and prices on the wall, fielding phone calls, and finally, setting out trays of snacks, glasses and the iced champagne. We had put out two stacks of glossy brochures about the show, featuring a partly true biography of the artist toward the back. It gave the usual information about background, education, aims of the show, and other important shows I had been in. It did not mention that I had come within ten seconds of being murdered by one of my customers in San Miguel, or that the beautiful model in many of the pictures was known by the police to be a killer, although with considerable justification. Don't mess with Maya. And don't make inaccurate remarks about her racial background. It's the basis of class in México. Maybe it was Perry's insensitivity to cultural nuance that did him in.

Inside, the gallery was both wide and deep, with a row of arches down the center all the way to the back wall. The long ceiling beams from the outer walls converged on top of the arches, which were alternately filled in to provide additional hanging space. The eighteen pictures of the show covered all these spaces and one long outside wall, and part of the back wall as well. The sales desk was in the back on the other side. Near the desk stood an easel with a photo of me standing, palette in hand, looking at an unfinished painting. Maya had taken the picture. I thought my expression seemed to say, "What now?" A truthful image, I still hadn't decided what to begin next. At the rear of the show side stood the refreshment table.

People were starting to filter in from the street and I was shaking hands and taking hugs and pretend kisses from customers I had known in the past. Maya and Cody had come down with me, and I know Cody was proud to not be limping any longer. It had taken more time for his gunshot wound to heal than he had expected, but it had also been fifteen years since he'd last been shot. Fifty-eight is not forty-three. Things change.

We made some sales right away and red dots began to appear at a few of the pictures. I watched this closely because knowing which pictures sold first always told me something about the show. The first one to sell had been the last one I painted. That was about right. Sometimes in doing a series I ended on a high note. Sometimes I just ran out of gas. I called this way of going on too long, "painting beyond the idea." But this series had legs and I could have gone on if it hadn't been for the show deadline. And I probably could have finished one more, if I hadn't been set back by the vandalized picture and the time it took to shovel the dead bodies out of my house.

Maya was working the crowd with her usual skill. Tonight she had her hair up as in the pictures and we had managed to find an orange hibiscus blossom for her just before the show opened. In one of the better shops in San Miguel she had found a pale blue bias-cut dress with suitable cleavage. It came just to her knees and had spaghetti straps. She brought over a glass of champagne for me. "See how well Cody is doing tonight! He doesn't limp anymore." His gait was smooth but slower than normal. He had put on a linen sport coat earlier for the show, but quickly discarded it in the heat.

The room was beginning to fill and there were many new faces. Evenings around the plaza in Mérida are vibrant on any night of the week. Suddenly in the crowd I saw Barbara coming toward us. So did Maya.

She wheeled around and faced me. The color went out of her face. "Oh my God! It's the *güera*! What am I going to do? I killed her *esposo*!" A woman in the crowd turned sharply to look at her. Not something you hear at every art gallery opening, but that's one of those special details that make a Paul Zacher opening night unlike any other.

Barbara reached us before I could respond. "Paul, Maya, the show is beautiful!"

I knew Maya hadn't seen her since Perry's death. She visibly steeled herself and turned to face Barbara.

What was the proper etiquette for greeting the widow of a man you had killed? I wasn't sure Emily Post covered this.

"Barbara, I'm so sorry for the way it all happened. I didn't mean to kill Perry, but he was going to shoot Paul and he had already shot Cody," Maya said.

Barbara smiled sadly and put her hand on Maya's shoulder.

"I know, darlin', It just had to happen. I would have done the same thing. I don't blame you at all. He would have killed you too, once he realized you were there. Perry never did anything half way. That was part of his charm, I guess, such as it was." It seemed like a subtle rotation had occurred in her attitude toward him in the four and a half months since his death.

Then she hugged Maya. I thought I'd never see it. I left the two of them; they were somehow connecting. Next they'd be borrowing each other's clothes, although Barbara's skirts, short as they sometimes were, would have been a bit long on Maya.

A couple from Wichita introduced themselves to me and said they were vacationing in Mérida and had wandered in on the way to the plaza. They had picked out a picture with one of the local dancers as their souvenir of the trip. After seeing the dancers at work in the plaza the night before, now meeting the artist had made it special for them. The $4,000 sale made it special for me. Francisco Ortiz, the gallery owner, placed a red dot next to it.

I looked at the first picture in the series, which had been done with a Yucatan girl wearing a folk dancer's white dress with the colorful embroidery, and compared it with the final one, which used Maya nude, seen from the waist up with her hands extended. I had saved a lot on costumes. She looked boldly into the eye of the viewer. I liked them both, but there had definitely been progress. The god behind Maya faced left and his hands were extended beyond hers. Barbara touched my shoulder and her fingers brushed my neck.

"I hope you're not redoing them in your mind." She and Maya were finished bonding. "They're perfect as they are."

"Thank you. I thought you'd be in mourning."

She leaned closer to my ear. "I'm still mourning inside, and I've got a very fetching *bustier* if you're into black." I found I was picturing it in spite of myself.

"How are you doing, really?"

"I'm OK, now. At first I was in shock at the idea that the man I married was capable of killing people who got in his way. I knew he had done things in business that were harsh and probably illegal from time to time. That's just part of being a wealthy man in the oil business. None of them are boy scouts. Then later, I was angry, humiliated that I could be associated with that. Not that I ever cared much about what people think. I went over all the people in San Miguel that we knew. Could I ever throw a party again? Would anybody come? Of course, you would."

"I know you can take rejection. Besides, they'd come just to see you."

"Oh that? I never felt rejected by you. I've always known you wanted me at least as much as I want you. I can see it in your eyes, even now. You just have a different agenda. I always respected you for it."

"Would you have respected me if I'd slept with you?"

"You mean, in the morning?"

"Something like that."

"I'm sure I would have respected you in a different way. And then suggested that we do it again."

"Let's talk about the show."

"OK." She paused as if gathering her thoughts, and looked around. "It's beautiful work, Paul, I mean it. It's impressive to see them all together. It's so coherent. Seeing them like this, I can understand your vision. The old and the new, both emerging from the jungle."

"Thank you." I wasn't sure I would have articulated it in that way, but then I never felt any need to articulate it at all. It was a visual thing. For me it didn't need words. "You look like a million tonight."

For a moment I thought she blushed. "Forty million, actually. I had to split it three ways with Perry's two kids by his first wife, but I'll get by."

"I bet you will. I'm glad you came."

"Well, life goes on. Perry would have wanted me to come."

"Really? I thought he wanted me dead."

"That was not Perry's best instinct, or his smartest. It must have made him a little crazy to think he'd been made a fool of. It's not so easy when your family comes from nowhere and then ends up with all that money. He was always careful to distance himself from his roots. But he was a true collector at heart and he loved the things he had. I plan to continue that tradition. I came down here to buy one of these pictures. I know I could have bought one up in San Miguel, but I wanted to see them all together, hung as a group. You know, they'll never be seen like this again."

"Which one do you like?"

"I'm not sure yet, but not one of Maya. That would be too odd. What would I say to Perry's kids, James and Rebecca, if they came down? 'And that's Maya. She's the one that killed your daddy.' I've put the piano picture away for a while too, but I'll put it back when the dust settles. Perry always loved that picture."

"Are the kids likely to come down?"

"No. James, the older one, has never quite gotten past the divorce. He's always thought I had something to do with it."

"Did you?"

"Now darlin', you don't really think that! I was only nineteen when I married him."

"You must have really been something at nineteen."

"Honey, I still am. You'll see some day. We still have to finish that picture."

We walked along the row of pictures for a time, not speaking. She held my hand. Then she stopped and turned to me. "I'm lonely now. I go through his coins like he used to do, and I found a tray of jewelry I hadn't seen before, in that rosewood cabinet. Emerald crosses, crude gold chains. Shipwreck stuff, I suppose. I'm frustrated, emotionally, sexually. I'm used to a little more fulfillment than I've been getting." I hugged her closely in sympathy, my hands moving on her back. It was all I could do.

Later Cody and I met at the refreshment table. I poured us each a glass of champagne and handed one to him. He sipped his thoughtfully. "I've been thinking about something."

"What's that?"

"Maybe it's time we sprung Delgado. He got busted in late January, now it's the middle of June. That's a long time to spend in a Mexican jail."

"Especially if you are a cop." Maya appeared beside us. "He must have a family, too. What about them?"

Around the gallery men were nudging each other, looking at the pictures and then looking at Maya. She smiled at them. Other men were looking at Barbara. She smiled too.

"Maybe cousin Luis with the ice cream truck is taking care of them," I said. The gallery owner walked over to the long wall and put red dots on two of the Maya pictures.

"Well, anyway," said Cody, "I think it's time to let the guy out. I have a certain sympathy for cops that get set up, even if they're not quite straight."

"You know that I owe him one for trashing that picture. Don't you think that was serious?"

"Yes, I do, but maybe four and a half months in prison is enough. All we have to do is send a note to the archaeology police and suggest they x-ray those ceramics. They'll see the coins right away. Maybe time served is enough for the theft of eleven fake pots."

"I agree with this," said Maya. "Let him go. He has a family and he is not a bad man. He was not a killer, for example."

"How about Valentín Guzman? If he'd been a little smarter I might be dead now."

"He can stay where he is," said Maya, "but maybe Barbara could help his family while he's gone. Here in México employers feel a little more obligated than in Gringolandia. Paul, why not say something to her?"

Later, Cody and Barbara and I met again at the champagne.

"You're doing well," Barbara said to him, "but I feel I should apologize to you."

"I'm OK, but thank you," he said. "I just had to buy a longer bathing suit to cover the scar. No more Speedos for me now." I was imagining a rhinoceros in a Speedo. She took his hand and held it in both of hers. "I'm just glad it wasn't four inches to the right," he continued.

"So am I," she said.

"I'm feeling rather foolish that he even got a shot at me. I took the chance that in the distraction of Rodriguez pounding on the door I might be able to wing him, if I could just get a shot past Marisol. He'd still be alive if it had worked."

"But Perry never could have gone to prison, especially here. That wasn't his style."

I took her by the elbow and led her off a bit. "Maya asked me to say something to you about Valentín Guzman's family. I'm sure the police told you the story."

She touched my cheek and then took a sip of champagne. "You're sweet, but it's all taken care of, darlin'. His wife is still on the payroll. She will be until he's out and gets on his feet."

That could be a while, I thought.

We closed the gallery at nine and left a gratified Francisco Ortiz totaling up the sales while we walked over to Plaza Santa Lucia for a beer. On a bandstand on Calle 59 a quartet was playing Yucatán *boleros*. The sky was black and the stars were dim over the Mérida lights. I had sold all but two of the pictures. We'd be able to eat for a while but I didn't know what I'd be painting next. That was OK. Something always came to me. DO MORE PICTURES Delgado had said. It was good advice.

Barbara had selected the first picture in the series, one with a folk dancer girl I had especially liked. She had posed for me one morning in the bright sun of the Plaza Hidalgo. She was only seventeen, and she was shy and uncertain of what else I might want from her, but her eyes had widened when I told her what I'd be paying her. We only had time for one session, so I focused on her face and just roughed in the rest of her body. I gave her 200 pesos and for the first time she smiled. Later that day I bought a dancer's dress in one of the shops and I used Maya in the dress to finish the body two weeks afterward in San Miguel.

Maya sipped her Negra Modelo. She was more relaxed than she'd been in a long time. I knew she had spent months stewing over Perry's death. Besides, the time leading up to a show can be hectic and she had spent a lot of time posing for the last of the series. From the way she sat, her skirt had moved up her legs and I suddenly noticed the midnight blue choker on her left thigh, just above her knee. She had reclaimed it and was wearing it like a garter.

As for the forty centavos, I had the two coins framed under glass and hung them in my studio, in the way many business owners frame their first dollar. My first earnings as a detective. Maybe some day I'd make bus fare. It could happen.

Feedback from readers is important, both in telling the author what he is doing right, and suggesting what might be done better. Please take a moment to post a brief review of this book on his Amazon pages.

Please visit the author's website at:
www.sanmiguelallendebooks.com

CPSIA information can be obtained
at www.ICGtesting.com
Printed in the USA
BVHW072048080720
583188BV00001B/85